Disappearing to Nowhere

Linnsy B. North

Copyright © 2024 by Linnsy B. North

All rights reserved.

No portion of this book may be reproduced in any form without written permission from the publisher or author, except as permitted by U.S. copyright law.

ISBN: 9798332484087

Imprint: Independently published

Illustration by Marty Bohnet, MBohnet Art Inc

Contents

Dedication	VI
Trigger Warnings	VII
Pronunciation Guide	VIII
1. Chapter 1	1
2. Chapter 2	11
3. Chapter 3	21
4. Chapter 4	31
5. Chapter 5	43
6. Chapter 6	51
7. Chapter 7	59
8. Chapter 8	69
9. Chapter 9	79
10. Chapter 10	87
11. Chapter 11	95
12. Chapter 12	107
13. Chapter 13	117

14.	Chapter 14	125
15.	Chapter 15	135
16.	Chapter 16	143
17.	Chapter 17	151
18.	Chapter 18	159
19.	Chapter 19	167
20.	Chapter 20	177
21.	Chapter 21	185
22.	Chapter 22	193
23.	Chapter 23	201
24.	Chapter 24	211
25.	Chapter 25	220
26.	Chapter 26	226
27.	Chapter 27	233
28.	Chapter 28	241
29.	Chapter 29	248
30.	Chapter 30	261
31.	Chapter 31	270
32.	Chapter 32	279
33.	Chapter 33	289
34.	Chapter 34	297
35.	Chapter 35	301

Acknowledgements 311

*To all those who've been tempted by darkness
and found their way back to the light.*

TRIGGER WARNINGS

This book may contain dark and disturbing depictions, as well as dark humour on the pages. It's a *dark, high romantasy*, the world is supposed to be dark. When that is said, some of the imagery described on the pages contains as follows:

    Mention of child neglect
    Mysterious disappearances
    Death
    People being burnt alive
    Gore
    Violence
    Mental health issues
    Near drowning
    Violent creatures
    Potential cannibalism, but not quite *(Not very descriptive)*
    PS: look out for the beetles, they may be hostile.

Enjoy.

Pronunciation Guide

Salem: Say-lem
Thestepi: Thes-te-pee
Amadeus: Ama-deyus
Riften: Rif-ten
Elodie: Ello-dee
Galen: Gay-len
Killian: Kill-ian

You will encounter letters like Æ, Ø and Å from the Norwegian Alphabet throughout this book.
Æ is pronounced similar to the "A" in: *Atmosphere*
Ø is pronounced similar to the "U" in: *Hurt*
Å is pronounced similar to the "O" in: *Or*

Chapter One

"Did you let the goat out?"

"What?"

I can't help the frustrated sigh as I turn to my sister. Thestepi is standing in the doorway with dirt all over her delicate face. Her light brown hair is flying in all directions from the gentle breeze, tangling the strands together in knots.

"Did you let the goat out?" I ask again, slowing it down for her.

She stares at me like I've grown two heads. "Of course I did. Just like yesterday, and the day before, and the day before that. I even milked her."

"I was just asking." I say, trying to calm her rising anger. Her temper has never been pretty, and even worse to endure. "Are you ready to go to the market? I want to pick up my new dagger before I head for sparring with Amadeus."

Again, Pipp stares me down like I've grown two heads. This time though, I'm not sure if she's annoyed with me, or just in a generally bad mood.

Probably both.

"Have you seen my face?"

I don't need to look at her again to know why she's asking.

She's filthy from digging in the dirt all morning and tending to our animals. "Why don't you go wash up before we leave? There should be a bucket of water by the shed," I say, picking up my mug from the counter to take a sip.

Just as the liquid hits my tongue I feel it.

The ground underneath my feet starts to vibrate, stealing the air from my lungs. My eyes fly open when I hear a voice I don't recognize invading my thoughts, whispering my name. My vision blurs. It's a struggle to take a breath, as the overwhelming feeling of something *other* presses against my psyche.

The sound of shattering ceramics interrupts the connection. The presence retreats slowly, and my mind is my own again.

I curse as I almost keel over, trying to catch my breath. A tiny beetle scurries across the stone floor from the disturbance, before it slips into one of the cracks in the wall, disappearing from view.

"Oh my Gods, are you okay?" Pipp blurts out, and before I know it, she's at my side.

"Did you.." I start, but stop myself when I see her concerned expression. She doesn't need this. I'm the oldest. I have to deal with this on my own. "Never mind. I'm fine," I say, dismissing her.

"Salem, you're bleeding," she argues as she tries to get closer to get a better look.

Am I? I look down, baffled to see crimson blood slowly seep into the fabric of my trousers.

Fuck. That's not good.

Pipp leans in even closer, seeking eye contact. "What happened?"

I'm not even sure what to tell her. That I temporarily lost my mind? Because that was what it felt like. It felt like... It's difficult to put into words.

But if I had to... I'd say it felt like some kind of calling. Like being invaded. But that can't be true. My mind is definitely playing tricks on me.

"It slipped out of my hand," I say, referring to the mug shattered on the floor, and immediately taste the bitterness of the blatant lie. Shaking my head, I crouch down to inspect the cut on my leg. It isn't too deep, but I need to bind it.

"Bullshit!" Her anger rises again, and I don't have the mental capacity to calm her down right now. Instead I pluck the shard of broken ceramics out of my leg and watch a drop of blood slide down my pale skin.

The hairs on the back of my neck rise from the strange whisper in the distance.

Saaaleeem.

The allure that's woven into the whisper is almost impossible to ignore, it tugs on something in my chest. This time, I know I didn't imagine it. And yes, it's most definitely some kind of calling.

"Did you hear that?" I breathe, shifting my gaze over to my little sister, fear seeping into my being.

"Hear what?" Pipp asks, concern etched across her features. I can't stand the look on her face.

"Nothing," I smile softly, tucking a strand of hair behind her ear. I push my own worry down, and force my strength to the surface. She gives me a look, the one that tells me that we're not finished with this conversation. But we are. "Go wash up and get ready, I'll deal with the mess."

Her face switches from concern, to a scowl, to rolling her eyes in record time, and it almost makes me smile. At nineteen she's not quite grown out of her adolescent phase yet, but she's close. Thankfully, she's still easily distracted. "Maybe we can splurge on some new threads for your tapestry?"

Pipp lights up instantly, softening her features once more and jumping to her feet. "Yes!"

Distraction complete.

She disappears through the front door and I can't help but smile. Pipp has always been a bright light, ever since she was a child. Despite being born of misfortune and hardship.

At a young age I had to step into the role as the responsible parent due to our mother's questionable profession. It's not been an easy task to raise my younger sibling when I was a child myself. I don't have a motherly bone in my body, and yet circumstances demanded otherwise.

Our mother disappeared on us for weeks at a time, sometimes even months, making us believe that she'd become a victim of the mysterious reaping that happens every five years during the summer months. We were terrified of it at first, until we learned she was too old to disappear. Then we actually wished she had.

Tearing off a strip of fabric from my tunic, I tie it around my wound, hissing at the sudden pressure. Then, I pick up the shards of ceramics from the floor and throw them in a bucket by the door.

"I'm ready." I jolt from the interruption, yet I'm grateful for the distraction of my line of thought. I don't like remembering the past, or dwell on it.

"Good," I force out a smile while I wipe my hands off with a wet rag. "Grab the basket and lets get on our way."

Walking down the streets of Terrby is one of my favorite things to do. They're always bustling with people going on with their lives, merchants showing off their goods, trying to haul in customers from the streets. Children running around laughing, playing games and causing mischief. Terrby isn't a big place, it's more like a tiny farm village where we mostly trade amongst ourselves. It's located in the middle of the country, boarded by a large forest off the main trading route, making it hard for travelers to find. Only the fewest dare venturing into the deep forest that is said to be haunted.

Today, the atmosphere almost seems to be subdued, despite the warm weather. It's mid June, not past noon yet, and normally there would be more people out in the streets at this time of day.

"Do you think someone will be taken this month?" Pipp suddenly asks, as her eyes roam the nearly empty street that leads to the market.

I take a deep breath and sigh, "You know they will."

"I'm scared it'll be you this time," she admits almost timidly.

"It won't be," I assure her. *Not if I have anything to do with it.*

It's rumored you can bargain your way out of the reaping, but nobody seems to know anything more than hearsay. All we know is that it happens during the three days of the new moon's energy in June, July and August. The people that disappear are never seen again.

Pipp's eyes gloss over, her bottom lip trembling as she halts in front of the blacksmith. "You don't know that," she protests. "And, you're in the right age group now."

She's right. Of course she's right. I have no way of knowing if I will be taken or not, and from that strange experience I just had in the kitchen...? I don't dare put too much thought into that.

"It will be fine." I take her hand, giving it a little squeeze to reassure her. Even if the only thing I can do is hope it doesn't happen to either of us. "Listen, we shouldn't talk about this here," I say, glancing around us to make sure no one overheard.

"But, Salem—"

"Thestepi," I interrupt with a stern voice. "Not here."

She rolls her eyes, but relents, and that's all that matters. Nobody talks openly about the reaping. It's not allowed.

Which I think is fucking stupid.

The bell rings as someone opens the door to the blacksmith's and exits the shop. I grab the door and hold it open for my little sister to enter first. The heat from the forge in the back comes rushing towards us and the smell of leather and heat immediately tickles my nostrils. The sound of metal being beaten into submission rings out in the room.

I give my sister a warning look as she walks past me, then I follow her, letting the door fall shut behind us.

The beating stops, and Heason looks up from his work, mallet in hand. His face brightens up in a huge grin. "Well, if it isn't my best fighter! You here to pick up your new blade?"

I roll my eyes, shaking my head. "For an underground pit master, you're horrible at keeping it a secret."

"Everybody in this Gods forsaken town knows about The Pits, it's not a secret anymore." Heason spins the mallet in the air before catching it and pointing to me. "You want to see your new blade or not?"

"Of course I do."

His grin widens, if that's even possible, before putting the mallet down on the working bench beside him. With surprising grace, he moves across the room, opens a cabinet drawer, and pulls out a small object wrapped in fabric. "This blade was an absolute pain to craft," He complains, but I know better.

"Oh, come on, you like the challenge," I press, quirking an eyebrow at him.

His boisterous laugh fills the forge and his shoulders move with the sound. "That I do," he confirms. "I will say though, it took me longer than I'd like to admit to get the balance right." He pulls the fabric to the side and reveals a small dagger with incredible leatherwork on the small handle. It's shorter than most other daggers, and the ridges that are woven into the hilt make it harder for someone to knock it out of my hand during a fight.

"It's..." I sigh, and a slow grin spreads across my face. "Incredible."

"Try it," he says, looking to me with expectation.

I pick it up with reverence, studying the craftsmanship Heason has put into the small weapon. "It's surprisingly light," I note, glancing up at the huge man.

"It's a new combination of ore I've been working on, a blend of iron, silver and," he glances around before meeting my curious gaze, then leans in lowering his voice. "Skystone."

My curiosity deflates. "Skystone? You've got to be kidding me..."

"I'm not," he protests softly, his eyes widening. Determination settles in his eyes as my skepticism grows. "You remember that burning star that came out of nowhere and landed in the forest a couple of months ago?"

Pipp snorts at my right before she moves away from us, seemingly to inspect some of his tools that are laying around. But she's still close enough to listen in to our hushed conversation.

"How can I forget?" I glance over at her before concentrating on Heason again. I remember that day vividly. In the middle of the night the sky lit up like it was mid-day, and the ground shook so bad that some of the stones of the fortress fell from the turret. It woke up the whole town, and people started running around like lunatics in the streets.

"Right. So, I went there a couple of days later and in the center of that crater, there was this huge lump of stone, it was lighter than any stone I've ever held, and had this incredible golden sheen that shimmered underneath the surface. I've never seen the likes of it before," He tells me, growing more enthusiastic the more he relays. "It made me want to experiment with the silver along with the iron."

Giving the dagger a closer inspection, I can actually see the golden pattern that's hidden into the metal. It almost looks to be alive, swirling around in something that reminds me of flora. Twines that blossom out into petals and buds.

Carefully, I trace the pattern with my fingertip, feeling the blade almost hum in response to my touch.

"I can't take this blade," I say, holding it out for Heason to take.

He steps back, crossing his arms over his chest. "I made it for *you*, and you alone." He lectures. "Take it. I insist."

I look into his kind eyes, feeling my chest swell with an emotion I'm not quite familiar with, then I give him a slight nod. Heason visibly relaxes before his face brightens with another grin. "Now, I've paired you up with Amadeus tomorrow, I trust you'll give him a run for his money with this kind of blade in your arsenal."

"Heason!" I scold. "We're not using weapons during a pit fight." It's fists only for a reason. If we did use weapons, we would end up killing one another. And our population is dropping quick enough as it is with the reapings.

Leaving the forge, I tuck the new dagger into the sheath at my ribs for easy access and tug my sister along with me.

"Do you think there's anything to it?" She asks, making me almost stumble a step.

"To what?" I ask, furrowing my brows at her.

"The Skystone," she emphasizes. "He made it almost seem magical."

I shake my head. "No, he's probably taken a hit too many to the head, despite his young age," I say quietly.

"Or the heat from the forge made all of his brain cells overheat and die," she says.

"Thestepi!" I scold, shocked at her words.

"What? It's true. It's stifling hot in there, I don't understand how he survives."

I poke at her side, rolling my eyes. "You shouldn't say such things, it's quite rude of you," I say, trying my damndest to reel in my laughter and failing.

So much for being a good role model for her.

"Stop it." Pipp giggles as my fingers dig into her side to tickle her. Laughter spills out like the smooth chiming of bells, making my heart soar with joy at the beautiful sound. She has the most incredible laughter.

If magic does exist, her laughter is the purest form.

We stop at Mary's cart next. The short, plump woman that supplies the town with all kinds of threads and needles. She also makes the most beautiful tapestries I've ever seen.

I know little of weaving, but Thestepi is a true master of the art. She makes all our clothes and other useful trinkets. Me on the other hand? I'm only good at fighting. Which is ironic since I've been raising both of us our entire childhood. I should technically be good at most of it, but the fact is that I'm just adequate enough at a handful of the more useful traits we need to survive. Pipp excels at everything, except fighting.

We are complete opposites, not only in skillsets, but also our appearance. Where she is dark, I am light.

My heart plummets as I get a good look at Mary.

"Ah, isn't it the two most beautiful girls," Mary says on a sniffle. Her eyes are bloodshot and puffy. It's like she's holding on by a thread where she sways from side to side by her cart.

Beside me, Pipp gasps. "Mary, what's wrong?"

Immediately, she's at Mary's side, steadying her as a sob wracks her body. Mary tightens an arm around herself, as if that's the only thing that's capable of keeping her upright. Silent tears adorn her weathered face, and her body shakes from the effort it takes her to keep in her sobs.

When she doesn't answer immediately, I make the effort to keep my voice soft and steady when I press. "Mary?" And take a tentative step towards her.

"My son," Mary hiccups. "He... He went to bed last night, but—" another hiccup, then a small sob shakes her body again. Pipp takes her by the shoulders, guiding her to sit on a crate at the side of her wagon.

The woman follows without protest and slumps down as she seems to lose all hope.

"What's happened to Mason?" I ask, stepping up beside her and placing my hand at her back to give her my support.

"He's gone," she sobs, collapsing against Pipp's side.

"What? What do you mean gone?" Dread floods my senses, and the hairs at the back of my neck stand on end. I meet Pipp's wide eyes over her head as we both come to the same conclusion.

Mason has been taken. "May his soul find his way back," I whisper and hear my sister echo the common prayer.

Heartbreaking sobs fall from Mary's lips, and all I can do is stroke her back. It's a pitiful attempt to console her, and my eyes brim with unshed tears.

"Salem," Pipp chokes out, tears brimming in her beautiful hazel eyes. "It's started." Her voice shakes and all I can do is nod.

"It will be fine," I say as I grab her delicate hand in mine.

It has to be.

I tremble where I stand when I sense it again, the strange presence that floods my mind. I hear it. The distant voice in the back of my head.

Like a whisper.

Like a siren's call.

Saaaleeem.

Chapter Two

"You're late," Amadeus snaps at me when I enter the arena ten minutes after we normally meet up for sparring.

"I'm always late," I smirk.

He's already damp from sweat. Most likely having been here for at least an hour to get warmed up. Apparently, that doesn't take away the frown on his face, and he keeps his eyes squinted. A line furrows his brow, making me question how much sleep he got.

"What's up with you?" I ask, stumped by his disheveled appearance. He's not the type to appear unkempt, no matter what he's doing. Amadeus has this annoying ability to still look put together after hours of training, or even after working in the fields all day. It's like his skin and clothes repel dirt.

"Nothing," he grumbles, the response almost incoherent through his trimmed beard. "Come on, we don't have all day."

"Ooh, grumpy are we?" I laugh.

Amadeus rolls his eyes at me, wincing slightly, before stretching his neck from side to side in preparation. The fact that he immediately takes up a stance of attack tells me he's not fucking around today.

He means business.

"Seriously?" sighing I drop my satchel to the ground and push the loose silver strands of my hair away from my face.

He grunts in response, and I mirror his stance.

Alrighty then.

Before I have time to get my bearings, his muscles tick. He lunges at me, almost managing to get the upper hand and knock me to the ground. I dodge, and he spins around my frame. I track him with my eyes, and my body follows thereafter.

Amadeus narrows his eyes in obvious annoyance.

"What? Thought you could trick me?" I taunt. His jaw ticks just as he rushes towards me. Again, I manage to dodge the attack by spinning around, narrowly avoiding his strike.

I know I can't keep this up for long, but I can play with him for a bit.

A growl travels up his throat, and he moves in the other direction faster than I anticipated. Before I know it, our bodies collide with a force that knocks the air out of my lungs and we go down.

I hit the ground with an umph, knocking the rest of the air out of me and I gasp in an attempt to regain the ability to take in oxygen.

As I thought. He's not fucking around today.

"Fuck," I gasp, struggling to expand my lungs, from both having the wind knocked out of me and the pressure of his weight.

"Come on, Salem." This time, he's the one taunting. His lips almost brushing my ear. I feel more than hear his next words. "You can do better than that."

I grit my teeth, meeting his warm brown eyes with my own frosty gaze. There's a flicker of gold appearing around his irises. I blink, and it's gone.

That's odd.

"Are you feeling okay?" I ask, noting his confused expression and widened eyes. I can't hide the uncertainty that laces my voice as I study his face more closely.

Amadeus has never been this... distracted before. I should know, we've been best friends for years. And when I made the decision to partake in the underground pit fights, he was quick to follow.

"Everything is fine," he snaps, gritting his teeth together before tightening his hold on me. "Now, you seem to be in a bit of a situation here, Salem." Pointing it out to me only makes me angry, and he knows it. "So, I'd suggest you shut your pretty little mouth and get out of it."

Asshole!

Lifting my right foot, I manage to hook it around his throat. With all my might, I straighten my entire body, pushing at him. He's not anticipating my move, and his hold slips, giving me the opportunity I need to roll away from him and jump to my feet.

He coughs out a laugh, shaking his head. "Fuck, Salem."

"You didn't see that coming?" I keep my voice light, and smirk.

"I did not," he admits, shaking it off and getting to his feet.

I take up my stance, still smirking, then I make the snap decision to go on the offense to get the upper hand on him.

I hate being on the defensive anyway.

"I give," he finally says, chest heaving. I release him from my chokehold after we've been sparring for almost an hour. Sweat drips from both our bodies, and dust clings to the pair of us for a change. Not just me.

"You sure you give?"

Amadeus trips on his own two feet, falling to the graveled ground on all fours. He twists around and leans his elbows to his knees as he works on calming his breath again.

"Yes, Gods, you're relentless today," he groans, making me grin.

"Now, what did you learn?"

His grumbled response makes it clear he doesn't want to answer, but I give him my patience and I'm rewarded with his loud sigh as he falls to his back on the gravel. "That you're a pain in the ass?" He tries, looking up at me with one eye open.

I scoff. "Try again."

"Fine, you are still the superior one in hand to hand combat," he mutters, flinging one arm over his face to cover from the scorching sun.

"And?" I push, putting my hands to my hips.

"And weapon handling." He groans, loudly.

"Thank you," I say, giving him a mocking bow.

"Arrogant asshole."

"I've been called worse things by better men," I shoot back. "Do I really have to prove to you that I'm better at insults too?" I ask, lifting a brow in question.

His jaw drops for a second, before he laughs. "You're insufferable."

"I'm well aware," I grin.

Sheathing my dagger at the hip, I extend a hand to Amadeus. He takes it, but he doesn't pull himself up. Instead, he pulls me towards him with a boisterous laugh and I tumble atop of him before I quickly scramble off.

"Hey!" I protest, and his laughter almost manages to make my anger boil.

If I'm not mistaken, I think he might be flirting with me. The thought makes me uncomfortable. Over the years we've become close, but he feels more like a brother to me than anything else.

Catching my breath, I let the silence stretch between us, until Amadeus shifts beside me. Clearly uncomfortable. I lean against my knees and pick up a handful of gravel in my hand. Letting stone after stone fall, I finally clear my throat. "So... I heard Mason was taken today," I say, looking down at my dusty palm.

Amadeus clears his throat too. "I heard."

"You scared?" I ask, almost hesitatiant.

There's a stupid smile hidden in the corner of his mouth. "For him? Or for you?"

I scoff. "Yourself, but okay, let's go with him."

Amadeus flashes me a quick grin that doesn't reach his eyes. "Nah. If I get taken, I get taken," he says with a shrug. "Not much to do about it really." He picks up a handful of gravel and tosses it in front of him, making pebbles dance across the sparring area. "Last night marks the first day of the new moon's energy. More people will disappear tonight and tomorrow."

He almost sounds wistful.

Which is understandable. His older sister was taken five years ago, leaving him all alone after their parents died a few years prior to that.

"Don't you think—"

"No," he cuts me off. "There is nothing to ward off the *boogieman*. We did every possible thing we could think of when Teagan was taken. Locked the doors, boarded up the windows, we even painted the doorframes with goat's blood for fucks sake. And... Despite all our efforts, she was still gone on the last day of the new moon energy in August." He sighs heavily. "We thought it worked, but... She disappeared anyway."

I take his hand in mine and give it a squeeze. "Hey, if you do get taken, at least there's a chance for you to see your sister again," I say softly, trying to give him the support he needs.

He smiles, but it doesn't reach his eyes. They don't glitter or shine. They're bland, overshadowing the warmth in the pigments they normally hold. "Maybe," he sighs, dragging a hand through his hair before letting his head fall.

"We're going to get paired up tomorrow," I say, changing the subject to lighten the mood.

He lifts his eyebrow, looking me up and down. "You're kidding?" He snorts. "So you're telling me that I have to deal with your insufferable gloating for beating my ass in public? For fucks sake." Groaning, he falls to his back again, covering his face with his hand.

"It appears so." I grin, but this time, it's my grin that doesn't reach my eyes.

I won't lie. I'm terrified for the next three months. There are approximately forty-six people in my five year age group. Nearly half of them will disappear by the end of the new moon energy in August, completing another reaping.

Honestly, I'm not quite sure if Amadeus will be taken this year, his twenty-sixth birthday is in July, but technically, he's still twenty-five years old for the first half.

The ones going missing are always in between the age of twenty and twenty five. Since I'm a year younger than Amadeus I'm definitely in the danger zone, and I do have a feeling that—

Nope. Not going there.

I can't. I simply can't disappear on my little sister. Mom isn't going to be there, since she's probably chained herself to her master again. I haven't seen her for weeks, and she rarely comes to our house in Ador's Cliff anyway. I'm sure I'd find her if I went to The Brothel in the Northern parts of Terrby.

We live in the southern parts which was named after some rich idiot by the name of Adornav that disappeared the year before I was born. It's considered to be one of the better neighbour hoods to live in, but then again, Terrby doesn't really have much to offer.

"How about you?" Amadeus asks, startling me out of my own stupor.

"What about me?" I blink away my emotions before looking down at him.

He removes his arm from his face, propping himself up on one elbow as he studies me. "Are you scared?"

I take a breath, and swallow. "A little," I admit. I sigh deeply before shaking my head. "I don't want to leave Pipp."

He nods in understanding.

"Have you talked to Heason about taking her in if... you know?" He asks, lifting one eyebrow.

I shake my head in response.

"You should. I mean, if it does happen, you would at least know she's taken care of," he says as he sits up once more. "Besides, Thestepi is resourceful. She will figure something out regardless."

"I know, I might. Or maybe I'll talk to Tegner about it," I say, smiling dumbly.

Amadeus snorts out a half laugh. "Tegner is a brute and an asshole. He'd be no good for your Pipp."

I shrug. "He's a good man," I argue, and the skepticism on his face makes me laugh.

"Really? So he's one of the better men that has called you worse things than an arrogant asshole?"

I shove his shoulder, rolling my eyes. "Oh, shut up, he's way too old for me."

"He's not even thirty," Amadeus grunts.

"No, he's not. But I'm not warming his bed either, if that's what you're fishing for," I say. "And whose bed I'm warming is none of your damned business anyway."

He sputters for a moment, opening and closing his mouth without finding the words. "I wasn't—You know what, it doesn't matter. I don't even want to know," he says, chuckling.

"That's what I thought," I look over at the other people sparring around us before my eyes drift to the area where the audience normally stands. It's empty. Come tomorrow it will be packed with people betting on the matches that will be held in the pit below.

The first time I came here as a thirteen year old child, I was desperate for even the smallest of scraps of any kind. It didn't matter if it was a piece of gold, a silver head or even a small knob of copper. We had no more coin for food, and we needed it badly.

I was prepared to beg for it. Anything I could get. I didn't care if the whole town knew of our situation. It didn't matter anymore at that point. Heason had just taken over the fighting ring at the ripe age of twenty-three. The former ring master got reaped the month prior, and Heason swooped in and saved the entire Underground from collapsing completely, even if there was a chance for him to also disappear.

Thankfully he didn't and ten years later, he's still the ringmaster of Ghostport's fighting arena. The Northern parts of Terrby has been littered with people living in poverty for as long as I can remember, but that is no longer the case. There's a whole underground of questionable activities that has risen in these parts of our town.

At one point, we were a permanent addition to these ghostly streets.

Until Heason. He gave me a chance, even if I was way too young to even step foot inside the ring. And he's been looking out for me and Pipp ever since, if not in an untraditional way from afar.

I've had my ass handed to me by almost everyone here in The Pits. But not anymore. Now I'm one of the best fighters in this organization. The only two people that are capable of beating my ass are Heason, and Tegner.

I get up from the ground, brushing the dust off my trousers. "Ready for round two?"

Chapter Three

*T*he entrance to the cave pulses with some kind of energy I've never encountered before.

A beckoning.

A calling.

A siren song.

It wafts towards me, going through my body, sending shivers down my spine as the hairs on the back of my neck rise in sheer protest. The sound of water droplets echoes from the mouth of the cave. Chills spread along my skin and the air feels damp as I take a tentative step forward.

I halt, as the sound of a whisper slithers towards me.

"Saaaleeem," a taunting voice calls out from the entrance. "Salem," this time, a whisper in my head, a different one. Deeper.

It seems to call out for me, urging me to come find the source of its voice. Just as I try to take a step away from it, I feel a tug on my chest, forcing my body forward. Like an invisible thread.

Everything in my entire being recoils from the darkness, and yet, it's the most alluring thing I've ever felt.

This energy is deadly, and I can't help the pull it has on me.

I take a step.

Then another.

Passing through the mouth of the cave, I sense a presence all around me. Glowing beetles scurry away from my feet, giving my steps their own visible heartbeat.

"That's it, closer. Come closer," the walls seem to whisper.

It feels like I'm walking for ages before the narrow tunnel opens up to a bigger space. I'm awestruck to see glowing beetles covering every surface around me. The cave looks like a moving constellation from the way they flap their translucent wings. Their soft glow illuminates the cave, revealing an old woman standing in the middle of the room with her long nose stuck in a petrified tree stump.

I blink, trying to make sense of what I'm actually seeing. The old woman stands there, almost like a statue. The only thing that tells me she's a living being is the soft grunting noise she makes as she slowly tugs on her elongated nose.

"Aaah, Salem Vanroda," *she sings, her voice reminding me of trickling water, hiding a bite of cold.*

A new wave of chills spreads along my skin, raising the hairs on my arms, legs, and neck in a flash. "What will it be, my child?" *She asks in her slithering tone.*

"Wh-what?" *I stutter. I fucking stutter! I've never stuttered in my entire life, and yet this terrifying old woman has me quaking in my boots.*

"What will it be—the needle or the mallet? Choose."

Confusion clouds my thoughts, making it hard to form words. I can't help but wonder if she's referring to the actual objects or is it a metaphor for...something?

"Choose!" *She screeches and I jolt from the sudden change in her impatient voice. A shiver runs down my spine in protest from all of it.*

"Needle!" *I gasp, the word comes tumbling out of my mouth without me having time to consider the answer.*

Suddenly, the feeling of free falling floods my body and I scream in utter horror as I'm swallowed by an endless darkness.

I bolt up in bed, gasping for air.

Sweat covers my skin and my nightgown clings to my body. I'm shaking from head to toe. Putting my hands to my chest, I try to calm my pounding heart that's trapped underneath my ribs. Scrambling through the darkness, I tremble as my fingers comb the cluttered nightstand to find the lamp. Clumsily I manage to light it and the illuminated room dances in brutal shadows before my eyes finally adjust to the light.

It was just a dream. It was just a dream. It was just a fucking dream.

The words almost tumble from my lips as I slowly manage to catch my breath again.

"You okay?" Pipp whispers beside me, and I tense.

She's curled up behind me in a tight ball under the blanket, her hazel eyes glittering from the soft glow of the lamp.

"I'm fine, Little Bird," I say quickly. Too quickly, and I wince.

She doesn't answer me. She lays there and studies me with sharp eyes as if she's trying to decipher my inner thoughts. My little sister sees so much, too much, and she knows I'm keeping secrets from her.

She always knows.

"I'm not a child anymore, Salem," she says softly, sounding so young, but so wise for her age. She's no longer that small child asking why our mother never comes home. I remember the way she used to crawl into my arms as she cried from the endless nightmares that knocked on our doorstep during the dark nights.

She's become that bright light I've always known her to be.

I swallow, but don't answer.

"You can talk to me, you know." She insists, trying to get me to open up to her.

I sigh. "I know."

Holding out my arms, I see the sad smile in the corner of her mouth before she tucks herself into my embrace. I nuzzle my face into the silky strands of her hair and allow her hazelnut scent to calm my fraying nerves.

"What would you choose...the needle or the mallet?" I ask softly.

"What?" She lifts her head to meet my gaze, confusion glittering in her eyes. "Are you sure you're okay?"

A soft laugh slips out of me before I nod. "Yes, Little Bird, I'm sure. Now, what would you choose? I'm curious."

She takes a deep breath as she contemplates my question. Then she says with a small smile. "The needle."

I'm surprised by the relief that fills my soul with her answer.

"Because a needle can mend, but can also be a great weapon," she elaborates. "Oh, don't give me that look, you know I'm right." Her face brightens with a smirk. "Think of it. A needle dipped in poison, hidden in the right place can be just as deadly as a mallet. Besides, a mallet needs strength, a needle needs stealth."

I'm taken aback by her violence and snort out a short laugh. "You've been holding back on me, Little Bird."

"What? You're not the only one that knows how to fight," she states in a matter of fact tone that is so like her I can't help but roll my eyes. My fingers prod into her sides at their own accord and a surprised giggle slips out of her.

"Clearly," I laugh, shaking my head. She struggles against my teasing before managing to grab my wrists and stop me.

"How about you?" Pipp tilts her head to the side as she studies my face and I fall back to the pillows, letting out a heavy breath.

"I chose the needle."

She's silent for a moment, clearly waiting for me to continue my explanation. "It was just a dream, Thestepi," I say softly, tucking her silky strands behind her ear.

"From the way you were thrashing around in your sleep I would call that a Mare, or even a Hulder," she scoffs, giving me a once-over.

"Oh, hush," I scold softly.

She gives me a pointed look, lifting one single eyebrow. "Really? Are you going with that tale? You know as well as I that Mares are real."

"Pipp, they are just stories."

I roll my eyes, and Pipp sits up in bed looking down at me with a stern look. "Mares are real. They are warnings from our loved ones of darker times."

"Pipp," I sigh.

"No. You are not doing this to me, not when it was *you* that told me about them in the first place!" Her anger simmers under the surface and I can feel her turmoil getting worse.

I need to get her to calm down before she's spinning into a panic attack. "You're right, it might have been a Mare, but it might also just have been a dream." *That felt very, very real.* "But I'm sure there is nothing to worry about, Little Bird."

Her breathing calms, but I know she's not satisfied with my answer. "Tell me about this dream." She demands, and when I don't answer she continues. "What did you see?"

I drag my hand across my face and groan. "A cave. I saw a cave, and an old woman. Beetles. There were lots of beetles and she wanted me to choose between a needle and a mallet. I chose the needle and then I woke up. Happy?"

Her brows furrow. "Were you able to move your body?"

"What in the Gods names does that have to do with anything?" I ask, lifting my hand from my face to look at her.

"Answer the question."

I don't appreciate her demanding tone, but don't argue. "Yes, I was, but only in the direction the dream wanted me to go."

Her eyes flare wide in shock. "Do you think—"

"I don't know, Pipp! I don't know, and I'm really fucking scared of it. I might—" I shake my head when my nose starts to sting and I know I'm just moments away from crying. "I don't know."

This is something that I didn't want to talk to my sister about, because I'm responsible for her. I'm the oldest, the one that is supposed to have everything under control, and right now? Right now I feel like I'm losing it.

Maybe I'm going mad. Maybe I'm being haunted. Maybe I'm even getting punished by the Gods.

Or maybe, I'm about to get reaped.

Pipp lays down beside me once more and curls into my side. "It will be fine," she whispers, tucking my hair behind my ear.

The stinging intensifies and tears prickle at the corners of my eyes, and take a shaky breath. I hate crying. Especially in front of my sister. There's a reason why I went to The Pits and not her, and there's a reason why I didn't let her join The Underground when she got a little older.

It was brutal, and I didn't want her to go through more pain than she already had when our mother refused to take care of us.

"Let's talk about this tomorrow," she whispers.

The hell we will. We are not talking about this subject ever again if I can help it. "Yeah." The word tastes bitter in my mouth. "Let's just sleep."

Sleep didn't come easily for me after my dream last night, and it feels like I've been trampled by a herd of cows. I'm sore from sparring with Amadeus, and a maddening headache has settled behind my left eye from lack of sleep. The bright light pouring in through the open window has me squinting in pain.

"Lock your doors! Board your windows! The end is coming! We are all doomed!" A man shouts from the outside.

"Gods, not again," Pipp groans beside me, rolling over to her back. She opens her eyes, meeting mine and I rub the sleep out of my face.

"Freddie," we say in unison.

Our neighbor has been raving about doomsday every five years for as long as I can remember, screaming his head off as soon as the reapings starts.

"Doomed I say! Doomed! They will come from the sky! Huge monsters will come to feast on our bones!" He continues and I roll my eyes, wincing from the increased pain it causes.

"Freddie! Come back here!" A woman yells, and I assume it's one of the Cobalt Priests. They always stick their noses in other people's business behind the guise of saving the forsaken souls.

"They lurk in shadows and misery! I've seen it! I've seen it in my dreams! They will ruin us all!" Freddie screams.

I roll off the thin mattress on our floor and stagger to my feet, feeling dizzy from the splitting headache. I stumble to the window just in time to see Freddie duck away from two Cobalt Priests that chase him after him. He leaps over our fence and into the chicken coop, making both birds and feathers fly in every direction.

"Really, the chickens?" Thank Gods it wasn't the goat though. She'd be nipping at his bare feet, or...worse. He's dressed only in a dirty cloth that he's tied around his waist and I can imagine Betty the Goat nipping at his precious jewels. That would be a sight to see.

"Freddie, you are embarrassing yourself!" One of the priests chastises the half naked man in our chicken coop.

Well, she's not wrong.

With a groan, I turn away from the window, head for our front door, unlatch it, and swing it open. "Oy! Freddie leave our chickens alone, they don't like strangers. Or I will set Betty on your ass. She will go straight for your dick if I tell her to!"

To my surprise he actually jumps out of the coop for once, barely escaping capture by the two women dressed in cobalt blue. He scrambles over a haystack like a professional before he continues down the street towards the market, both women at his heel.

Huh, maybe it wasn't pointless after all.

"Poor Betty," Pipp sighs behind me, rubbing her red rimmed eyes. "I doubt she'd enjoy nibbling on his dick to be honest."

I laugh, shaking my head. "I don't think anyone would."

Pipp yawns loudly as I close the front door. "I'm sure mom would."

The day goes by in a blur.

I let out the animals, collect the eggs—the ones that Freddie didn't crush in his scuffle with the priests—and milk Betty the Goat. Then I board up the windows.

Yes, I've decided to board up the windows like a fucking coward.

Pipp keeps asking if I've lost my mind, but I ignore her questions like the plague. Occasionally, I hear the whispering voice in the distance. And by the third murmur I make the call to grab the planks from the shed.

I'm not the only one, I hear banging of hammers and nails in the distance a few places in town too.

The reaping makes everyone suspicious and on edge, even the ones that don't believe in magic or the disappearances. *Like me, though—No, stop that. It's not true.*

As soon as all the windows are boarded up, it's nearing the time when I have to get to The Pits for my upcoming fight with Amadeus. But first, I need to talk to him. I'm shaken and unraveling from it all and I have to talk to my best friend about it. Besides, our match isn't supposed to be until the end of the show, as we are the main attraction for tonight.

I have time.

"Where are you going?" Pipp asks behind me, and I almost jump out of my own skin from the sound of her voice.

"To Amadeus," I say, rubbing the center of my chest.

"You're fighting tonight aren't you?" Her presence comes closer with each step she takes and her slim body radiates a warmth I desperately need. I'm chilled to the bone from the constant dread.

I nod once in answer and pick up my new dagger, sheathing it at my ribs. Even though I won't use it, I can't stand the thought of not having it nearby.

"You knew that I was going to fight tonight though, you were there," I say, quirking an eyebrow at her in suspicion.

She just shrugs. "I was hoping you'd say something."

"About what?"

"About you, dumbass. What's going on with you? Why have you boarded up the windows? Why do you jump from every sudden noise you hear? Don't you think I haven't noticed how you rub your chest and tense up. I'm not blind, nor am I stupid. Something is going on with you and you're keeping secrets."

Breathing in deep, I consider telling her everything, but the words won't form. They get stuck in my throat and the pressure feels overwhelming, so I keep my mouth shut.

"Salem, please! Talk to me!"

My nose stings once more and I shake my head. "I got to go," I say, then I leave.

Chapter Four

"Oy, Amadeus!" I yell at his front door, banging my fist on the old wood so hard it rattles the hinges. "Open the damn door, I need to talk to you!"

I ignore the scowling people that pass by me and continue my furious assault to the door. My fried nerves are running on fumes, and I desperately need to talk to him. At this point, I might actually talk with anybody. Even my mother.

There is no answer at the door.

"Amadeus!" I yell again, banging some more.

I wait.

And I wait.

The door doesn't open. There's no sound coming from the inside of his small house. I try the door handle, but it's locked, so I peer through one of the windows at the front. Only to find the place vacant.

By the Gods...

"I'm kicking the door in! You better be decent!" I warn, giving him a moment to open up before I take several steps back to gain momentum. One kick later and the door lays in pieces on the weathered floor.

I ogle the destruction I just caused. "What the actual fuck?" My voice is no louder than a whisper.

I know I'm strong, but I'm not *that* strong. *His house is old, it's probably rotten.*

"Oy, dick head, where are you?" My voice almost seems to echo through the darkened house, which is absolutely spotless. There is no clutter anywhere, no sign of a struggle. As soon as my foot crosses the threshold, I know the house is empty.

In fact, he is nowhere near *here.*

I can't explain how I know, I just do.

I've always been able to sense him if I concentrate, ever since we made that blood pact between us all those years ago, he's somehow been a part of me.

For each step I take, my stomach sinks to the bottom of my being. My skin is slick with sweat and my tunic sticks uncomfortably to my skin by the time I reach the bedroom. I pray that my gut feeling is wrong.

"Please, please, please don't let me find him dead. Or worse..." I whisper into the stillness of the house. Finally I turn the knob and open the door to his bedroom.

It's empty, just as I feared.

The bed is the only thing that isn't neat. The blanket is thrown to the side. It almost looks like he got out of bed and then disappeared into thin air.

He's gone. He's actually gone.

Shaking, I step further into his room to have a closer look. Maybe I'll be able to find some clues of where he's disappeared to, but there isn't much to go off on. In fact, there is *nothing* to go off on as far as I can tell.

The frustration wells up in me and I walk briskly over to the bed and rip the blanket away. The blood drains from my face so fast I get dizzy when I spot it.

A single beetle lays motionless on the sheets.

I gingerly pick it up, holding it in my hand. "Amadeus?" One of its leg twitches, and the wildest thought passes through my crazy imagination.

What if—*Nope. Not going there.*

I have to be raving mad to say his name with so much hope to a fucking *beetle*. I'm staring down at it with such ferocity that I'm almost surprised it doesn't seem to have more of a reaction to my voice. "Are you—"

Shut that thought out of your stupid brain, Salem.

That beetle is just a beetle. A totally normal beetle. *That glows.* It is not, and will not ever be some kind of magic that has turned your best friend into a fucking insect.

But where the hell is he?

I wrack my brain and flip through my memory from yesterday. He seemed... *fine!* Yes, he seemed a bit more tired than normal, but nothing out of the ordinary? He might have been a bit more snappy than usual, but that's not uncommon when he has a lot on his mind. I think back to the way he was stumbling over his legs, and the way he squinted his eyes. So much so that he had to cover them from the sun. He didn't mention any headaches, but when we talked about the possibility of him getting reaped, it almost seemed like he didn't care. Or maybe...*he knew.*

My nose starts to sting, and tears prickle behind my eyes. I'm shaking from the effort not to cry. *I will not fucking cry.* Desperation has me scanning the room for *any* clues to where he might have disappeared to.

He's gone.

My best friend is *gone.*

He's been chosen by...what exactly? We know *not nearly enough* about the disappearances that plague this cursed land, other than it happens every five years during the summer. It, whatever *it* is, targets the young adults from the age of twenty to twenty five. That's also the reason why most people don't get children, get married or enter any type of committed relationships until *after* we know for a fact we're *safe!*

Amadeus was supposed to be safe! He wasn't supposed to get taken!

It's unfair. Especially since his sister got taken five years ago.

I won't stand for it.

Panic tugs at me, pushing at my ribs as I stagger back a step, almost stumbling into the doorframe. I drop the beetle to the floor and watch it scurry away from me.

I feel sick. A rush of nausea washes over me like a tidal wave and I have to bend over as I dry heave through my sudden panic.

He's gone. He's actually gone.

The tears win, and they start to flow freely down my pale cheeks.

Rage crashes into me right after, and I grab a hold of the nightstand beside the bed and throw it half way across the room. It breaks into multiple pieces, a drawer spills open. The contents scattering across the floor.

Amongst them I spot a quill, a vial of ink and a journal. My eyes zero in on the journal and my heart seems to halt in my chest before it starts to pound uncontrollably against my ribcage. Within that journal lies his most inner thoughts. It feels so wrong to read it, but by this point I'm desperate.

Slowly, I walk over to it and pick it up. My hands are shaking. Maybe he recorded something that can give me any clues to where to find him, or figure out what happened to him.

I open the journal and read from the last page. I feel the blood drain from my face and ice floods my veins.

"She's back. The Old Lady from last night."

Quickly, I flip the page to the entry before the last one and start to read. By the time I'm finished reading it...I'm one hundred percent sure that I'll be one of the chosen ones to disappear.

And I know exactly who I need to talk to.

The horrid smell of incense and drugs permeates my nostrils, overwhelming my senses. The atmosphere here is vastly different from my neighborhood in Ador's Cliff, but that has always been the case of the slums of Ghostport.

Here, the streets no longer feel welcoming and lively but dingy and abysmal. Occasional grunts and moans fill the air as I walk closer to the alleyway.

I tune out the simmering emotions that stir under my skin as I reach the entrance to the brothel. Next to the front door a man is caging a woman in with his big frame. Her skirt is haphazardly bunched up around her waist from his hand. Her corset loosened to give better access to her voluptuous breasts, showing off her inviting cleavage.

I look away, holding my head high to make sure I won't back out of what I have to do—the conversation I need to have.

As I push open the door, the stench becomes more intense, and I stifle a cough. Wrinkling my nose, I try my best to ignore it.

The brothel isn't packed, it never is, and yet there are more people here than I would expect there to be. Most of them are either high, or drunk off their asses. I try not to look too closely at anyone as I enter, but I have to admit that it's a little difficult to ignore all the naked women in the room. They all seem to bask in their own sensuality, something I've always envied these women for. The way they move like water nymphs in a gentle stream.

At my right, a woman moans loudly just as the door closes behind me. She's bouncing on a burley man's lap with her back turned to him, squeezing her breasts as her face twists in pleasure.

It's not real.

The pitch in her voice is all wrong.

My eyes move involuntarily to where they connect. I can see the base of his cock when she lifts her body for a second before she slams down again, pushing his length deeper. The obvious force she uses to push down onto him tells me that he's too small for her liking.

Another naked woman comes sauntering up to me, pushing her tits in my face.

"Can I be of any service to you today?" She slurs, and I lean my head away from her. She's so close that I can almost taste the musk smell of seed on her.

"I'm looking for Diana," I say to her, standing my ground.

I meet her glassy eyes, as she looks me up and down with interest. I see a glint of hunger enter her gaze.

"Oh, isn't she a little old for you?" She smirks as she takes a lock off my silvery hair and twirls it around her finger.

I raise an eyebrow in response.

"Is she here?" I ask.

Pouting, she tugs a little on the lock and I grab her wrist and squeeze down on it. "Hands off. Now, tell me where to find my mother."

Her eyes widen and she immediately stumbles a step back, wincing a little from my grip. "Salem," she breathes, finally recognizing me. Letting go of her wrist, I quirk an eyebrow and wait.

"Yes, yes, of course," she says hurriedly, shaking herself a little. The whore straightens, turns and motions for me to follow after her. I do just that and she leads me to the back. Now and again, she turns her head to the side to look back at me, which is understandable considered my reputation. But I'm not going to hurt her. Not unless she gives me a reason to.

We enter a hallway with row after row of beaded curtains. Here, the sound of moaning and grunting is almost too much. Closing my eyes for a moment, I take the time to compose myself.

I hate this place.

We walk down the corridor and I glance to a couple of openings where men empty themselves into the whores as they moan for the sake of it.

There's a reason why I try to stay away from this place as much as possible. Not just because of all the gross smells, or the unwanted attention I get from the women. It's mostly because of the mother I loathe.

This is where she wanted me and Pipp to *work*.

I'm fuming by the time the whore in front of me stops at a curtain and I can hear my mother's fake pleasure fill the room as an older man fucks her. The chain around her ankle clinks as it hits the floor from his thrusts. I drag the beaded curtain away and step inside the tiny room.

I glare down my nose at them in disgust.

"Get out."

The man doesn't stop, he just pounds into my mother even harder.

"Oh, for fucks sake," I growl as I lunge and grab the man by the back of his neck. I yank him away from her and he slips out with a nauseating pop.

"Hi, *mom*."

My mother screams in utter horror from seeing me, confusion lacing her hazy eyes until recognition finally settles in.

"Salem," she says, slurring over my name. She covers herself with a silk robe, which probably is the only decent piece of clothing she owns. The room she's chained to is utterly disgusting. "What are you doing here, *dear*?"

"Looking for you," I snort.

"What the fuck do you think you're doing? I paid for an hour, I'm not done," the man protests in anger.

Slowly, I turn to look at him with a frosty gaze, my glacier-colored eyes piercing his terrified stare. "Look, I don't give a flying fuck if you paid for a week with my mother. I need to talk to her, and you need to get the fuck out of my sight."

His angry growl doesn't scare me. I know who he is, and I know he doesn't stand a chance against me.

Still, his common sense seems to be slow to kick in, because he fists his hands and opens his mouth to speak. I interrupt him before he gets the chance to even finish the first intake of breath. "Listen, Steve, I know very well who you are and how you chose to spend your money. And whilst you make poor decisions by burying your small dick inside my mothers cunt, you do in fact have a wife and four young children at home that deserve better than the likes of you. I'm sure you have better places to be, don't you?"

He sputters for a moment before he shakes his head slowly and gets up from the floor. He's grumbling angry words underneath his breath that I don't care to register as he puts his trousers back on and leaves.

I scoff after him before I turn to my mother.

The silver bracelet around her ankle that has her chained to the wall clinks softly as she pulls her robe closer around her. It doesn't help, it slips down one of her shoulders immediately to reveal several bruises on her pale skin.

The chain rustles, and I stare down at it with disdain. "How long this time?"

Diana lifts the garment up her shoulder, trying to cover herself up some more, but she can't really hide the fact that she's naked underneath the robe. It's incredibly short, it barely covers anything at all.

"A month, maybe two?" Her voice is hesitant, but she lifts her head just a fraction in defiance.

I narrow my eyes. "How long?"

My mother swallows, avoiding my eyes.

"Six months," she finally says, crossing her arms across her chest indignantly.

"For fuck's sake, mother...six months? What about Pipp?" I ask her.

"What about her?" My mother retorts, curling into a ball on the dirty mattress on the floor.

"What about—mother, she's nineteen! Not to mention the reaping has started," I say, flinging an arm out to get her attention, a reaction. *Anything!*

My mother pales, her eyes flicker to one direction before she pins her gaze at my feet.

I sigh, and crouch down, tilt my head slowly to the side and seek eye contact.

"Mom," I say in a softer tone, and she flinches.

"You're better off without me," she says, diverting her gaze away, fixing it at some random spot on the wall.

I close my eyes, leaning my head back in defeat. Fighting traitorous tears.

"Mom, I'm going to be taken," I say to the ceiling.

I sense more than see my mother clench up, then she nods. Once.

"I know." There is some bite to her voice now, but barely. "Why do you think I've been such a shit mother to you girls? You're both going to be taken," she says, still staring at the wall. "I've known since the day you were born."

The air seems to leave my lungs and I struggle to find the words. "What? You–you knew?"

"I didn't see the point in telling you."

"You didn't—What the fuck, mom? Why didn't you tell me? I could have—" I break off, not finding the right words. Anger billows inside me, hot and furious. Still, I force myself to ask. "How did you know?"

"It doesn't take a genius to note that every even number reaping takes all the people born on an even number, and the odd numbered reaping takes the people born on an odd numbered day." She finally meets my gaze...her eyes feel distant, though not as hazy as before. Now they almost seem to shine with malice.

"There are exceptions though. You see, I'm an odd number. I was supposed to get reaped in 1305, but I was already pregnant with *you*. Your father on the other hand was reaped, because men don't get pregnant, obviously," she spits.

Clenching my jaw, I inhale deeply as my body starts to shake from the effort of holding it all together. My mother doesn't seem to notice my struggle and continues. "You see, the magic that transports the chosen one can't take them both. Instead of killing off the abomination in the womb, it takes none."

My heart breaks from her harsh words. The pain comes gradually, like a simmering fire spreading through my veins. Is *this* the reason my mother always resented me? Is *this* the reason she always hated me? Why she neglected me almost to the point of death?

I struggle to breathe through the pain and the rage, and it is no longer just my nose that stings, but my eyes *hurt* from the unshed tears.

It dawns on me that my mother might have wanted to replace me with my sister, but apparently when she was born she was— "What did you say? Is Pipp also going to get reaped?" My voice spills over with emotion.

Looking at my mother, I see the glee in her eyes. Her posture has changed, and she looks almost elated. Like she hasn't allowed herself to be...relieved at the fact that both of her children will get reaped. Then it dawns on me what she implied.

"Why didn't you tell me that there was a loophole? Why didn't you tell me that there was a chance of not getting reaped?" My voice has become almost shrill from all my pent up emotions. "You never gave me a choice!"

My mother stands up so fast that I don't even realize her movement until she slaps me hard across my face. My head whips to the side, leaving me dizzy. When I finally manage to look at her again, her eyes brim with barely controlled anger.

She reeks of sweat and cum and she has a tiny split in her bottom lip that I didn't see until now.

"Because I wanted to get rid of you both."

The taste of iron crosses my tongue, as the heat from the sting burns my cheek. Slowly, I turn my gaze to my mother. She's breathing heavily with her own emotions. The fact that this woman is my mother has bile rising in my throat.

"Then what about Pipp?" I whisper, and a single tear trickles down my cheek, soothing the sting her hand left.

"I'm not suited to be a mother," she snorts. "Besides, my Master won't allow me to have children."

"But you do have children! Two of them, in fact!"

"Not anymore," she responds. "Get out."

It's like another slap to my face. My lip trembles, and unshed tears blur my vision as I somehow manage to stand up straight. When I'm finally composed enough to move, I turn around and walk away.

Chapter Five

As soon as I enter the arena I can hear the buzzing from the crowd, it's muffled through the chamber wall, but it's still loud enough to hear that the fight that's already going on is entertaining enough for them.

"Where the fuck have you been? Never mind, you are up next, with Tegner since I haven't seen Amadeus," Heason says as soon as he sees me.

"He's not coming," I respond, and I can tell that it throws him off by his expression.

"What do you mean, he's not coming?"

I take a steadying breath before I speak. "He got reaped." My voice breaks, and I just want to scream. I hate the fact that I'm teary and shaken from the events of the day. I don't know how long I can keep everything contained.

The man blanches, and his face goes a shade paler. A moment later he clears his throat and hands me two strips of fabric. A curse leaves his lips, and it makes my heart ache even more.

"Yeah," I breathe. With shaking fingers I wrap the first strip around my knuckles, then the other. Wait, what did he say?

"Back up a bit, are you matching me up against *Tegner!?*" I protest on a squeak.

"Yes, that's what I said. Are you able to fight?" His voice has softened, and I clench my jaw before nodding.

"Of course," I say. I was late, as I always am. It's not that I have much of a choice really.

Tegner. I'm up against fucking *Tegner.*

"Then what are you waiting for? Get ready."

I'm frozen to the spot, my heart starts pounding in my chest with nerves. I haven't gone up against Tegner in over three months, and that time I got my ass handed to me so bad I wasn't able to take on another opponent for almost five weeks. I'm not ready to take him on again.

Heason gives me a reassuring nod.

Well, shit. Just, shit.

I hitch my shoulders up, inhale deeply and let it out in a slow calming breath. "Fine, where is he, is he ready?"

This is not going to go well for me, and I'm already preparing myself for a defeat.

"Ready when you are." A low gravelly voice says behind me, and I can hear the smirk on his smug face. Slowly, I turn to meet his gaze, trying my best to not reveal the tremble in my body. I swallow and nod.

"Good," I force myself to smile. "Let's give them a show they will remember shall we?" I ask, looking up at him. The slow grin that spreads across his face makes a shiver run down my spine.

"That sounds like a perfect plan."

I'm so fucked.

"Ladies and gentlemen, the moment we have all been waiting for," The announcer shouts to the crowd, railing them up for the main event. "A fighter we all know and love. She's ruthless. Our own little Grimm Reaper," He continues, and I roll my eyes.

As soon as my foot touches the first step my stomach lurches and the sensation of ice runs down my spine.

Oh, no.

Saaaleeem.

No, no, no.

That voice. I know that whisper.

Not now. Not now. Not now!

"Salem Vanroda!" The announcer shouts, ending my presentation as he turns in my direction.

For a moment I just stand there, frozen. Not remembering what I'm doing there. My vision blurs, and I can feel some sort of tug to my core.

The same sensation from the dream last night pulls on my chest, making that invisible thread tighten. It feels like it's about to yank me out of my own body, and I have a sinking feeling that it will. I also have a strong suspicion of *where* it will take me.

My splitting headache gets even worse, and I gasp.

Not now, old lady, I'm busy!

The deafening sounds from the crowd fall away slowly, fading into the background and are replaced with water droplets echoing inside my head.

On the other side of the ring, I see Tegner walk up his steps as the announcer makes his introduction. His arms lifted in the air he encourages the crowd to cheer even louder, a cheer I can't hear. All the sounds have faded away to nothing, replaced with the ominous echo in my mind.

Slowly, the thread holding me gets pulled even tighter, making me stumble a step.

By the Gods, this is such bad timing for a visit to the cave. As soon as that thought hits me, the thread gets pulled taught, and I gasp in horror as the image of Tegner and the arena dissolves in front of me. It morphs into the dark entrance of the cave from my dreams.

Well, fuck.

The pulsing energy from The Cave wafts towards me in waves. It almost feels like a heartbeat coming from the deep.

This time I don't hesitate as I take the first step, forcing the glow beetles to scurry away from my furious steps.

The sound of dripping water envelopes me, along with the echo of my feet as I walk the long passage into the heart of the cave.

It opens up to reveal The Old Lady with her elongated nose stuck in the tree stump.

"This is fucking bad timing," I complain to The Old Lady, flinging my arms out.

As I study the woman, I realize that beside her, there is a basket filled with half molded bread and a mug of something that looks like mead.

"So, what will it be, Salem Vanroda?" The Old Lady ignores my complaints. I just look at her patiently. But the lady doesn't continue.

I groan in frustration. "What?"

The Old Lady smiles down towards the petrified stump. "Short tempered, are we?" She chuckles softly.

"Yes, today I am. Everything is going to shit, so, please get to the fucking point."

"Fine," her voice sounds as old as she looks, or, older, maybe.

"The map or the valley? Choose," she says, and I can hear the smile in her voice.

"The what or the what?" I'm stumped. What does that even mean? Is there a reason behind her choices or are they random objects she's forcing me to choose between. I try to give it some thought, but don't get far in my thought process as she interrupts it with a screech.

"Choose!"

Frustrated I pick the first option, because I can't fucking deal with this annoying woman right now. I have a man's ass to kick back in my own reality, or rather, he's about to kick mine.

"As you wish," *she chuckles and reaches for the half molded bread in the basket beside her.*

"Oh, Gods, please don't," *I start to say but before I'm able to finish my sentence the feeling of free fall envelops my senses and overwhelms me. The darkness rises, and pulls me under.*

Just like last time.

Unlike last time, I'm met head on with a fist to my face from Tegner's right hook. I stumble backwards, almost tripping on my own two feet. Thankfully, I manage to keep myself upright, just in time for the next attack from the enormous man in front of me.

A growl of anger and frustration comes tumbling out of me as I fucking lose my shit.

Tegner is almost twice my size, he's stronger and has more experience than I have, naturally he does. Not to mention, he's much, much taller than me. I don't even reach his collarbone. I don't quite understand why Heason paired us up tonight. He could have chosen literally anyone, but he just had to pick Tegner, of all people. What was he even thinking?

With Amadeus, it makes sense. We're pretty equally matched. Yes, he's taller than me, but he's leaner. Not to mention our skill level is pretty much the same. Tegner is a fucking bull of a man compared to my best friend.

Before I know it, I have one of his arms hooked around my neck and his chest pressed up against my back.

"Where did you go?" He hisses into my ear.

"What?" I grab his arm with both of mine, trying to get out of it. I struggle against the hold, but I can't escape.

"Where did you go just now?" He repeats, and I get the sense he doesn't like having to repeat himself from the way he slows it down and ennunciates every single word.

"I didn't—"

"Don't even start with me. Your eyes went all golden and weird, and you didn't react to anything. It was like you weren't even here," he almost growls into my ear.

I try my best to break from his hold, I throw my head back, clocking him in the jaw. He gives an annoyed grunt in return, but I'm absolutely helpless in his hold.

"Don't lie to me, Salem," he bites out.

"I have no idea what you're talking about," I grunt, as I wriggle against him, trying to hit back at him. Throwing my legs up, but there is no point. Tegner is just too big, too *good*.

I'm suddenly aware of the crowd. They're booing and throwing objects and food down to the mat where me and Tegner are fighting. No, he's handling me. Because I'm not fucking good enough to beat him.

"Be truthful with me, Salem. I'll ask this once more," He warns through his teeth against my ear. "What's up with you?"

My body goes slack in his bulky arms and dread settles in my bones. This might be nothing to worry about, but if I'm right...

"I'm going to get reaped." It comes out as the defeated whisper it is. "And I need to win this for Pipp," my voice doesn't even sound like my own with all the pleading lacing my words.

Tegner doesn't react with words though. Instead, his other arm slides across my midsection and he squeezes me gently towards his chest. Like a...hug.

Is he really *hugging* me? I think he is.

This huge beast of a man is actually hugging me, instead of continuing this fight we're supposed to have, he's in fact showing me affection. I refuse to put too much thought into that. Honestly, I'm not sure how to handle this kind of behavior. It's not natural to me.

Then he loosens his grip, making it possible for me to twist away from him, and a cheer erupts from the crowd. I swing around to face him, taking up a defensive stance. He gives me a minuscule nod, and it throws me off for a second.

Is he...?

Oh, shit.

He's tossing the fight, giving me the win.

I just have to work for it, and give the crowd a show.

And that's exactly what I do.

Chapter Six

"There you are, I've been looking everywhere for you," Pipp says when she finds me, hours later. "Thought you would come straight home after the fight, what are you doing—," She takes a sharp intake of breath. "What's wrong? Why are you *reading?*"

I look up from the book I'm holding, and her eyes are wide with concern. She takes a step towards me, almost like she's approaching a wounded animal.

"Salem," her voice is calm, and I can imagine the picture I'm making. I'm sitting hunched over stacks of old books and ledgers of the disappeared ones, tucked in at the tiny library in our town. Which to be fair isn't much bigger than half the size of our small house, with a few shelves and a handful of books.

"How hard did you hit your head tonight?" She asks. My frown deepens, because I didn't actually hit my head tonight. At least not *that* hard.

"I'm fine."

"And still. You're holding a book," she stares at the book I'm holding in my trembling hands. The paper is damp and smells a little stale. I'm pretty sure the roof is leaking.

"Did you know that there are dragons in this world?" I ask, pointing to the drawing on the open page. "It's says here that they existed alongside us over a thousand years ago, not only them, but all sorts of magical creatures that roamed our world and—,"

"What in the Gods' names are you talking about? Dragons?" Pipp takes the book from my hands and flips the pages before looking to me with a strange expression. She blinks, and I frown when I realize that she's looking at me with...pity. "Listen, dragons aren't real."

"Oh, but Mares are?" I retort, pinning her with my angry glare. She blinks, opening her mouth before closing it shut. Her jaw ticks and I scowl at her when her expression softens.

"Have you ever seen a dragon?"

"Have you ever seen a Mare?" I ask immediately.

Pipp sighs before she shakes her head. "Listen, Mares are said to be shadows that come to you at night. They sit on-top of your chest while you sleep and force warnings to you while you dream. Dragons on the other hand are said to be huge creatures that fly in the sky and destroy villages. Tell me, have you ever seen a whole village burn down? Ever seen a huge creature in the sky?"

I shake my head slowly, because I haven't. But that doesn't mean they don't exist. Looking down at my feet I force a steadying breath into my lungs and fixate on a tiny beetle crawling over a book on the floor. Before I'm able to open my mouth to tell her anything at all she starts speaking again. "Besides, there's nothing written on these pages."

I freeze.

"What do you mean?" I take the book from her and flip the pages, thoroughly confused when I see the tiny scribbled handwriting, as well as the depictions of different creatures on the page. "What on earth are you talking about? It's all here," I say, flipping to a page and pointing to a drawing of a creature that looks to be half bird-half lion.

Pipp looks from me, to the page, and back to me again. "There's nothing there, Salem. They're blank," she says softly, and the tone in her voice almost makes me flinch. There's definitely pity in her voice.

"It's not, I swear!" I flip to another page and show her a horse with wings. I see her eyes flicker to the book, then to me again. And her expression is like a punch to the gut.

"Look, you were in a fight, you hit your head pretty hard," she says and takes a tentative step towards me, lifting her hand to my temple. When she takes her hand away from my skin I see crimson blood on her fingertips.

Maybe...maybe she's right? Looking down at the book, my vision goes blurry for a moment. No, it's not my vision that's the problem. The text seems to blur together into shadowy blobs on the page before slowly disappearing, then there's nothing. Not even a shade of ink left.

I can hardly believe what I'm seeing, did I just imagine everything? What is going on here? Am I losing my mind?

Fear settles in my bones, and chills spread down my back. I'm on the verge of tears yet again. I feel like I'm about to unravel at the seams of my own sanity. First the shaking ground and the voice in my head. Then the dream that sent me into a near panic attack. Not to mention the hallucination in the fighting ring, but... Tegner *did* say that my eyes went all golden and weird. And now this vanishing text.

"Let's go home," Pipp says softly as she slowly takes my hand.

"I talked to mom," I blurt, surprising even myself with the words. The grimace on her face makes me almost feel guilty, but I have to tell her about this. "There is a way to not get reaped."

"What do you mean?" Pipp tugs on my hand again, trying to pull me along, but I stand my ground.

"Mom told me that she was supposed to get reaped, and that she didn't because she was pregnant with me. I think that might be why she's been like...you know..."

"Sure, but what I don't understand is why you're telling me all of this," she sounds almost scared. "I don't understand Salem, you're not making any sense."

My eyes snag on a second beetle, crawling along one of the shelves. Then a third on one of the chairs. There's a nearly perceptible glow to them as they slowly flap their translucent wings.

"Oh, here," I say and push the leather pouch filled with coins into her hand. She tries to push it towards me, but I shake my head. "Take it."

"What is going on with you? Tell me!" Her eyes are wide and brimming with fear. It breaks my heart to see her like this, but I can't focus on that right now.

In my peripheral I see another beetle on one of the ledgers on the table.

"Listen to me, Thestepi," I shake her shoulders, pain shooting up the arm of my abused body. "*You* have a choice. If you get pregnant before your reaping, it won't take you. Then you will be safe." My words come fast now and her face gradually shifts from fear to sheer terror as what I'm telling her slowly dawns on her. "The first winter will get hard if you don't prepare for it. I know it's too late now, but do as much trading as you can when the fall comes. Okay?"

She starts to shake her head, and I gently cup her face with my trembling hands. I let my eyes trace her beautiful face, memorizing her features. Her porcelain skin. Her hazel brown eyes. Her light brown hair. The small bow on her upper lip. The dimple in her cheek.

"You will be fine, you hear me?" A low hum of small wings gradually fills the room and I know I don't have much more time with my sister. "If you need help, go to the underground—"

"No! No, you're lying!" Pipp interrupts me and a sob breaks out through her lips.

"Oh, my Little Bird," I pull her in for a hug, trying to calm her. She trembles in my arms, and tears trickle down my cheeks. "I wish I was. I wish with all of my heart that this was a lie."

Something touches my leg, and I feel it crawl upwards.

"If you don't want to get reaped, get pregnant before the next one, and you will be safe. I promise," I say.

"I don't care...you...you can't leave me," Pipp cries. "I need you."

I manage to stifle a sob that threatens to break free. "You don't need me, Little Bird, I'm the one that needs you." My feet are covered in the same tickling sensation, and as I look down, they are covered by crawling insects. They're making their way up my body and I can no longer see my lower half.

Sensing that Pipp's gaze followed mine, I look up again and see that I'm right. "Don't look down, eyes on me," I say, forcing strength into my voice.

A sob wracks her body as the beetles slowly engulf me, and I know I can't get away from them. I know that this will be the last time I see my sister.

"Survive without me," I whisper.

"I can't—,"

"You can, and you will," I interrupt her. "I love you."

The beetles have reached my face, and the thread at my core is pulled taught, before something yanks on it.

Panic fills her eyes. She screams my name just as my stomach drops, and I fall through the floor. I'm free falling through Nothing for what feels like ages. Her scream echoes through my head before I come to an abrupt stop.

The sound from my fall bounces off the rugged stone walls along with a steady rhythm of water droplets. Pain shoots through my body, and I struggle to take a breath. I'm dizzy, disoriented and utterly heartbroken.

She's gone.

And all I'm left with is the memory of her fear, and the sound of anguish in her parting scream.

Slowly, I get to my feet, feeling my body tremble from exertion and pain.

The book that I held is laying beside me on the ground. I didn't realize it came through with me since I dropped it when I held my sister. As I bend down to pick it up, I sense that I'm not alone and look up to see the old crone from my dreams.

My stomach sinks.

The Old Lady stands in front of me, smiling down at her tree stump, chuckling softly. I take a deep breath to steady myself. Grabbing the book, I cradle it against my chest like it's a lifeline, and a tiny sob slips out from my lips.

"Why?" It comes out as a mangled scream, my knees almost buckling beneath me.

"You were chosen," she explains with a smile. "Along with all the others." Her voice still hides that tiny bite of cold. A menacing sound that gnaws on me in all the wrong ways.

"Now my child," she says. "One last question, Salem Vanroda, what will it be?" she asks in a withering voice.

"Both," I say immediately, not even bothering to listen to her question. If there is in fact a way to not get reaped, this might just be it.

The Old Lady chuckles in response. "Are you sure?"

"Yes. Both," I say with confidence.

The smile in her voice is evident, but I don't understand why. And I get the feeling that I won't like the outcome. "Have it your way."

"Wait, what is the question?" I ask, but The Old Lady just waves her hand and a searing pain engulfs me. Golden threads of light shoot from her fingertips, latching onto my left arm.

A scream of absolute agony is ripped out of my chest as the threads tangle around it, wrapping themselves around the limb. Then they bore through the skin. It burns, like what I imagine a branding would. Pain is all I can focus on, and the scream that leaves my body is almost deafening.

When the pain finally dissipates, a golden pattern is left behind under my skin. A swirly pattern in different shades of gold. It moves like a living painting of floral depictions creeping down my forearm.

Wind picks up around me, and I stumble. I try to keep my footing but it's impossible.

"Hold your breath, Salem, and fight for your life," her cackling laugh fills the cave, making my hairs stand on end.

"Good luck," she sings, then she waves her hand at me. A strong gust of wind sweeps me off my feet and I'm blown into the cave wall, going through it.

Before I can take another breath, I'm plunged into ice cold *water*.

Chapter Seven

The cold hits me like a shockwave.

It's a painful reminder of my bodily state. The wounds sting from the algae in the murky water, and I realize that I do in fact have more injuries than what I initially thought. There is one in particular that has me worried—the one at the back of my shoulder blade.

While it normally isn't allowed to use weapons in the Underground, now and again we do end up bending the rules. Since I knew I would get reaped anyways, we made the snap decision to be rebels. At this very moment, I regret that. Not the fight, just the getting hurt part.

Forcing my eyes open, despite the blurry vision it gives me, I try to orient myself. All around me there are moving blobs with flailing arms and legs. The realization that I'm not the only one that is fighting the icy waters gives me some semblance of relief.

Above me, I see shimmering lights. The surface. I have to reach the surface.

Kicking my feet I start to swim upward, I move my arms over my head to help push through the water. My lungs start to burn along with the annoying sting at my back.

Suddenly, something wraps around my ankle, and I scream. The remaining air in my lungs disappears in huge bubbles in front of me before I feel myself being pulled down.

My heart jumps, and my gut sinks. Fear follows, accompanied with an understanding that I might very well die in this murky water. I try to kick at whatever has me trapped. It's soft and slick with small rugged spikes that almost tickle without hurting. Why that is important to my brain while I'm drowning I have no idea, it just is.

I need to breathe.

Something huge obscures my vision and this enormous circle gets closer to my body. Terror grips me, as the glowing thing *blinks*.

It's *alive*. It's a fucking creature.

Oh, holy Gods, I'm dead. I'm absolutely dead.

I need to breathe.

My left arm starts to burn, and all of a sudden the golden threads underneath my skin light up, illuminating the enormous creature in front of me. It's blackish in the murky water, and huge tentacles spurt from its body.

Holy Gods. It's a kraken.

I need to breathe.

Black spots dance in my vision as the enormous creature drags me deeper. Frantically, I try to tug my leg out of its hold. Grasping the new dagger Heason made that I keep at my ribs, I see the shimmering gold pattern in the metal. A pattern that stirs my memory, but I don't have time for that now.

I need to breathe.

My lungs are on fire.

I take the dagger and slice at the thing holding me. The grip loosens and I manage to yank my foot free from its grasp. The water vibrates around me, and if I'm not mistaken, that attack just made everything much worse. Something grabs my arm, and I feel the pull, then the stretch of the ligament.

I need to breathe, but instead I scream silently through the pain when it's wrenched out of its socket.

I can't breathe, but I *have to*.

Icy water rushes down my throat, filling my lungs.

I'm so fucked. I'm so utterly fucked I can't even... *The pain is blinding*. It radiates from my shoulder, the multitude of wounds on my body, and my lungs. I can feel my fingers start to tingle. Frantically, I somehow manage to sheath my dagger, even if my movements have turned sluggish.

I try to stay conscious, I really do, but the darkness engulfs me in the end, just as something grabs my arm and pulls.

Air.

Precious air floods my lungs.

There's a slight pressure against my numb lips, a tingling sensation that lingers as the air is pushed down my throat. Water rattles inside my lungs.

Solid ground digs into my back, biting into my flesh as someone press down at the center of my chest. Over and over again. This body doesn't feel like my own, but I know that it is.

More air, and again that tingle settles on my lips. Something intangible slides into place far away.

"Breathe damn it." The low growl above me makes the hairs on my arms rise, and how I'm able to register that sensation I have no idea. "Breathe woman!" Another push at my chest and water drips into my face.

As my senses slowly trickle back to me, I feel the pressure from inside my lungs and I think I gag, but I'm not sure. Something hard slams into my chest and it jolts me back to reality.

Turning to my side, I heave the churning water out of my lungs. It sputters out of my mouth in large blotches of liquid.

Beside me, I sense someone slump back in relief. "There you go. Just breathe." A firm hand settles on my back, patting me. Somehow, the touch is comforting and soothing. Two things I'm not used to feeling.

The skin on my left arm feels tight, like someone has bound it with rope and tugs on it. I gasp in pain and his hand disappears like I hurt him. It sure sounds like it from the pained hiss he makes. "What the fuck..?"

I turn my head to look at my savior—ugh, that thought makes me want to cringe. I don't like the idea of needing to be rescued in any way, shape or form.

I'm caught off guard from the sight of him, and a chill runs down my spine.

In front of me is a stranger that feels so familiar I almost want to cry in relief. Everything from his jawline to his deep forest green eyes feels familiar to me. Even the scar on his chin, it's almost as if I can picture what left it. His hair is wet, wild, and has a coppery shade to it, even soaked. His clothes cling to his body, revealing wide shoulders and muscular forearms.

I blink.

"You," I breathe. Then I shake my head. Because I don't know this man. I have never met him before, I would have remembered him.

"You," his jaw slackens as he seems to get lost in my eyes. The moment is stretched to an infinity, spinning around in a circle and I get the same feeling as before of something intangible sliding into place.

"You saved me. Why?"

The moment breaks, and he stares at me like I've lost my mind. "Excuse me? I do believe a thank you would suffice." He tugs down the sleeve on his left arm, and my eyes snag on the golden flora adorning it. I blink as it moves under his skin.

Somehow, the depiction is a perfect blend between masculine and feminine.

The same pattern swirls under my own skin.

Before I'm able to get a better look at the impressive mark, it's already hidden under his sleeve. As the spell is broken, I look up at him, drowning in the green of his eyes.

With a frown I say. "Thank you?"

He scoffs and mutters something that sounds an awful lot like "ungrateful bitch", and my hackles rise.

"Excuse you?" I glare at him, and his eyes grow cold.

"Yes, I do think I should be excused," he says, but it feels like he's slapped me across my face for some reason. "You just had me jumping back into that water to save your sorry ass."

I recoil from his words. How dare he?

I'm about to start yelling at him that it was absolutely not my fault that he jumped back into that lake, how the fuck could I have known what he would do? I was busy drowning. But my body chooses that moment to register the trauma it just went through.

The pain flares like a kindle to a flame, and the burning in my lungs makes me bend over in a coughing fit.

Lovely.

Someone slaps me hard in the middle of my back, probably the stranger that saved me, and a choked scream escapes my throat. The pain from my dislocated shoulder is so bad it almost has me immobilized.

Shame colors my cheeks, and yet I manage to force out a response through my fit. "I didn't make you do shit." It sounds strangled, weak, and it only makes me angry.

"Oh, really?" His voice is so low that it resembles a growl, close to my ear and as I look up he's crouched down beside me with a hand at my back. "If it wasn't you, then that golden curse on your arm did."

The audacity of this man!

Boiling with anger, I move without thinking. "Take your hands off me." My threat is dripping with venom, and I press the tip of my dagger to his throat. "Or you bleed."

I sense more than see his slow smirk, before he chuckles softly against the side of my head. "Trouble…" The word is spoken so softly that I feel it on my skin like a whispered caress.

A familiar voice calls out my name, but I don't take my eyes off the stranger, or the dagger away from his throat. Instead I press the tip fractionally upward, until I see a bead of crimson gather where it touches the skin. "Back. The. Fuck. Up."

His lips are just a breath away, and I watch with horrid fascination as a smile slowly spreads across his face, revealing a slight dimple at his right cheek. It makes his eyes glitter with an emotion I can't quite place.

Hatred? Fascination? Adoration? Lust?

To be fair, it could be all of the above, but all I can think is… Fuck, he's got a dimple.

"My, my," He murmurs as his gaze drops to my lips. "This is going to be fun."

What. The. Fuck.

Again someone calls out my name, closer this time, and I turn to look in that direction, only to feel my heart stop. Relief slams into me as I see him. "Amadeus!" He pushes through the crowd of people, and I manage to get to my feet. My knees threaten to buckle under my own weight as my best friend sweeps me off my feet in a bone crushing hug.

"Shit, Salem, are you okay?" He puts me back to my feet and surveys my face, and his expression softens. "Oh, Salem, I'm fine. Don't cry," he says, mistaking my tears for concern for him and not the excruciating pain he just caused. "Fuck, you got reaped too, how... Do you know how many? Do you have any idea of where we are? What—What the fuck is that!?"

I watch his jaw fall open and his eyes go wide. He's staring at something behind me and I turn to see a huge tentacle shoot from the water, and in its grasp...a screaming girl. We're frozen in place as the enormous creature surfaces and a gaping pit opens up in the middle of the lake.

Then the girl falls.

I shut my eyes as her screams bounce off the surrounding mountains.

"By the Seven Gods," I hear Amadeus whisper behind me.

Not everyone makes it.

Some drown.

Others get killed by a monster.

No wonder the stranger was so pissed after jumping into the water for a second time to save me. But I didn't ask him to. It wasn't my fault.

I dare a glance in his direction, only to see that his attention is solely on me. A muscle ticks in his jaw, and for some reason his glowering stare and furious expression are so breathtaking I have to concentrate on my next inhale.

"Did the old woman come to you too? She plagued me for two days." The interruption breaks the moment and I look to Amadeus before I nod. "She did. It started the day you disappeared."

A crease appears on his forehead. "I just got out of the water a minute ago."

I shake my head no. "You were reaped two days ago, at the new moon's peak."

"That can't be right, I—" he shakes his head, as if to get out of some kind of fog. "I swear I was just shoved through that wall..." He trails off, and really, it doesn't matter.

We got reaped.

Our lives back in Terrby no longer exist. All we are to them now are memories, and a name on a scroll.

Heason, Tegner, Freddie, my mother...Pipp.

I will never see them again.

"Congratulations," a male voice booms over our heads. Gusts of wind pick up around us and our gazes move upward. I can no longer feel the connection to my jaw, because it now lays on the ground.

Three, huge creatures come into view from above.

They are all winged and utterly beautiful.

I can feel my heart halt in my chest as my brain manages to make sense of the winged creatures and what they are.

One of them looks like a horse, with huge feathery wings attached at the top of its shoulders. A woman is seated on its bare back, no saddle or halter in sight. I briefly wonder how she communicates with the animal, but push that thought to the side as my gaze goes to the next incredible creature.

It looks like a cross between a bird and a lion. Snowy white feathers cover its body. It's double the size of the winged horse, and has a large beak that I just know is as sharp and deadly as my dagger. On its back sits a man with the most icy blue eyes I've ever seen. A piercing gaze that seems to lock onto me, pinning me in place. It's like he sees everything all at once. My past, present and future. All of it.

But the most terrifying thing about him, might be the fact that he looks familiar. I just can't place him.

When I'm finally able to tear my eyes off the man, I'm able to look at the last incredible creature making its descent. It's even bigger than the other two beasts. It has scales all over its body and resembles a lizard, with leathery wings and a long spiked tale. When it lands, the earth underneath our feet trembles and shakes.

It's a *dragon*.

A living, breathing dragon.

These are all creatures depicted in that book I found back in my village. From the fables of the old tongue. The book that fell through the portal with me, the book I picked up and—. The blood drains from my face as my eyes slowly go back to the lake behind me.

Fuck.

Scorching heat blasts behind me and I turn to see the dragon letting out a huge breath of fire from its massive jaws, the scales at its chest glows from the heat gathered inside.

Seated on the back of the dragon is a woman with short, blond hair. Both sides of her head are shaved short, and she has a grim expression on her face. A gruesome scar marks the right side of her face, giving her a wild look.

She's not one to mess with.

We all collectively shudder.

To my left, two people scream, and start to run.

It all happens so fast. One moment, they're there. Then, a blast of endless heat and their scorched bodies drop to the ground. Smoke wafting from their corpses.

"Anyone else that wants to get barbecued?" She asks, and her face splits into a grin so wide it makes shivers run down my spine all over again.

We all stay silent, unmoving.

"Good." She tilts her head to the side as she surveys us all. "Let's get a move on. More people will arrive from the July reaping in a few days."

I glance over at Amadeus in confusion. July? This was the June reaping, wasn't it?

Amadeus looks just as confused as I feel. He meets my gaze and shrugs.

"Silence!" She shouts as a collective murmur starts to spread through the crowd. "I don't have time to hold your fucking hands, you either live, or you die in this place. And it's all up to you. And the creatures that live here."

Chapter Eight

"This is so surreal."

I concentrate on putting one foot in front of the other, and *try* to ignore the amazed tone in his voice. Every step I take jars my shoulder as I cradle it in my other arm.

It's still dislocated, and I just can't seem to get a break from this fucking line.

We were told to line up and follow the dragon to our new home, and since no-one wanted to become the next living torch we did so without much protest. Not to say there weren't some, and they... Well, they had a blast, you could say.

"This is so surreal," Amadeus repeats and I inhale deeply, trying not to groan in annoyance. Sure, I'm happy to see him again, but I'm also pissed from here to eternity over this entire situation.

I got reaped. There was a chance of not getting reaped and my whore of a mother didn't even give me a choice in the matter. To be fair, I would probably be a shit mother, but not as bad as my own. What I can't understand is why no-one knows about this loophole. It should be common knowledge.

"This is so—"

"If you say that this is surreal one more time, Amadeus, I swear I will cut your fucking tongue out of your mouth and feed it to the dragon," I snap. He whirls around to look at me, walking *backwards* on the narrow path. He doesn't even seem to mind that one side of the trail is a deadly drop. "Eyes forward! This path is dangerous enough as it is without you walking it backwards!"

"Come on, Salem, don't be such a grump," he smirks, and I just glare at him in return. "Tell me, what crawled up your ass and died?"

"Seriously, Amadeus, do you really want to fall to your death?" I hiss through clenched teeth, ignoring his obvious dig. Grinning he turns around, skipping a couple of steps over the rugged stones. What on earth has come over this man? It's like a complete flip of his personality. The Amadeus I know never skipped around like a carefree child. He must have hit his head.

"I can't wait until we get there," he says. *I can't for the life of me understand why.* "Do you think we will be able to ride dragons too?" Why on earth would he want to do that? They torch people for fun. "Or maybe, maybe I'll be able to see my sister again."

That explains everything.

I let out a trapped sigh before answering. "Maybe?" I don't want his hopes up, only to watch them crash and burn if it turns out his sister isn't here. Or...dead. Which is a huge possibility in this place from what I've already seen.

As I look up I'm sure there must be at least a couple hundred people in front of us, and at least as many behind us. It's rumored that the reapings occur across the entire continent. And if what my mom said about it taking people born on different dates from the age of twenty to twenty five... that leaves an enormous pool to grab from. This simply can't be the only place we disappear to.

My thoughts drift towards Pipp, and her parting scream. It still echoes through my mind. The heartbreak, the panic. Her hazel eyes wide with fear as the beetles covered my entire body and ripped me away from her.

My foot slips as the stone I put my weight on tilts from its place. I gasp and fling my arms out to steady myself, feeling my dislocated shoulder protest. My eyes roll back into my skull for a second, and I have to force them open to not pass out from the pain. A heavy stone tumbles down the stony cliffside to our right and my stomach turns.

That could have been me.

"You okay?"

Thankfully, Amadeus doesn't turn around to look at my pained expression as I struggle to collect myself and calm my racing heart. "Yeah..."

The incline of the path gets rapidly steeper the further we walk, and my muscles ache and burn, along with my blistered feet. I'm miserable, agitated and annoyed at pretty much everything at this point, wondering why they have us walking this path for no fucking reason.

"Holy hell," Amadeus whispers, halting. Forcing me to stop as well. "Salem, look."

"What?" I snap, looking up.

The blood drains from my face.

"Shit."

"Yeah, that's for sure," he says in a mixture of shock and awe.

In front of us, lies a cliff. It's more or less a vertical climb, with dangerous stairs carved into the cliffside. It's so narrow they have to climb one at a time.

My blood freezes when I hear a piercing scream cleave the air, and I watch in terror as a person slips on the steps and falls. They tumble down the hillside, knocking five more people with them to a certain death.

I gulp.

I can't do anything other than stare at their crumpled bodies, long after their screams stop echoing around us. It's not until the final echoing thud disappears on the wind that I'm able to tear my gaze away.

My face twists in a pained grimace, and a small gasp tumbles out from my lips.

Fuck.

This...is suicide.

I gasp when I spot a person break from the line and start running. *No, no, no, don't run!* Chaos erupts, and I watch in horror as more people start running too. I'm about to open my mouth to shout at them when I hear a furious roar from above. Automatically my eyes fly to the sky, and the massive dragon that swoops down.

"Get back in line!" I scream to the deserters, but I'm too late. The scales at its chest start to glow, then its jaw opens wide. Heat pours out of its mouth as it glides over us. The temperature rises in an instant, scorching the side of my face. Yet I can't tear my eyes away from the raging fire that overtakes the other side of the path. Trapping us.

When the fire calms, burning corpses litter the hillside. The nauseating smell of burnt bodies assaults my nose.

"Well, at least I'm dry now, that's something," Amadeus mumbles in front of me. I whip my eyes to him, and my jaw falls slack. "What?"

"I can't...How can you be so calm about this!?"

"Well, they started running, what did you expect?" He levels me with a glare and I take a slow step away from him.

"Not that!" I shriek.

He shrugs. *He. Fucking. Shrugs.*

I shake my head. "Just walk," I mutter. I'm stunned. I have no idea how to react. First of all, the brutality of this place is absolutely atrocious.

Second of all, I don't recognize my best friend at all. This is not like him. And third, there's all the death.

I just feel numb at this point.

Suddenly my feet hit the first step. I didn't even realize that my body had started moving again, but now that I'm here I let my head fall back to get a better look at the climb. It's so far up, it almost disappears into the clouds. The steps are double the height of normal stairs, and there are two handholds carved into each step. They're evenly spaced the whole way up.

And just to add insult to injury, the steps are wet and slippery. *Of course they are.*

I swallow the lump in my throat, trying my best to collect myself before I embark on the upcoming misery I'm about to endure.

I can't climb these stairs. There is no way my dislocated shoulder will hold. I'd have to climb them one-handed. And the pain would momentarily blind me if I even tried. Unless...

I unbuckle my belt with my left hand, somehow managing to loop it around my entire body and fasten it. Strapping my arm close to my body and hissing through the pain, I twist my arm around the belt. Locking it in place.

It will have to do. If not...*I can't go there.*

Then I start to climb.

For what feels like forever the pattern is the same.

Left arm up, locate the handhold, one foot up, then the other.

Over and over I repeat it in my head.

Left arm up.

Locate the handhold.

One foot up.

Than the other.

"Where do you think we're going?" I hear Amadeus ask right above me as we climb.

I take a moment to make sure that I have a firm grip on the step leveled at my chest before answering. "I don't know, and I don't care. Please concentrate on climbing instead of talking to me." It almost sounds like a snarky growl, but I don't have the energy, or the mental capacity to check my attitude at the moment.

"This is easy," He says, and I can hear the smug grin on his face. His overconfidence will get him killed. I look up in agitation, about to tell him to get a fucking grip when the guy above him slips on the steps.

"Brace!" I yell. My knuckles go white from the firm grip on the handle and I flatten my body against the wall, tucking my head down. Just in time too. Moments later a hard body slams into my back with so much force I feel my grip slip. I hold on for dear life, and pray to the Gods that this won't be the end of me.

I hear the body tumble down the cliffside, and my eyes involuntarily trail after him. His slack form crashes into the sharp stones like a puppet without strings. The broken body eventually disappears from view.

A shudder runs through me when I see numerous bodies scattered along the entirety of the cliffside in unnatural positions.

"Don't even think about it," A familiar voice says and I freeze. Where the fuck did that voice come from? It sounded like...No. That's *impossible*.

And it wasn't like I was about to—

"You weren't? Then keep moving, Trouble."

It's the stranger. The one that pulled me from the lake. He's...*in my head*.

Why is he speaking in my head?

"I don't fucking know. Move along. Make sure you don't slip on the steps."

Does he think I'm an idiot? Of course I'm going to make sure to not slip on the fucking steps. I don't want to die.

"If you don't want to die, Trouble, then what was that fleeting thought passing through your pretty little head?"

Chills spread down my neck, and my cheeks heat.

The fact that he's inside my head makes this interaction so much more intimate. But how can he be? My gaze snaps to my left arm.

Shit.

Am I somehow connected to this man? But how? Why? Why *him*? I spot the mark swirling around my wrist like liquid gold. It's beautiful, and…intricate. I stifle a small whimper that threatens to escape my lips.

This kind of connection is unheard of.

Somehow the mark feels both feminine and masculine. It's somewhat familiar to me as well—just as the stranger was. But the memory eludes me. It feels like it's on the tip of my tongue…but the memory is foggy. Almost like it's covered in a layer of mist.

My foot slips on the step underneath me. My grip falters and I fall.

I don't scream, I just grit my teeth as my life flashes before my eyes. I brace myself for what comes next. I'm about to die.

My knees smash into the step underneath me, stopping my descent. I fling out my good arm, hooking my elbow to the step in front of my chest. My breaths are quick and shallow as my body comes to a stop.

"Fuck," I gasp.

"What happened?" I barely hear Amadeus's question over the deafening roar inside my own head. Blood surges through it, and I feel nauseous thinking about what just happened.

"Uh, nothing," I lie.

"Bullshit."

Shut up, I wasn't talking to you. A soft chuckle vibrates through my mind.

"What's wrong with your face?" Amadeus asks, and I look up to meet his puzzled gaze. "You're white as a sheet. It looks like you've...Why the fuck is your arm strapped to your body?"

Gasping, I look down. Unsure what to say, I go with another lie. "Needed the challenge," I mumble, feeling utterly pathetic.

"So you decided to climb this trail with your non-dominant hand? You look green Salem," he notes, like I don't already know that.

"Can't you just focus on yourself, and let me worry about me?"

"*Liar,*" The stranger chimes in, and I roll my eyes.

"Well, nobody asked you, did they?" I mutter.

"What was that?" Amadeus asks, and there is no way I'm able to get out of this. Sensing that Amadeus isn't going to let this go I open my mouth to explain, but the words get trapped in my chest.

I don't want to tell him.

"*Don't panic, I'm underneath you.*"

I startle, and make the dumb mistake of looking down. And sure enough. The red tinted hair of the stranger is now underneath me. My stomach plummets when it dawns on me the reason why he's there.

The people between us must have already fallen.

I've completely tuned out their screams in favor of my own survival.

"Stay still, Trouble," the stranger says, and I see his lips move this time. For some reason I actually do as I'm told.

My eyes widen when I see him continue to climb. "What are you doing?" I blurt. When he stops, he has me caged in by his warmth.

"I'm trying to help you," he grunts. "You're bleeding."

I slow blink. "Am I?" I didn't even notice.

The stranger quirks an eyebrow at me. "And your shoulder is dislocated."

That I did know.

I turn my head around to look at him better and I'm met with his striking green eyes. They remind me of the color of damp moss that you find deep in the forest. He even smells like it. Like fresh basil and dewy moss.

"Lean back into me," he says.

"What?"

"You heard me. Now, please do as you're told. I'll guide you through it." Guide me through what? The warm breath at my ear has my mind completely muddled, goosebumps breaking out across my skin. And that's just pathetic.

I never swoon over men. No, I don't swoon. Period.

He rolls his eyes. "Come on, your pride can't be that stubborn. Let me help. Lean into me."

I do as he asked, and lean back. One of his arms finds the belt buckle I've fastened around myself. It slackens as he unbuckles the strap and all the while I hold his stare.

"Grab your arm and guide it back into the socket," he murmurs to me, and my eyes flick down to his sculpted lips. "Careful, not too fast." He instructs gently in my ear.

"Good. Now, take a deep breath, and on the exhale, push your elbow up just a fraction. It should pop back in," he continues.

And he's right.

It pops back in place.

Just as the shoulder slides back in place I groan in relief and let my head fall back to his shoulder.

"Good girl. That wasn't too hard, was it?"

My eyes pop open at the same time my core clenches from his words. What the actual... Did he just? Did I just...?

"Who are you?" I whisper, trying to ignore the odd sensation he just evoked in me.

Slowly, his head moves towards the side of mine and I feel the way his smile stretches. "You can call me Riften."

Shivers race down my spine from the soft brush of his lips against my ear and I stifle a moan by biting hard down on my lip.

"You good to continue climbing?" He asks me in a whisper.

I nod, hesitantly.

"Good."

Gingerly I start to climb again, meeting Amadeus's ankles after just a couple of steps. I look up and find him glaring down at me with anger edged across his handsome face.

"What the fuck was that?"

Chapter Nine

The words get stuck in my chest, like I physically can't tell him what's going on. I shake my head in confusion. "Just move," I mutter, and show him that I'm about to continue climbing.

I cut him off when he opens his mouth to speak. "There is nothing going on, Amadeus, and if you don't move this instant I'll grab your ankle a throw you down this fucking cliffside."

The threatening tone in my voice is thankfully enough for him to continue climbing. *Thank the Gods.* Taking one step at the time I concentrate on the movements of my body, making sure I have a good grip before continuing.

"You're aware that you're bleeding on me, right?"

I wasn't, but frankly, I don't give a shit. I can't do anything about my bleeding wounds at this point anyway. It has to wait until I'm on solid ground. The only thing I can do at this very moment is to climb and pray I don't slip and fall, or pass out and fall to my death. Or get scorched by dragon fire—.

Fuck it, by now there has been way too many options with certain death as a result for me to even care.

We were right to fear the reaping.

I'm so over this, but if I don't want to die, I don't have a damned *choice.*

The moment I crawl over the ledge, I collapse in a heap of limbs on the ground. My breath comes quickly and tears threaten to break free from the corners of my eyes. The deafening sound of my blood rushing through my head makes me dizzy, but that could also be from stress.

Who cares.

Just as my body starts to tremble, a shadow falls over me, startling me. My eyes pop open and I stare up at Riften's huge form. "Get up," he says, holding out a hand for me to take.

Why does he *continue* to help me?

And why do I continue to accept it?

The moment I'm back on my feet, I stumble into his chest like a clumsy fawn. "Sorry." The breathless apology makes me wince. Did I really make that sound? I think I did. And the knowing smirk on his face has me blushing like a complete idiot.

What is up with this guy? He's not even that attractive!

He chuckles as he shakes his head. Like he knows what I'm—fuck, I forgot. He *can* hear my thoughts.

Perfect.

On reflex I shove him away from me, and a full body shudder runs through me. "Stay out of my head." It's just as much a threat as a plea. And how those two contradicting actions go together, I can't explain.

"I told you that this was going to be fun. You can't fool me, Trouble." His gaze locks on mine, and he taps the side of his temple twice before he turns around and walks over to another guy. They shake hands and clap each other's backs like they're old friends. Maybe they got reaped together or something.

There's certainly more people gathered than I'm comfortable with.

Mentally, I build a wall between me and Riften in the hopes of blocking him out of my thoughts. And from the way he turns around to scowl at me, I might have accomplished just that. My attention snags on the guy he just greeted, he's dressed like the riders were, and adorning his left arm is a black mark that stretches up to his neck in the form of snakes.

And they're *moving*.

I look away, feeling my stomach twist.

Taking a breath, I try to orient myself.

We're standing in the middle of a large flat area on top of a mountain, and still we're surrounded by more mountains. An enormous stone structure juts out from one of the cliffsides. Large watchtowers loom over the courtyard, I don't know what else to call it. Four large stone buildings with simple details surround us on all sides. A fifth building towers in front of us, with a tunnel going straight through the center.

Somehow, it feels like this place was built to be temporary, but over time it evolved into something permanent and functional.

In front of what I assume is the main building, a line of people dressed in dark leathers stands with their arms crossed over their chests. They all have a black mark crawling up their left arm. Every single one of them is equally beautiful and terrifying.

My heart stops in my chest when I spot someone I actually recognize.

His eyes no longer hold that light they used to. They're colder, and almost feel dead. But his face is exactly the same as it was ten years ago when he disappeared. His ashy blond hair looks to be longer.

"Amadeus," I hiss, tugging at his arm. "Look," I nod towards the front. "To the right side, under the banner."

At my side I hear the sharp intake of breath. "No way. He looks just the same..."

"Right?" I whisper back.

The last time I saw Thorian he'd just taken a brutal beating in the Underground. After his disappearance, the ring in Ghostport almost collapsed. And it would have if it hadn't been for Heason.

"He doesn't look a day older," I whisper, staring at the man. Looking closer at the assembly at the front I frown. Out of the thirty or so people standing there, only one person looks to be over the age of fifty. And he's the only one that doesn't have a black mark crawling up his arm.

The ground shakes behind us and I whip around to see the huge dragon perched on the ledge. Small stones crumble under its weight, and the woman on the beast's back slides down. With a gentle touch she lets her hand glide along its jaw, and the crowd parts for her as she moves closer. Then the dragon flies away, and the other two creatures land in its place. The man and the woman dismount from their backs and follow.

"Not too bad," The dragon rider says as she passes by. But my stare is on the man. There's something about him that I can't put my finger on. His hawk-like eyes pin me in place as his gaze lands on me. A muscle ticks in his jaw, and I feel raw. Exposed. Like a child being reprimanded for doing something they shouldn't.

"You're probably wondering where you are, and what I can tell you is less than I'd like to," the dragon rider continues. Tearing my gaze away from the ice of his stare, I look to the female that now has reached the front. "My name is Yara LeRouge, and this is the land of Nowhere," she gestures around with a hand. "Welcome to the compound of The Dover Mountains. Your new home."

I look around at the crowd, and my heart skips a beat when I see that our numbers have drastically diminished. Almost half of the people I saw at the stone beach by the lake aren't with us. A pang of sorrow slams into me, but I have to shake that thought away.

"You've just survived the path of Howling Souls in the Valley of Howlsten. Congratulations." she says, folding her arms across her chest. Shadowy flames lick up her arm and I tilt my head in thought.

I wonder if the depiction of the black mark is significant.

"Over time," she says, gaining my attention once more. "Some of you will experience changes. Some of them will be subtle, others will be outright dangerous either to yourselves, or others. They will be dealt with when the time comes." She tilts her head as she surveys us.

"I will give you all a word of caution—this land is cruel. It's nothing like our old world and if you don't have the stomach for it, the cliff is there." She points behind us, then pauses. As if she's giving us a moment to...what? Jump? "You are all stolen soldiers, and there is no mercy to be found within these walls, and certainly not out there." Her voice has a finality to it that makes my gut clench.

"Most of you will die. Already a large number of you have." Her voice booms over our heads and someone beside me shudders. "This land is at war with evil creatures, and it's up to us to defend it. The Old Lady came to all of you and gave you three questions. Based on what you answered we will now let the beetles decide which of the two devisions you belong to. Later, the dragons will choose who to bond," She takes a step back and we all stand there, confused.

"What did she say? The beetles?" A girl says, and I can hear the fright in her voice. I have to admit, I'm not thrilled to have a beetle make any kind of decision for me.

"Why not a griffin? Or a pegasus?" Someone yells in the crowd.

I sense something brush my leg. Looking down, I stifle a scream when a single glow beetle crawls up my leg. My feet are frozen to the spot, I'm utterly immobile, and all I can do is watch as it moves up my torso, along my arm, and down towards my palm.

Someone screams, and I clench my teeth in preparation for...I don't even know what. A sharp sting stabs my left palm, and I whimper from the slight pain. That wasn't too bad?

Then, the burning settles in. I stare at the beetle as it burrows itself into the wound it just created. To my horror, the wound closes up immediately. The invisible force that kept me immobilized disappears, and I turn my hand over.

A black symbol is placed underneath my skin at the center of my palm.

My heart is pounding in my chest. I feel nauseous. Beside me a guy actually pukes. I don't blame him.

There's a freaking beetle under my skin.

Why the fuck does it have to be *beetles?*

"What was that for?" Amadeus yells beside me, and I glare at him with fear in my eyes. He's cradling his arm, and I see that we have different symbols on our palms. "What's the meaning of this," he bellows, ignoring my warning glare.

"It's your beetle mark. Now, there are two different marks. Everyone with this mark," she gestures to one of the banners on the left side. "Puts you in infantry, and this mark will put you in the stealth unit." She points to the banner above Thorian, and my eyes go wide.

Does that mean he will be some kind of instructor to me? I have no idea.

"All the reapings have different marks because you bond different creatures. June reapings bond dragons, July—griffins, and August bonds with the pegasi. And if you do bond with a dragon, your mark will grow," Yara says, indicating her own left arm.

I glance down at my left arm, and the golden pattern that peeks out from under my sleeve.

I haven't seen anyone else with a mark like mine, other than Riften that is.

"I'm in infantry," Amadeus says and I snap my gaze to him, tugging on my sleeve. "What about you," he asks, and I look down at my palm. Like I need to look to double check, when I really don't.

"Stealth," I say, frowning when a memory stirs in my mind. What did Pipp say again? *A mallet needs strength, a needle needs stealth.* Looking at our two marks, I can clearly see that his is more bold and forceful, whilst the one in my own palm almost feels delicate and...precise.

"The dragon regiment is located in that building," Yara says, pointing to a large stone building to the side. "You all will be located on the first floor, there is a shared area for sleeping. That will change over time depending on what happens to you. Now, get to the building. Find a cot. Get some sleep. Tomorrow we meet here at dawn," she says, dismissing us.

Letting myself follow the crowd, I walk in a daze. A person can only take so much brutality, and I've reached my limit for today.

Chapter Ten

"I'm stuck," I grumble from the inside of my clothing.

We got woken up this morning by a thunderous roar that made the whole building vibrate, then the tell-tale sounds of wings could be heard from outside. It felt like multiple dragons landed on the top of the building by the way it quaked.

"How the heck did you manage that?" I hear Amadeus laugh from the outside of the tunic. Then I feel his arms on my hips as he stops me from turning around.

"Woah there, careful with those arms," he chuckles.

"Are you going to help me or not? I'm not interested in being your damn entertainment," I growl.

"Calm down, I'm just messing with you," he says and tugs on the garment, somehow managing to make it even worse.

"Did you really just tell me to calm down?" I'm not sure if he buys the dangerous undertone in my voice.

He doesn't. "Yup, it's not a big deal, let me just—ouch!" My fist connects with his face.

Somehow I managed to get my arm and head through the right holes without his help, and sent my fist flying. And I'm not even sorry about it.

"What was that for?" He stares at me, and I glare right back with anger brimming under my skin.

I point a finger to his face and hiss through clenched teeth. "You know better." Tucking the tunic into my trousers, I hold his stare with my furious gaze.

His facial expression slackens and his eyes start to wander. I'm about to throttle him when his eyebrow lifts in surprise. "What's that?"

"What's what?" I grunt, and look down to my arm and the rolled up sleeve. Why are the sleeves rolled up?

Amadeus clears his throat, and I snap my gaze to him again. "Um, Salem...that's my shirt." A slight blush creeps up his neck.

"No, it's not." I look down. "Oh, shit. You're right."

"It's okay, I can take yours," he says, and I just glare in return, wondering how he's going to pull that off with me being smaller than him.

He takes a step towards me and gives a slight nod towards my arm. "Or would you like to explain that marking to the people around us?" He whispers.

"What marking?" I whisper back.

He lifts an eyebrow at me. "I'm not stupid. That's almost the same as the one that the dragon rider had, but in the wrong color," he says. "I just don't know what it means, yet."

I roll down the sleeve to cover it, avoiding his unasked question.

We stand there awkwardly, as he looms over me. He exudes a demanding energy, waiting patiently for me to tell him about the bond. It's almost compelling me to open my mouth to speak. I fight it. With all my mental strength I build a fortress in my mind to block the sudden urge to spill my secrets to him.

"Is there a problem here?" A male voice asks beside us, and shivers trickle down my spine. I know this voice. Intimately.

Turning my head, I already know Riften is standing there. And the look he gives Amadeus? Let's just say I wouldn't like to be on the receiving end of that particular look.

Amadeus takes a step back, and suddenly I can breathe again. I didn't realize the pressure that had been there until it was gone.

"No," he says, gaining a frosty facade as he gages Riften. "There's no problem."

The tension between the two men is palpable, and I watch them in perverse fascination as they mentally butt their heads together.

"Guys, guys," I say, taking a step between them, putting a hand on their chests. "Roll in your titties, there's no need for a cock fight just yet," I grumble.

"Yet?" Amadeus blanches, horrified. "What makes you think...? No. Not ever, thank you."

I lift an eyebrow at my best friend, tilting my head to the side. "Didn't know you were such a prude. I think you've spent too much time with the Cobalt Priests." It's too fun to rile him up and make him flustered. It almost has me cackling with laughter.

Riften snorts, shaking his head. "Roll in your titties," he repeats under his breath, ignoring Amadeus's protests, and the corner of his mouth twitches as if he is trying not to show his amusement.

"Do you think they plan on feeding us? I'm hungry," I say, attempting to change the subject.

"Salem!" Amadeus protests. I look over at him, blinking innocently. "I'm not a prude," he growls, and I bite my lip to not start laughing.

"Sure you're not, because arguing about this doesn't just prove my point?"

The guys move simultaneously, Riften taking a half step in front of me just as Amadeus takes a step towards me. Tilting his head, Riften looks at

Amadeus from head to toe, and up again. "I wouldn't if I were you," he says. I can't help the smile that tugs on my lips.

"He wouldn't hurt me," I reassure him, placing an arm on Riften's arm.

We both tense as if sparks shoot through our bodies, or, at least my body. He snaps his gaze to my hand and swallows. He almost looks puzzled for a moment, but shakes his head slowly.

"You sure about that, Trouble?" He asks softly.

"Amadeus would never hurt me," I chuckle. "He's my best friend."

His jaw ticks, and his eyebrows jump in surprise.

"Dude, what's your problem?" Amadeus asks, pushing at Riften's chest.

I pinch the bridge of my nose. "I'm out, you two have fun. I have better things to do than watch you act like toddlers." I don't have time, nor the energy to deal with their territorial bullshit.

At dawn we're gathered in a clusterfuck of unorganized chaos in the courtyard.

No longer exhausted by death and pain—having blocked that part out in favor of functioning—I have time to take a better look at our surroundings.

The open space is located on the ledge of the cliffside, surrounded by five buildings in a semicircle. Four of the buildings look to be almost the same size, including the one we just exited. A narrow road leads through a tunnel in the main building, leading into another valley beyond.

In the light of day, everything looks to be in poor condition. Some of the windows are boarded up, others are cracked. The tiles on the rooftops are mostly loose, and some places look to be burnt.

That might be courtesy of the dragons.

Heason would have knocked me over the head for not paying more attention last night. Tegner too. They always talked about the importance of being aware of your surroundings at all times.

Perched on the ledge around the courtyard sit a dozen dragons in different shades of blue. They range in color from deep navy to light teal. Their beady eyes narrowed and pinned on us. Occasionally warm puffs of air and smoke waft toward us, making my heart rate spike and my body tremble.

They are *huge*, and absolutely terrifying.

The largest spike on one of the teal blue dragons must be the same length as my leg, I don't think I would reach their elbow. And I'm tall for a woman.

Are they really going to sit there and watch us? I have no idea what we're supposed to do.

"Is this what you call a formation?" A male voice booms. Locating the source of the voice, my eyes widen. It's Thorian. He walks slowly from one of the dragons on the perch. The only one of the bunch that isn't blue. It's green. As soon as he dismounts the dragon, it flies off again, and he walks up to the front with slow, deliberate steps.

"Infantry to the right, stealth to the left." It's not a request.

We exchange confused looks. I'm already standing to the left, so I don't have to go anywhere, but everyone else looks too hesitant to move.

Thorian runs his hand through his ashy blond hair. "I'd suggest you start moving before the dragons start to light up the place." He smiles, a sinister grin that scares me.

We don't move, but in my peripheral I see some people shift on their feet.

A dragon puffs out a breath of fire at the same time that Thorian yells, "now!"

That makes everyone jump, and in no time and plenty of chaos, we divide ourselves on the correct sides.

Thorian runs a hand across his face. "You are soldiers, stolen or not, you are soldiers!" He booms. "Act like it."

"And what if we don't want to?" Someone yells back from the infantry side.

I flick my gaze in his direction, and see a blond guy standing with his arms crossed over his chest.

"Well, in that case, you will meet your maker pretty fast," Thorian replies, pinning the guy with his stare.

"You said that yesterday, but I thought that was only if a dragon didn't want to bond with you," he retorts, sticking his nose up in the air.

Slowly, Thorian turns his body towards the person, and his face twists up in that terrifying grin once more. Shivers run down my spine. This is not the Thorian I remember from the Underground. He's...much scarier.

A rumbling breaks the sudden tension, making the air around us vibrate as one of the dragons behind us starts to growl. Thorian laughs, but it sounds more like a cackle. "There is no way out of this. You either live or you die in this place. This is the new normal. Get used to it."

There are so many things that don't add up.

Thorian disappeared ten years ago, I'd expect him to look the same age as Heason, who's in his thirties, yet he doesn't. It's like the timeline is warped here, like time moves differently for some reason.

The guy that asked the question tilts his head in thought, looking slowly over his shoulder at one of the blue dragons. The smile on his face widens as the air starts to vibrate with another low growl. The earth shakes as one of the dragons behind us takes a step in his direction. The people around him takes a step back.

Oh, please don't...I don't think I can handle more death, especially before breakfast. It would totally kill my appetite.

"That's what you're thinking about?" Riften's sudden appearance in my mind makes me jump, and I look around for him with wide eyes.

I don't appreciate the invasion of privacy either. It's rude.

"It's not my fault you project your thoughts like a beacon..."

I just roll my eyes. Trying my best to ignore him as another shudder shakes the ground under my feet when the dragon takes another step.

The crowd parts for it like a fire has been lit under their feet. Everyone but the questioning man moves away. He looks up at the dark blue dragon with wide eyes. It's got him pinned with a stare. Either in awe or fear, I can't tell which.

The air starts to crackle with energy, when the dragon lifts its head skyward, letting out a menacing roar that makes me wince.

And the guy laughs.

Chills trickle up my arms, raising every single hair on my skin.

"Look." Riften says in our mind link, stopping me from closing my eyes.

Golden threads seep out from underneath the scales at the dragon's chest, stretching towards the guy that lifts his left hand towards them. He almost looks to be in a trance, with glossed over eyes and a vacant expression on his face.

Shit.

The dragon is... is it going to *bond* with the guy?

I blink, and the golden thread is gone. As if it were a trick of the light.

The man shudders. His head falls back, and his mouth opens wide. It's so silent in the courtyard you could hear a pin drop. His eyes roll back into his head.

Then, he screams. Loud, and filled with tortured pain. It knocks the breath out of my lungs. It's as though his agony courses through me as his body starts to shake. He stiffens, and topples over, falling to the ground, he continues to twitch.

This feels wrong.

The mark on his left palm flares up, red thorns spreading underneath his skin. It stretches up the length of his arm and along his neck, circling it with thorns that seem to cut deep into his soul.

The dragon roars, lifting its head to the sky as it lets a stream of fire into the air.

A girl screams, and my focus lands on the twitching body in the courtyard. His very essence seems sucked out of his body.

First, his skin starts to crack. Almost like all the water has evaporated from within him. His cheeks hollow, and his eyes bug out of his face. It's like watching someone grow old in seconds.

When it finally stops, he's no more than a husk.

All I can do is stare.

Gods...

What the actual *fuck* was that? *This* is what we're facing if...I don't even want to know what just happened.

For once, Riften doesn't seem to have anything to say. He seems as stunned as everyone else.

Movement from the front makes me jump back. Thorian takes deliberate steps in the direction of the dead stranger. When he reach him, he stops and uses the tip of his boot to tilt his head to the side. He tsks in obvious disappointment.

"Shame," he sighs. "He was quite pretty."

Chapter Eleven

Amadeus grunts when my elbow connects with his jaw, he stumbles back a couple of steps, still managing to keep himself upright. His hand flies up to grab his face, eyes bugging in aggravation.

"You could ease up on me, you know?" He grumbles.

"I could," I say, spinning around as I sweep my foot under him, making him fall to the ground. "But I won't."

I grind my teeth together through the jab of pain in my ribs. Not wanting to show any weakness in front of these people. Even Amadeus.

He moves, my feet are kicked from under me, and I fall on top of him. He turns us over, pinning me to the mat with his larger body. "If you're not easing up on me, you should ease up on yourself."

A low growl of frustration leaves my throat.

"I'm fine." I push at him, but my shoulder threatens to buckle under his weight.

"Right." He looks me over and something sparks in his eyes that makes me almost uncomfortable. And I don't know why. His eyes gloss over, and I swear there's a flicker of gold appearing in his eyes. He shakes his head and frowns. "Wha—" He rubs the back of his neck with a shaking hand. "I haven't seen Teagan anywhere." He says, and a crease of concern appears between his brows.

A couple of days have passed since the failed bonding in the courtyard, and our numbers continue to dwindle. The most visible proof is the fact that the sleeping hall isn't as crowded. It's impossible to know everyone's names still, and for the most part, I don't bother asking. Neither does anyone else, really. Chances are we won't see them again the next morning.

Just for that reason it takes me a moment to understand who he's talking about.

Teagan.

His sister.

Using my legs, I manage to push him off me since he doesn't have the best hold. "Wasn't she an August reaping?" I ask, panting a little when I get to my feet again. Brushing myself off I cock my head to the side and study him more closely. "You feeling okay?"

He runs his hand through his hair before nodding. "Yeah, sure." I frown from his dismissive tone, but before I'm able to ask any further questions, he continues. "She was."

I can tell that he's trying to change the subject, and I let him. "So, if she is here, she will be over at the Pegasus division," I say as we circle each other.

"She might not be there," he prompts.

He's right. She might not have survived.

"Don't give up hope yet, she might be here somewhere," I tell him, trying to comfort him.

A muscle ticks in his jaw, right before he charges. I pivot, avoiding his attack. Spinning around, I lift my leg and send him flying when it connects with his midsection. The air gets knocked out of him, and a long groan tumbles out of his throat from where he writhes on the ground.

"You're a menace," Amadeus says through gritted teeth and pushes himself to his feet.

"Tell me something I don't already know, would you?"

Grunting he brushes dirt off his body. "I'm done." His gaze moves to a spot behind us, and my attention follows. A lump forms in my throat when I look at the dragons gathered on the perch. These are in all shades of green. Their scales glint in the sunlight, and their attentive focus chills my bones.

One of the darker green's is missing one of its front claws.

This is their routine, I've realized.

They arrive in groups of twelve, sit on their perches, and watch us train in the courtyard in groups. For the most part, they just watch. But sometimes they find someone lacking and barbecue them on the spot. There is no way of knowing what or why they do what they do, but so far, I've managed to stay alive. I plan to keep it that way for as long as I possibly can.

We've teamed up with my bunk neighbors, for lack of a better term. Elodie and Killian. They know each other from back home, and got reaped on the same day, at the same time. Thank the Gods they were both clothed, or else that would have become awkward real fast when they emerged from the lake.

"Come on, Amadeus, are you really going to let her speak to you that way?" Elodie asks, and tosses her silvery hair over her shoulder, trying to hide her laugh. She is failing spectacularly, grinning from ear to ear.

Amadeus grunts in response.

Killian starts to laugh, a full belly laugh.

"Ignoring us, are we?" He teases, and rises to his feet as he enters the square that marks our space. "So, am I kicking your ass, or hers?" Killian asks Amadeus.

"Hers," he says, then he grins, and I roll my eyes.

"You're such a sore loser," I sigh.

Both Killian and Elodie already had some combat training coming into this, which makes it more fun to spar with them.

I study Killian's posture and notice that he favors his right side. It's obviously his dominant side. Which makes it easier for me to gauge his attacks and plan my own.

Killian lunges, and I'm about to dodge his attack, when a blast of heat suddenly fills the space beside us. I lose my focus. Killian's punch hits me straight in the chest, forcing all the air out of my lungs.

It feels like being kicked by a horse, without the added momentum. Just the immense pain from it. I fall to my knees, gasping.

"Fuuuck, that hurts," I grit out.

Killian blinks.

"What...I barely grazed you," he says.

"Seriously?" I glare at him.

Killian stares at his hands, blinking. "Yes." Frowning he balls them into fists a couple of times. "I pulled back my punch, I swear."

"What do you mean?" Elodie asks, walking over to him.

"I got distracted by the live torch over there, and pulled it back, I barely touched her," he says.

I glance over at the scorched body in the square beside us. I think her name was Trish, maybe? Really, it doesn't matter. She's dead now.

"Holy shit, holy shit, holy shit," the guy nearest the corpse breathes, looking terribly green.

"You okay?" I ask, gasping a little because of the lingering pain in my chest.

"Uh," He stares at the charred body in front of him. "I...think so?"

I can't for the life of me remember his name, I know I've seen him before, probably in the sleeping hall, or maybe even the mess hall.

His body starts to shake as he's trying to keep it together.

"I have a sister," I say.

"What?" The guy stares at me.

"I have a sister, she's five years younger than me, and she will get reaped during the next reaping," I rub my chest in discomfort. I'm not even sure why I'm telling him this. "Unless she gets pregnant."

"Unless...wait, is there actually a way to not get reaped?" Elodie asks all of a sudden, looking horrified. "Why didn't I know about this?"

"I didn't either, my mother told me the day before I got reaped," I sigh. "Apparently, we could have prevented all of this crap if we would have been pregnant during the reaping," I grumble, kicking at a stone on the ground.

"Now that's just sexist," Killian says.

"Agreed," Amadeus chimes in.

"Yeah, is there any way for us men to not get reaped?" The guy asks.

"Not that I'm aware of," I say to him. "Anyways, I don't think we can get out of this now that we're here. What's your name?" I ask the new guy.

He blinks for a second, as if he needs to process that I asked him a direct question. "Uh, Galen?" He says.

"Okay, Galen, you good now?" I ask him.

He blinks again, rubbing his neck. "I think so? The smell is killing my nostrils though."

"Agreed," Amadeus says.

I wrinkle my nose. "You just had to point it out, didn't you?"

"Sorry," Galen rubs his neck again, and a light pink color creeps up from under his shirt towards his jawline. It's sharp and well defined, and so is the rest of his face. Honestly, he's kind of disgustingly pretty. And he's blond. He has this tough guy look, but he seems to be a real softy at heart. I just hope he doesn't lose himself to this horrid place.

"Weren't you sparring with two other people?" Amadeus suddenly asks.

Galens mouth drops open. "I was. They..." He takes a deep breath through his mouth and lets it out slowly. "They got torched."

We all look over at the two bodies on the ground not far from his spot.

"Well, at least they had a blast in their last moments," Killian mumbles under his breath.

We all look at him with dumbfounded bewilderment, and exchange looks with each other. "What? It's true!" Killian laughs. "Look at them, they're totally lit."

"Your humor is pitch black sometimes..." Elodie rolls her eyes, trying to hide a smile, and failing.

"Anyways," I clear my throat. "How many is that now?"

"Today or since we got here?" Killian cocks his head to the side.

I glare at him.

"What? It's a valid question. I can't fucking keep up with the deaths. They are too frequent and too brutal for my brain to grasp this new reality." Killian drags his hand through his dark brown hair, whilst forcefully blowing out air from his mouth.

"Good point," I say. "Well, at least three today. There were a couple of failed bondings yesterday."

"What? When? Who?" Elodie asks suddenly.

"I don't know. Do you really think I have the energy to keep up with all of this? I'm doing my best to stay alive at this cursed mountain camp, my schedule is full," I say, rolling my eyes.

Killian snorts. "I hate to say it, but I get it."

We all look at each other, then we break out in laughter. It's short, and it dies down in an awkward silence between us. The reality of this place is finally sinking in for us. I can see it in their eyes. They're scared. All of them. Me included.

None of us want to die.

"Hey, should we continue the sparring session?" Galen asks. "I want to get this day over with and get to bed, and hopefully not die tomorrow."

An hour later we're all exhausted, covered in sweat, dust, and muck from the courtyard. But alive. We head towards the mess hall to grab something to eat. Not that they have much to offer really. The options are porridge and bread, and most of the bread is half molded and dry. It all tastes like sawdust and misery.

I grab a bowl and scoop up some porridge with a wooden ladle. It is so dry it sticks to it and I have to whip it forcefully down towards my bowl a handful of times for it to even let go of the wood. The clump of porridge makes a gut turning splat as it hits my bowl, leaving me nauseous.

If it wasn't for the fact that I'm starving, I wouldn't even consider eating it.

Dragging my feet, I head over to a table and sit down. As soon as I'm seated, the other people that are already at the table take one look at me and the others. They wrinkle their noses at us and I blink in confusion.

I take a moment to survey our state.

We are all covered in ash, soot and dirt. Mud to be exact, and maybe a little gore.

Shit.

None of us even thought about cleaning up before heading for dinner and I suddenly realized that we all reek of the smell of burnt flesh and death.

Great.

I open my mouth to say something, but ultimately decide not to bother. We're all miserable here, why not make it just a little bit worse?

The other people at the table make a unanimous decision to pick up their bowls and leave the mess hall all together.

I'm too tired to even care.

"You got something there," Amadeus says, reaching out his arm across the table to brush something off my face.

I pull back from his touch in annoyance. "Stop it."

"It's right by your mouth," he insists.

"Leave it."

I lean even further away from him, despite the pull I feel in my chest. In fact, I lean so far back from him, that I graze Killian that sits beside me.

Pain.

Pain like nothing I've ever felt before shoots through my body from the contact and I gasp out in shock. Pain and confusion jar me as my entire body freezes up. The table rattles as something hits the underside of it, but I'm not sure if it's my doing or someone else's. At the moment, I don't give a flying fuck about it. I'm busy with the excruciating pain that pulses through my body.

"What the fuck, Salem?" Amadeus blurts out in horror.

Probably from the expression on my face.

I don't make a sound. I *can't* make a sound. My body is completely locked up. My muscles are cramping together, and I can't quite catch my breath.

"Salem? What's going on?" Killian asks beside me. His voice is filled with terror and fear.

I can't breathe. I can't speak. I can't do anything! What the fuck is going on!?

Suddenly, someone grabs my shoulders and yanks me off my chair away from the table.

The pain is still there, but it's as if a layer of cotton has been placed in between me and the excruciating pain.

Finally I can breathe again, and I force air down into my lungs as my body starts to shake. Not in pain this time, but out of fear.

I stare at Killian, feeling like my eyes are about to roll out of my skull as I glare.

He has his hands lifted in the air, as if he's afraid of touching anyone or anything.

"You," I gasp towards him. Then, someone gently grabs my jaw, forcing my head to look his way.

I'm met with deep mossy green eyes, filled with worry. His chest is moving up and down with his deep breathing. It's shallow, and pained. As if he's the one hurting. Red tinted hair falls down his forehead, almost covering his enchanting eyes.

"You okay, Trouble?"

I'm held up by Riften's strong arms, who is currently preventing me from falling to my knees.

Gaping, I just stare at him.

"I, eh," I start, but cut myself off, letting my eyes slide back to Killian that looks utterly horrified.

"I'm so sorry, I don't know what..." He looks at his hand, fear clouding his eyes. "I think I hurt you."

His voice is barely above a whisper.

"You what?" Amadeus growls in anger, and Riften's hold on me tightens.

"I don't—" Killian tries.

"You don't touch her!" Amadeus snarls.

"I don't think he did it on purpose," I say hurriedly. "I don't think he meant to hurt anyone, it's like in the courtyard," I say quickly, looking between them all. "Your punch hurt more than it should, and you said you pulled it back."

"I did! I did pull it back!" Killian sounds terrified now.

"I'm not accusing you of anything—" I'm cut off by a furious snarl.

"Well, you might not be, but I certainly am."

"Amadeus!" I exclaim.

"*I am too.*"

Quickly I turn my gaze to Riften in warning and mentally push at him. Killian did *not* mean to hurt me. It must be some kind of magic.

I take a step back, pushing Riften away from me, stand on my own two feet, and gather my confidence. Thankfully, the pain is almost gone now.

"It's like the dragon rider said, some of us might develop powers. That must be what's happening now," I say, looking from one to the other.

"So...Killian has what?" Elodie asks in confusion.

"I don't know. Pain infliction by touch?" My voice sounds unsure and full of questions, but it's also the only thing that actually makes sense to me.

"Okay, but...how do I stop it?" Killian questions. "I don't want to hurt anyone just by touching them."

I understand him completely. I wouldn't want to hurt the ones closest to me either.

We all exchanged glances with each other before looking at Killian.

"I don't know." I bite my lip in contemplation, trying to find a solution and finding none.

"You train," a male voice suddenly says behind us. We are so engrossed in our conversation that we jump in surprise at someone walking up to us.

We turn to see a tall man, probably in his early thirties, scrutinizing us. His icy blue eyes seem to pin us in place. He meets my gaze, looking me up and down. I get the same feeling I did the first time I saw this man. Like he sees too much of me. My past, present, and future at the same time.

There is something so familiar about him.

It's on the tip of my tongue, but I just can't figure out where I've seen his frosty gaze before.

"I what?" Killian asks, turning to the man.

"You train your newly sparked power of, what was it? Pain infliction by touch?" He looks to me for confirmation.

I nod. "It seems like it."

"Huh, that's a handy one," the man says.

"Who...who are you?" For some reason, it bugs me that I don't know this man.

He snorts out a short laugh.

"My name is Orvin Adornav," he says and lets his hand run through his beard as if to soothe it down.

"Adornav," I say slowly. I recognize that name. My neighbourhood was named after a wealthy guy with the same name. Allegedly he got reaped twenty-five years ago. It made it possible for a lot of people to buy property when his money was distributed. "You're from Terrby," I exclaim.

"I am, born and raised. Same as you I believe."

I narrow my eyes and tilt my head to the side, blinking in suspicion. "How...how do you know that?" I ask.

He huffs out a laugh. "You're the spitting image of her." He says. Running his hand through his beard once more. Suddenly looking sheepish. Nervous maybe?

"Of who?" I can't help raising the question through my obvious confusion.

He sighs. "Your mother."

The blood drains from my face as it slowly dawns on me who this man is...or...no. It can't...It just can't be. I stumble a step backwards, glaring at him. "How..." I start, but trail off.

"Yeah," he says, laughing humorlessly. "I'm your father."

Chapter Twelve

The laughter bubbles out of me without warning. I simply can't hold it, it bursts out of me from the absurdity of it all.

"You're like...what? Thirty-two, thirty-three? My father was supposedly reaped twenty-five years ago. The math is not mathing, my friend," I laugh.

He takes a deep breath, and bobs his head slowly. "Yes, and no."

"What's that supposed to mean?" Amadeus suddenly interrupts, making himself a part of the conversation. I clench my jaw for a second, biting my tongue.

"Time moves differently here," Orvin says to him. Looking like he wants to do anything but talk to my best friend. "Tomorrow is the July reapings."

"That—no. We've just been here for—what? Five days or something," Amadeus argues.

Orvin rolls his eyes. "If you could just shut up and let me explain, you wouldn't piss me off that much. Gods. I was reaped five years ago in this realm. I was twenty-four years old when I got reaped, making me twenty-nine years old actually," he shrugs. As if this is a normal conversation to have.

"You look older," I note, tilting my head to the side and I take a moment to really study him.

His face is scarred where his beard isn't reaching on his chin. The sides of his head are shaved short with longer hair on the top, and you can see the scar reaching all the way across the side of his head on one side. He looks rugged and angry, with deep creases in between his brows. There's also five perfectly circular scars curling from his cheekbone and up around his eye, giving him a menacing look. Then there's his eyes. They're so blue it's almost jarring.

"You're bonded to a griffin, aren't you?" Elodie asks, jumping into the conversation too.

"Yes," he nods. "I'm an Aerial Griffin Scout."

"What's an Aerial Griffin Scout?" Galen asks, relaying the last part slowly to better understand it.

Orvin, my supposed father, groans and makes a face. "It's just my role. I'm bonded to a griffin, making me able to be airborne. Everyone that is reaped during the July reapings are sorted into the Griffin regiment, like all of you are in the Dragon regiment because you got reaped in June. Scout is my beetle mark. There are scouts on foot too," he sounds bored.

"I don't care about all that—" I do, but that's not what's important right now. "What do you mean you're my father? You can't be!" Could he?

He studies me for a long moment. "Diana's your mother, isn't she?" He asks, and I blink, once. "You have the same heart shaped face, and that silvery hair." He sighs, smiling to himself. "You got my eyes though."

Shit.

He might actually be my father. "But you're too young!" I protest.

Orvin rolls his eyes. "Didn't I tell you that time moves differently in Nowhere? Besides, this is information you already knew. If you didn't, I wouldn't be able to tell you that," He says cryptically.

"Not to be selfish or anything, but what the fuck do I do about this newly sparked power of mine," Killian growls. "Train? How? What do I do with this kind of power? It's—I don't want to hurt anyone, but it seems like I'm doing it without meaning to!" I can tell that he's about to lose his shit, and I have no idea how to comfort him. I've got enough on my plate.

"Oh, yes. You have to do the mental training to try and block it. Visualize your power and put up shields." He says it like it's obvious, and it really isn't. It seems like Killian agrees with my assessment because he looks about ready to burst into flames.

Orvin rolls his eyes. "Look, there is no set way to train your power, because they are all different. Yes, you do have similar powers like water welding and earth control that are more common, but even they are different from person to person."

"By now I kind of feel like I'm just repeating myself, but...I'm confused," I say. I'm fully aware that I haven't said it out loud that much, but I've said it multiple times in my head by now.

"*I know.*" Riften says, and I glance at his expressionless face.

"*Shut up.*"

"The beetle mark in your palm unlocks the hidden magic in you. Some people don't have magic, but, to be honest...most people left from my reaping year do. Obviously, because in this hostile environment, having some kind of magical power helps keep you alive." Orvin looks over at the table and he lets his finger glide along the table top as he picks up a spoon, twirling it between his thumb and pointer finger. "Some people that don't have magic in them or develop some kind of power linger for up to a year, maybe two. But out of the six thousand that got reaped during my year, I think..." he leans his head back and looks up at the ceiling. "Roughly two hundred survived, and that's with all three regiments. I do believe there is one person that is unbonded and powerless, but I don't know when he got reaped. Never talked to the man, I honestly try to keep to myself for the most part."

That gives us a survival rate of what? Less than five percent?

Basically, we're all fucked.

Great.

"Does every bonded person get powers?" Amadeus asks eagerly.

"From the ones that survive?" Orvin spins the spoon between his fingers, letting it slide through each of his fingers. "Yes. I haven't heard otherwise. The creatures choose their bonded riders by their potential within a month or two after the reapings, but I've also seen a bonding happening as late as a year later. The creatures are the ones ruling here, we have no say until we get chosen and successfully bonded."

"What's your power?" Amadeus asks.

Orvin gives him a slow once over, tilting his head to one side. The side of his mouth twitches. "That's none of your business," he says, breaking into a grin that makes his eyes gleam with mischief. Then a dark laugh breaks free from him. "Oh, don't you even try to pry that information from me. My shields are too strong for that. Besides, I'm giving you guys more answers than I ever got after my reaping."

"Thank you, we appreciate that more than you know," Elodie gives him a small smile and bows her head slightly.

"You're welcome," Orvin puts the spoon back onto the table top and straightens. "Maybe I'll see you guys around. You're an interesting bunch." Again his attention falls onto me and a shiver runs down my spine. I resist the urge I get to shift my weight.

"Ta-ta," he says, giving us a half bow before striding away, disappearing in the crowd.

I let out a long heavy breath. Glancing over at Riften who's been lingering in the background like a shadow, I meet his thoughtful stare. His mossy green eyes rest on me through furrowed brows. There's a tingling sensation that settles in my stomach, and I feel a slight blush creep up my neck from the intensity in his eyes.

"*What?*"

I shake my head to answer his question, making everyone's attention land on me, before they look to Riften.

"What are you doing here?" I don't like the accusing tone in Amadeus's voice. It truly grates on my nerves.

"Would you just stop?" I grit out through my teeth, shooting daggers at him with my eyes.

"He's always around you. He's being creepy."

"He is not! If it wasn't for him I'd be dead right now! Leave him be, Amadeus, I mean it."

Riften snorts, shaking his head before he turns around and walks away from us.

"*I can feel your hungry eyes lingering, Trouble.*"

The blush creeps up my neck, heating my cheeks. "*Fuck off.*"

His laughter rings out throughout my mind, and I watch his shaking shoulders as he leaves.

"Oooh, do I pick up some tension there?" Elodie's teasing tone makes my cheeks heat even worse.

"Stop it."

As we trot across the courtyard after dinner I can feel the day catching up to me.

The sparring was brutal.

As usual.

The dinner was shit.

As usual.

I have no idea where the guys went, and honestly it doesn't matter. I need sleep. And right now, I have a lumpy bed with scratchy sheets screaming my name. Everything in this shithole sucks.

The food. The living conditions. The training. The constant dread and fear. The daily deaths and the constant possibility of becoming a living torch.

The dinner was informative though.

I still can't quite grasp the fact that Orvin's my father. The age difference is totally throwing me off to be honest, but if there is some merit to what he explained about the time moving differently, it won't be five years until I'm able to see Pipp again.

If she decides to get reaped, because she *does* have a choice. In some ways. The Gods might have something to say about it, but there is a way. Then again, when I think of all the horrible deaths I've witnessed since my reaping, I don't want her to endure any of it. This place is cruel, and it truly has the ability to destroy anyone. No matter how skilled you are prior to your reaping.

The lake.

The stairs.

The dragons.

The sparring.

The failed bondings.

"Holy shit, look at that!" Elodie suddenly exclaims. "It's fucking *huge*!"

I bump right into her back as she stops abruptly in front of me. "What?"

"Is that a dragon?" She sounds confused, and it makes my curiosity peak.

I look in the direction her attention is, not finding anything at first. "What the fuck are you on about, I don't see any—" The breath catches in my chest as I spot it. It's absolutely *stunning*.

Perched on a ledge on the side of the mountain far above us sits a stark white creature. It has the body of a dragon, but the wings are different. They resemble the wings of a pegasus more than the leathery wings of a dragon. They almost look to be covered with feathers, shimmering in the golden light from the oncoming sunset, making them look translucent.

And he's enormous, even from afar. He takes up the entire space on a ledge that I've seen both two and three dragons share quite comfortably.

My mouth falls open.

Holy crap. I've never seen a more beautiful creature.

"I wonder if it will bond with anyone," Elodie breathes, holding her hand to her chest.

"Oh, no. He won't bond with anyone," a female voice says behind us, and we both whirl around.

The dragon rider from the first day is standing there with her arms across her chest, looking up towards the mountain. I think her name is Mara? Tara, maybe? It was something Ara, I'm sure of it.

Fuck, I'll learn it eventually, right now I'm more focused on the white creature on the mountain ledge.

"Why is that?" Elodie asks, disappointment oozing from her voice.

"He's never been bonded before," she drops a big satchel to the ground with a thud, making what's inside rattle and clink. "Don't ask about the content," she says, giving us both a stern look.

"I wasn't going to, actually. I have some questions about the bonding," I say.

"Oh, what about it?"

"Do the creatures bond multiple times?" I query.

"Well, yes, some do. Others don't," she shrugs, brushing it off like it's nothing. She doesn't continue either, making this whole interaction awkward.

Peeking over at Elodie tells me that she's uncomfortable with the silence. She shifts her weight and twirls her finger around the hem of her too big tunic. I take a breath as I contemplate how to continue the conversation. "So," I start, exhaling the trapped air inside my lungs in a long breath. "What happens if the creature you're bonded to dies?"

"Well, you die." The answer comes so abruptly that I can hardly catch my breath.

"What? You just...die? But how? Why?"

"They make the rules, not us. You share a life force with your bonded creature, but they are their own source of life and magic. If they die, your life force will cease to exist, killing you almost instantly. Yes, on rare occasions some people are able to hold on for up to a day or so, but most die within the hour. That's why so many people die during the bonding process. Their bodies can't handle the additional magic. It's quite simple, really."

"It's not. Not at all simple," I protest.

"Yeah, well. After a while you learn to just roll with it," she snorts. "Anyways. The White Dragon? He's never bonded as far as I'm aware, and he's sworn not to bond with anyone. Either way, you don't have a say in which dragon chooses you, if they even decide to bond. Like I said; *they* make the rules."

"Honestly, I don't even know if I want to bond with anyone," Elodie mutters, making the dragon rider laugh.

"It's not up to you, you better accept it sooner rather than later and prepare for the worst," she says in a terrifying and emotionless tone.

I. Don't. Want. To.

I want to survive.

I want to live.

"Yara! Could you come help me?" A man on the other side of the courtyard yells, and the rider in front of us turns her head to him.

Yara! That was her name.

Right.

"Coming! Now, get to your bunks, rest up. Tomorrow is another day of misery." She picks up the satchel from the ground, throws it over her shoulder and stalks off towards the man, leaving us stunned once more. I swear this place will make me go crazy.

Chapter Thirteen

The days blur together in the Dover mountains.

July and August reapings come and go through the haze of constant dread and misery. Our numbers continue to drop steadily, and I still know next to no names. My friend group is enough names to keep track of.

There seems to be next to no structure to our training schedule. Most of the time it feels like we're just showing off for the dragons. They continue to watch us from their perch. Maybe that will change once more people go through a successful bonding. So far, that hasn't happened yet.

"My blisters got blisters," Elodie groans as she pulls off her boot and inspects her mangled foot. She's not the only one that has blistered feet. "Look," she says, sticking her foot in front of my face. I lean away from it.

"El, I'm not blind, and your feet smell like death, please keep them as far away from me as you possibly can," I chuckle, shaking my head at her as I watch her stick her foot into the stream of icy water.

There have been plenty of attempts at bondings. At least one or two every other day, but none have been successful a month and a half into our new reality.

"Sorry," she says and blushes slightly, her pale gray eyes dimming.

We're on laundry duty for the day by the hillside behind the cluster of buildings we occupy. It takes us about ten minutes to walk here, which makes this task extremely labor intensive. We have to carry all the laundry to the stream by foot.

Having a dragon help us carry it would actually be quite practical all things considered, so a bond wouldn't be too bad right about now.

On the plus side, our small group of oddballs has stayed together, getting closer and more tight knit. I haven't seen Orvin since he left us in the dining hall. He might have been stationed somewhere else, but I can't be sure.

Glancing over to Elodie, I see deep emotions swirling in her eyes.

Killian has been doing his very best to control his power of pain infliction, but he struggles to get a grip on them. It's difficult for him to not make physical contact with anyone. He doesn't want to unintentionally hurt them, and if he's not careful he might end up killing someone. A power like his, should in theory make us all wary of him. Yet, none of our small group seems to care at all. The chances of us dying from pretty much everything are sky high anyway, so what's a little more danger?

I take a deep breath. Elodie runs her hand aimlessly through the water in the stream, making small water whirls with her pointerfinger. She hums a tune I'm not familiar with, most likely a tune from her home town. I can feel myself getting annoyed by her stalling and my patience runs out. We've been at this stream for well over two hours, and she's barely touched the laundry. "Could you please do what you're supposed to do and wash the damn sheets so we can get inside? I think a storm is coming pretty soon," I say looking up to the darkening sky.

The clouds have a blue-ish shade, almost fading into dark gray. Heavy rain is definitively coming our way.

"Yes, yes, I'm sorry," she mumbles, pulling her foot from the water and putting on her boots again.

I've noticed that Elodie is struggling too. How she gives Killian lingering looks filled with pain and hurt. I can tell she wants to be with him, and not being able to touch him is slowly eating away at her. She hides it well, but not well enough. We all see it.

No one seems to want to tell us anything about this land, and every time we try to ask a question it's like their words get stuck in their throats. Somehow I've figured out that there is a kind of spell that blocks them from speaking about the history of the land going past the most basic information.

Which is extremely inconvenient.

"You know, if you had a layer of clothing in between. Like stockings or something you wouldn't get so many blisters," I say.

"Yeah? And where do you suggest I get a pair of those?" She asks, huffing out a breath. "If the dragons hadn't scorched half of the people they find unworthy, their clothes would still be usable after they pick us off like livestock."

I sigh from her angry tone. "El, I get that you're angry but—" I gasp when water is splashed in my face, and I'm immediately soaked in icy cold water. "What did you do that for?"

"I didn't do anything!" Elodie protests, sounding horribly confused, scared even.

"Yeah, right. So you suggest that the water just magically decided to jump out of the stream and into my face?" I snap through clattering teeth.

"I—I don't know," Elodie whimpers, and I see tears in her eyes. I'm about to open my mouth to console her when my words get trapped in my chest. Heavy gusts of wind suddenly break out around us. I look up to the sky, dread flooding my veins as an enormous teal dragon is headed straight for us, making its descent.

"Oh, shit, oh shit. Salem!" Elodie screams. Our bodies lock up in terror as the dragon lands, its yellowish eyes pinned at us.

It came out of Nowhere! How in the Gods names did it manage to sneak up on us like that? The teal dragon in front of us is absolutely massive. As it opens its jaw, gleaming white teeth as big as my palm comes into view.

We need to hide, but there is Nowhere to fucking hide. Anywhere. By the stream we're totally exposed to both the elements and the creatures around us.

The earth underneath our feet quakes as the dragon touches the ground, and we both struggle to stay standing.

Maybe it just wants to drink some water from the stream. Yes, that seems plausible. It's just thirsty. Fear enters into my body as I see the golden threads seep out from underneath its scales at its chest.

"It's going to try to bond!" I yell over to Elodie.

"What!? How do you know that!?"

"The golden threads!" I scream.

"What threads!?" She shrieks, her voice filled with panicked.

"The ones coming from its chest. It—they—can't you see them!?"

The golden threads reach out towards us, and I back up from the teal dragon on shaky legs. "Elodie, you need to move!" I hiss.

"I...can't," she gasps, her voice shaking.

"What do you mean you can't?"

"I can't move!" She whimpers through gritted teeth. And I watch in horror as the tendrils of golden light reach for her body, latching on to her left arm.

I've seen this too many times by now.

Golden threads reach for someone that seems frozen in place, clamping down on their left arm, seeking the beetle mark in the palm of their hand.

I see their bodies start to shudder and shake, eventually making them topple over. The skin on their bodies crack open, flaking away from the bone. Their cheeks hollow, leaving their faces gaunt and gruesome. Wide terrified eyes bug out from the eye sockets, eyes that will forever stay empty. Leaving them as a mare husk of what they once were.

Drained of all life.

"Please," I beg, falling to my knees as I again watch in horror as this happens to my friend.

Only...there is no scream of agony coming from Elodie as the golden threads find their mark. Her face is twisted in pain, but she doesn't scream. Her body doesn't shake or shudder. She stands perfectly still.

The mark on her palm starts to glow with a golden light. Then it begins to grow. It looks like a stream of water and golden smoke circling in intricate patterns along her arm, towards her neck.

Elodie gasps, her chest lifting from a deep breath before she lets it out in a relieved sigh. Her pale gray eyes start to glow, circling her irises with a golden ring that seems to move and settle in her piercing gaze.

Then the golden threads break loose from the dragon. They flow into her arm, and settle underneath her skin. Slowly, her golden markings start to darken, turning black, still moving like water her skin.

"Are you okay?" I breathe in her direction. Almost afraid of raising my voice, in fear of pissing the dragon off and turning me into a living torch.

Elodie blinks rapidly, seeming stunned and deep in thought.

"Did...did he hurt you?" I ask, trying my best not to freak the fuck out. "What happened? Elodie, talk to me," I beg breathlessly.

"I—" She frowns. "She didn't hurt me," she says. "She...we...she bonded with me," she breathes. Turning her head to me, she lets out a relieved laugh as her knees buckle and she collapses to her knees.

Tears start to run down her face, and she turns her gaze to the dragon. Her eyes are filled with love and understanding. She utters a sentence I can't understand, and I glare at her in confusion. It sounds like a language, but I have no idea what she's saying.

I watch as she lifts her hand up to the teal dragon, and my eyes almost bug out of my skull as the dragon takes a gentle step towards my friend and places its snout to her outreached hand. A golden shimmer shudders over the dragon's scales as the beetle mark comes into contact with her.

"What...what was that?" I'm hesitant to ask, but I want to know. I want to understand.

"Their language," she says, blinking rapidly again. "But I'm not able to repeat it, or translate it," she says on a swallow, turning her face to me.

So that's how it is. Their language. It's not possible to translate it into our tongue.

"But I understand now," Elodie mutters, her eyes filled with sorrow. "I understand why they called us here."

I watch as her eyes clear in determination. Elodie brushes the tears off her face. She swallows hard, and a soft laugh breaks out from her. "This is the best feeling I've ever had. She's...she's such a gentle creature, despite their violent behavior."

I blink.

"That statement makes absolutely no sense," I mumble, flinching suddenly as the teal dragon huffs out a warm breath in my direction, making smoke waft from her nostrils.

Laughter slips out of Elodie, and she shakes her head.

"She's amused by you," she explains.

"What's her name?" I'm almost afraid of asking, in case the dragon finds it offensive in any way.

"Her name is Euna," Elodie says, biting her lip before her eyes brighten in joy. "That's a pretty name," she says, directing it to her dragon. Because, essentially, it is *her* dragon now.

"This...this is incredible," I breathe. "You are the first successfully bonded pair."

Euna huffs, and a rumble breaks out of her chest, making Elodie laugh.

"What did she say?" I push gently, but Elodie shakes her head.

"I can't translate it. It's like it's on the tip of my tongue, but the words elude me. I know what she means, but I'm not able to tell you what she's saying." I can't hide my disappointment by her answer. That makes it difficult to explain pretty much anything the creatures say.

"Oh," I breathe, unease trickling along my spine. I wonder how they're going to rule us if they're not able to relay what the rules are.

Well, probably the way they already have.

By torching us if they don't like us.

I wonder if it would be different if I were bonded. If Elodie would be able to tell me what Euna says then, or if there is a curse or something that prevents it. And if it is a curse; how to break it?

"All I can tell you is that she won't hurt you," Elodie says, and I breathe out in relief.

"Thank fuck for that," I mumble, but for some reason it doesn't ease my worry.

I look at the markings on Elodie's bare arm—how they move and twirl around it like trickling water. It's incredibly beautiful to watch. I wonder if it will reflect her power, if she gets any. Or maybe she already has, considering the ice cold soak I got earlier.

"I have to go and tell Killian," she says suddenly, turning to me in a flash.

"Yes, you should absolutely do that," I respond, and watch as Elodie darts down the path towards the cluster of buildings again.

My thoughts go to my own golden markings and I wonder if there are different types of bonds. So far I haven't come across any other person with a golden marking like the ones Riften and I share. Every other rider I've met has had black markings, and they appear to have a life of their own by the way they move and swirl around under the skin. I wonder if the size of the mark have anything to do with the strength of the bond, or is the bond as strong for everybody?

Now that Elodie is bonded to Euna, I have so many questions about it, and how it works. Unfortunately, it doesn't look like I will get those answers unless I bond with a dragon myself, and...honestly I don't know if I want to. Even if I don't have any choice in the matter. The dragons make the rules, we just have to adapt to them.

I'm so caught up in my own thoughts that I don't notice that I'm left there, alone, with the teal dragon. And a trickle of unease has me choking up completely.

In slow motion I turn my head in Euna's direction, feeling the color of my cheeks drain away in a heartbeat.

I gape at her huge form as she studies me with knowing eyes.

I swallow, struggling to breathe. Slowly, I bow my head to her, because at that moment it feels like the most logical thing to do.

Euna chuffs, and warm steam surrounds my body. Making my hair fly in all directions.

I hear her move, but I stay motionless.

Then a strong gust of wind whirls around me, knocking me over as she takes off. I fall on my back, eyes wide as Euna flies off towards the mountain.

I stare after her, holding my breath. Not daring to move.

Then, it starts to rain.

Chapter Fourteen

The news about Elodie's successful bonding travels around like wildfire, and everyone's spirit seems to be lifted a fraction by it.

I get it.

After so many failed attempts everybody dreads the bond. Now they see that it's possible to survive it, the tension has diminished. It's like we all breathe a little easier. As far as I've gathered, the two first months here are the most deadly, and we're almost at the finish line.

Me, on the other hand? I'm more tense than ever.

The days that follow Elodie and Euna's bonding, more attempts occur. It's almost like the dragons have started to rush into it. Rumour has it that the other creatures also have started more frequent attempts too, and as far as I know most of them fail.

People die. In huge numbers.

I'm sick of seeing the golden threads whip after people, and turn the majority of them into husks. It's like I can feel their lives getting siphoned out of their bodies and see their souls leave their fragile remains.

It's nauseating.

"Can you believe that they don't care to even write down our names until we pass the bonding? What about the foot soldiers?" Elodie grumbles at lunch and slams her wooden bowl on the table. The content wobbling from the force, despite how dry it is. "None of the older riders even asked about my name, but now? Everyone knows it. I even had to write it into a book," she mutters.

Amadeus looks up from his bowl of sawdust to listen in to our conversation, but I ignore him. Instead I give Elodie a sideways glance without turning my head more than a fraction. "Why do you even care? Nobody cares about our names here, Elodie," I turn to her, leaning back in my chair.

"We're taken from our homes. Forced to climb up a deadly cliffside where most people fall to their deaths. Then we're shoved into an overcrowded building with poor living conditions and put on display in front of a dozen dragons who frequently torch the ones they don't approve of! And we're just supposed to accept that? Fuck no! I'm sick of it."

"What crawled up your ass?" She makes a face like I've slapped her. "I was just wondering why no-one cares about our names until we're bonded. I mean, don't they have magic in this land, someone must have the ability to know everyones names or something. Have you been asked for your name?"

"No." I clench my jaw for a second. "But what we all share is this." I lift my left hand to her, showing her my palm. I want to shove my hand into her face, but I refrain. "We all have the beetle mark, and how did they know what symbol to put there?" I roll my eyes, because to me it's starting to get kind of obvious. "The fact that we're not aware of the system doesn't mean there isn't one present."

Elodie growls under her breath, shaking her head as she tries to get a hold of her frustration. "I'm just saying that someone should care, that's all."

"Would you bother to write down every single name of all six thousand people getting reaped and killed every year?" I survey her for a minute before continuing. "How would they identify us if we drowned in the lake on our first day? We just got here, and if we haven't interacted with anyone, there is no way to tell our names or who we were. And who are they going to notify? Our families?" I start to laugh a bitter laugh, feeling my anger rise. "How would they do that?" I slam my hands to the table making everything on it in my vicinity rattle. My cup falls over and spills the contents across the table.

"Salem?" Suddenly, Elodie sounds concerned.

I cut her off before she can continue. "I'm fine."

I don't know what's gotten into me. My feelings are going haywire for some reason. It might be because I've had enough of this place. I feel sick of this land. It's a living hell being here, and all I want is to get home.

The longing for home is getting stronger and stronger every day that passes. It clenches around my chest and all I want to do is to crawl into bed beside my sister and hug her.

"I need air," I say as I push my chair away from the table, making it screech horribly against the floor. If I didn't already have the attention to every single person in the mess hall, I certainly do now.

The pressure in my chest is almost crushing, and I need space to breathe. I grab my bowl of disgusting slop, and carry it to the cleaning station, shoving it forcefully into the sink before leaving the hall altogether.

The fresh air that hits my face doesn't help, but the rain does.

Kind of.

I try to shut off my brain, but it doesn't work. I can feel my mood getting worse by the minute, to the point where I can't stand it anymore and I start to run. At first, I run around in a circle in the courtyard, but eventually I realize that my feet have carried me further.

Confused, I look down at the ground, seeing moss and dirt. I look up, and find myself standing in front of a cave.

It pulses with energy.

Glowing beetles crawl around my feet as I stare at the entrance.

"*Salem.*"

Fuck no.

I turn on my heel, and start in the other direction to get as far away from the creepy cave as possible. I have no time for that hag.

And how the fuck did I even end up here? I was running in the courtyard just a minute ago.

"*Salem!*" The whisper comes out sharper this time, and a prickling sensation runs down the back of my neck. It's impossible to tell who the voice belongs to, it sounds both masculine and feminine at the same time. Which is kind of unnerving.

"I said no!" I yell back to the voice as I continue walking. I blink, and force my body to halt when the entrance to the cave is in front of me again. I realize that my feet have found their way to the exact same spot as before.

"*Salem...*" The cave calls.

"What don't you understand? I'm not interested! I'm done. I'm so fucking done with this place, I just want out!" I scream at the entrance hoping the hag hears me.

I turn around once more to walk away, but my feet won't move. As I look up, the entrance is there.

Mocking me.

"Fine!" I growl and lift my arms in defeat. Golden threads shoot out from my fingertips flowing aimlessly through the air. A scream pushes up my throat. I shake my hands, watching in horror as the golden threads of light whip around. One of the threads wraps around a dead branch of a nearby tree and I yank my hand away.

"What the hell is going on!?"

"*Salem..*"

"Give me a minute!" I growl back, and I swear I hear someone chuckle on the wind. I shake my hands again, and finally the threads disappear into thin air and I can move my feet again.

I glare at the entrance of the cave with murder in my eyes and stomp through the entrance, getting swallowed up by the darkness.

Slowly the cave gets illuminated by glowing beetles along the walls and ceiling, and if I hadn't been fuming mad, I would stop and admire the beauty of the incredible insects. Despite my dislike of bugs in general.

I'm not scared of them.

I just don't like them.

As the cave opens up into the familiar space I take a deep breath, closing my eyes. "What do you want?" I snap, sounding as rude as I intend to be, but when I finally open my eyes to look at the old hag I expect to find, it's not her.

"How in the world did you get in here?" I gasp, looking around at the cave. "How did you even fit? You're huge!"

A rumbling sound makes the whole cave shake, and a couple of stones fall from the ceiling and along the walls.

"*With some difficulty,*" The sound filling my head is male, deep and growling, but not the same as the whisper I heard. It's catching me totally off guard. I look around, blinking rapidly in all directions before my eyes land on the White Dragon.

It spoke to me. Or, rather *he* spoke to me. But how? The dragons can't speak.

It huffs at me, and a deep rumble of amusement emanates from him. "*You're a funny one, aren't you?*"

"I'd disagree with you if I could, but right now my entire body feels funny and is buzzing. I'm so confused..." I whisper. "Did...did you do...are we bonded?" I ask the dragon.

He inhales slowly. *"No. I just wanted to talk to you."*

"Okay?" I drag out the question, narrowing my eyes. "I'm so confused," I repeat on a breath. It has been my most common emotion since getting here.

"Do other dragons do this too or just you?" I squeak.

"No. Just me. As far as I know."

"Okay, good to know." I blink.

Nothing makes sense, and even the bits and pieces that actually do make sense...don't.

"What did you want to talk to me about?" My voice is shaky, and to be honest I'm not feeling too confident at the moment either.

"I know you've felt a disconnection here, and I can admit that the tree is dying. You will play a much bigger part than you were prepared for in this war, Little One." He moves his head closer to where I stand, and I can feel the warmth from his huge head as he studies me with eyes filled with so much knowledge.

"The sky will burn until dawn. The rain will fall after the drought and give life to the shadows. Monsters will come, and you will lose what you hold closest to your heart, Salem," He warns, his unique voice filled with sorrow. *"I'm sorry, Little One. Your fate has been altered by your choice. A choice you made without every piece on the board. Be wary of the one who lurks in the shadows; for he will do what it takes to get his way."* He finishes, letting the silence between us drag on for a long while.

I stand there. Glaring at the White Dragon.

Blinking.

What. The. Fuck?

I gape at the dragon and my body shudders. "Okay, thank you for...that. I'll keep that in mind," I say, taking a hesitant step backwards.

Riddles.

I *hate* riddles.

I can never figure out those petulant, nonsensical word-spewn sentences for the life of me. If this dragon is warning me about my death, I will end up running smack into it, face first. That's for damn sure.

And now I have no idea what to do. Should I just go? Will he even let me? Does he have anything more to say?

I take a hesitant step backwards to make my leave, wavering for just a moment to see if he will let me go.

He just watches me with his intelligent eyes, giving me the sense that he's pleading for something I can't give him.

"Um, goodbye then," I say with my voice shaking. "I'll, uh, see you around, I guess." I back up for a few more steps before I turn on my heel and leave the cave, feeling my chest grow heavier with each step. As I escape the cave, I catch a glimpse of a blooming tree to my left before the whole world tilts in front of me. The sensation of my soul being yanked out of my body hits me in a flash.

I stumble.

Falling to my knees on the cobblestone, I gasp for air.

Looking up, I'm in the courtyard again.

Disoriented, I straighten and look over my shoulder, unease settling in the pit of my stomach. I was just in the cave, talking to the White Dragon but now? I'm not so sure it really happened. Did I just imagine it all?

"There you are." I look in the direction of the voice not recognizing it at first. Amadeus emerges from the darkened space between the buildings of the Dragon and Griffin Regiments. "Are you okay?" He asks, tilting his head to the side.

I swallow as I look over my shoulder to see if there is any trace of the cave. There isn't.

"Yeah, I just...nothing, never mind." I get to my feet as Amadeus reaches me. "What's up?" I ask him.

"Elodie's looking for you, that's all," he says, clenching his teeth, and I get the sense that he's not telling me the whole truth.

"You know me too well," he mutters when I narrow my eyes at him.

"I sure do, now spill," I demand, crossing my arms over my chest.

"No...I was just thinking about something," He says, then he stays silent for a moment, chewing on his lip.

I wait.

"I can't find her," He says.

Confused, I ask, "Who?" And look around, as if the one he's looking for is right there.

"My sister," he rubs the back of his neck in a jagged motion. "And with you finding your father and everything..."

"That's what's been bothering you?" I ask, and immediately realize that I'm being rude.

I backtrack. "I know you had high hopes of seeing your sister again, Amadeus, but...she's gone. And she has been gone for five years—"

"You don't understand, Salem! She's here, I can feel it in my bones!" He explains, grabbing me by the shoulders in a tight grip.

"Amadeus," I say in a softer tone. "I'm really sorry."

"I swear I can feel her! She's here, but no one has seen her. No one even knows her name. And there's the—" He cuts himself off, shaking his head. His eyes shine with unshed tears, and it breaks my heart. Cracks it right open.

I feel like a horrible person for the way I snapped at him, of course he has his own problems to deal with. I'm not the only one in pain or misery in this place.

We all suffer, and the worst part is that we don't know *why* we suffer. It all seems pointless. Like, suffering for the point of suffering.

"Maybe—" He interrupts me.

"I need to find her, Salem!"

"I understand that," I say, taking his hands and removing them from my shoulders. "And I will help, just...breathe, okay? It doesn't help being impatient," I soothe. Or, try to. Soothing others has never been my strong suit. "What kind of leads do you have?"

Chapter Fifteen

Turns out that he doesn't have much of anything. In fact, he hasn't been able to find anything written anywhere.

The book I'm currently staring at is blank. There is nothing on the front, and nothing inside. I look from the book to Amadeus, then down at the book again. I take a deep breath and look up at my best friend. "It's blank." I say slowly.

"Yes."

As I turn the page I glance up at him. "Like...there is *nothing* written here."

"I know."

I turn to another page, and I don't even know why I bother. It's not like the words will magically appear the more I flip through the book. Yet there are multiple people scanning the shelves and looking through seemingly blank texts. "What's the point of a library if the books are blank?" The book makes a thumping sound as I close it and put it back on the shelf.

"Do you understand my frustration now?"

I do. I absolutely do.

"Why are we even here if you knew there was no information to be found?" I ask, picking up another empty book. Leafing through the pages

I see this one also suffers the same ailment, so I put it back. "Let's split up," I suggest.

Honestly I'm not too confident of finding anything helpful within these shelves, but I said I'd help him look; so that is what I'm doing.

Even if all of the book spines are bare, they are still pretty to look at. I've never been to a proper library before. Here, there are shelves upon shelves with books from floor to ceiling. The leather bindings are stained in different shades of brown, red, blue and green.

Gently, I let my finger brush the weathered covers. It's so odd. All of these books look old and well read. The spines are slightly cracked in some places, and the pages are yellowed. Some of them even look to be bulging from moisture, like the space they've been kept in is too damp.

"Are you finding what you're looking for?"

My fingers halt their progress along the spines, and my heart skips a beat. I know who I'll find if I turn around.

That voice.

The intimacy of it.

"I haven't seen you around lately," I say through the lump in my throat. "I would have thought you were avoiding me."

Is my voice shaking? I hope it isn't.

His chuckle whispers along the sensitive skin of my neck, and goosebumps erupt from the ghostly touch. "I have been."

The admission coming from his lips makes me turn to him, but before I'm able to even open my mouth he holds up a finger to silence me. "No, no. None of that." His finger brushes my bottom lip.

"I didn't say anything," I whisper against his skin, and his pupils dilate.

"You didn't have to, Trouble." His voice holds a vibrant rasp that feels like velvet in my mind. He taps the side of his temple, and his eyes glitter with mirth.

A blush creeps up my neck, and I look away from the green of his eyes. He cups my jaw, directing my gaze back to him. "I didn't take you for being shy."

"I'm not," I say in a whisper.

His thumb brushes along my bottom lip, and I release it from between my teeth. Why is it that this man has me reacting like this? It doesn't make sense.

"Then why are you looking away?"

I take a deep, steadying breath to steel myself before I meet his amused expression. I take his hand in mine, and the golden bond between us is pulled taught. "I'm not." At least, not now.

"Right," his amused murmur makes my body tingle. "Let's pretend you're telling the truth."

"Riften, I don't have time for this, I'm looking for something." I brush his hand away from my person.

I need distance.

"Really? And you thought it would be a good idea to go to the Library of Stubborn Books?" He laughs.

"Is that the name of the library?"

He inhales heavily. "No idea. I just know that the books don't normally reveal their content unless you're worthy of their knowledge."

"How does that work?"

"Like I said, I don't know, and even if I did," he pauses and surveys me for a moment. "I wouldn't be able to tell you."

"What does that even mean?" I stare at him in absolute confusion, and when he tilts his head to the side and smiles knowingly, I get the urge to slap him.

He leans even closer. "I think you already know."

I turn to face him properly, and narrow my eyes. Stepping towards him I level him with a glare. "Do you ever back down?" I ask, standing my ground with him.

"Oh, I have no problem getting on my knees for you. The question is..." He brushes a strand of hair behind my ear before he continues. "Would you be willing to do the same for me?"

I take a sharp intake of breath, feeling my core clench. Then his voice vibrates through my mind. "*I don't think you would...yet.*" He takes a step back, leaving me almost breathless.

"Don't get into too much trouble now." His deep voice is absolutely unfazed by any of this, or so it seems.

I want to change that.

I want to watch him quiver.

I want to watch him break.

"Prove it."

He stops mid-step. "Prove what?" He doesn't turn, but he tilts his head so I see his profile.

"Get on your knees." I quirk an eyebrow, feeling a mischievous grin take over my features. "I want to see you bow before me. Maybe even beg for my attention."

The corner of his mouth twitches. "You gotta earn that, Trouble." And with that he walks away, disappearing between the shelves. Leaving me trembling with—I don't even know what!

It's not that I haven't been intimate with anyone before, but this feels different. It feels deeper, more...significant.

I let out the breath I've been holding, feeling my hand cramp up from the tight grip on the shelf beside me.

Shit.

This man...

"Did you find anything?" I jump from the voice behind me, and turn around. Amadeus crosses his arms over his chest as his eyes narrow to slits. A muscle ticks in his jaw, and I'm not sure what to say. "About Teagan," he supplies, reminding me what we're doing in here.

"Oh, right," I breathe. "No. No, I didn't find anything."

"Were you even looking?" He asks, and a sudden pressure settles on my chest. Coaxing a response from me. It feels foreign.

I don't want to give him an answer, so I fight the urge to speak.

"You guys are impossible to find!"

"Killian," I heave a silent breath of relief at the sound of his voice. Thankfully, the pressure I feel disappears with the interruption.

"What do you want?" Amadeus snaps, and I jolt from the rudeness in his tone.

"Amadeus!" I dig my elbow into his side. "Don't talk to him like that," I say, which only earns me a glare.

Killian pauses for a second. "Dude, the tension between you guys smells bad. Anyways, look!" I don't even have the opportunity to react to what he said before he rolls up his sleeve with a huge grin on his face.

On his forearm is an elongated black mark of thorns swirling under the skin.

"What? You bonded a dragon?"

He nods vehemently to my outburst. "This morning, after formation."

My eyes widen. "Damn, did it hurt?"

"Like a bitch! I thought I was dying! Have you seen Elodie? I gotta tell her!"

"Um, I think she's out flying on Euna with the other bonded." To be fair I can't be sure, I haven't really seen much of her since she moved out of the sleeping hall. You only get your own room after you bond. She's also started working closer with her dragon and we don't see her nearly as often as before. And in true fashion of this place, nobody wants to tell us anything—or rather—they can't.

"Cool. By the way," Killian says, bouncing on his toes. "Galen and Mason made some mead, so we were thinking—" He leans closer, and both me and Amadeus instantly shy away from him in favor of not getting inflicted by his touch. "Shit, sorry! We were thinking that we should have a bonfire." He says, grinning like a fool.

"That actually sounds pretty fun," I laugh. "Wait. Mason? Mason Ghostport?" I look at Amadeus, who looks equally surprised.

Killian contemplates for a moment. "I think he's from Terrby."

I'm shocked.

Killian clears his throat, grinning. "I'm gonna go look for Elodie. You guys have fun with whatever you're doing." He says, and walks away.

I take in a deep breath, sensing an awkward silence settling in the room. Biting my lip I look over to my best friend. "So, do you think it's our Mason?" It's difficult to gauge his expression, so I continue. "I mean, it very well could be, couldn't it? He's a good fighter."

"Maybe. I don't know too many people with that name. Wouldn't it be too much of a coincidence?"

I frown, looking at him with confusion.

"That so many people from our town end up surviving in Nowhere. We've seen Thorian, your father, us and now Mason? I'm pretty sure I've seen a couple of girls from Terrby too," he says, then he grabs a book from the shelf beside us.

He's got a point. Maybe there's a connection between the two places. There has to be some sort of explanation to all of this. How can it be that so many people from our shitty small town end up here? Well, it might be that it's the few I recognize that stick out to me, but still.

"What did you say?" Amadeus suddenly asks, and I look to him with a frown.

"Nothing, I was just thinking." *Shit, can he hear my thoughts too? I really hope not.*

"Hm, I thought I heard...Never mind, let's go. There's nothing to gain from these shelves." He says, leafing through the pages of the book he's holding before putting it back.

I follow after him out from the library, still deep in thought. If it is, in fact Mason, and he actually survived the reaping it makes me relieved for his mother.

Even if she will never know his fate.

Chapter Sixteen

The taste of mead hits my tongue and I sigh. "How did you get this?" I look down into the mug I'm holding. The quality is actually quite good. Rich and flavourful.

Galen laughs. "Mason and I made it."

"Oh, you did?" I ask, a small teasing tone slipping into my voice. A blush rushes up his neck and cheeks, giving his feelings away.

"Wait," I drag out the word, squinting. "Oh my gosh!" I gape, and my face lights up. "Galen!"

"Shh!!" Galen waves his hands in the air, finally settling on placing it across my mouth to stop me from talking. I'm having none of that of course. I grab his hand, grinning like a fool. "I didn't know you liked guys," I whisper with a grin.

Galen makes this incredible sound, it's a cross between a giggle and a snort and it has my drunken heart soaring.

I am, in fact, a bit drunk. "This is some potent stuff." I glare at the cup in my hand, through my lashes, because I can't keep my eyelids open more than half...something.

Even my brain has forgotten how to word. Or how to use them.

Yes.

Let's go with that.

It didn't take much to convince the others at the camp to have a bonfire. In fact, they jumped on the opportunity, especially when mead was brought into the mix.

It seems like everyone in the entire camp has turned up for the event. I can even spot some of the older riders and foot soldiers. The foot soldiers are actually the rarest people to spot at the compound. Maybe because their markings are smaller, but considering that it's rumored that there are more people becoming foot soldiers than riders, I find it odd that I don't see them more often than I do.

I suspect they get sent out on missions, or get posted at other locations across the land of Nowhere. I tried to ask around, but never got a straight answer, so I gave up on trying to make sense of it all.

In the end, all that matters is survival.

"I know," Galen says, taking a swig of his mug. When he sees my face, he almost chokes on his drink through laughter. "It is potent stuff," he clarifies.

"Oh! Yes, indeed! My thoughts took me places," I giggle.

"Which places?" He smirks, probably thinking my mind went somewhere dirty. I wish that was the case.

I make a face before I let out a huge burp. No fucks given.

"Damn, that one was pretty good," Galen snorts, then he takes in a huge breath in preparation for his own burp.

"Hey, that's cheating!" I argue, but it's unnecessary. Because the sound that comes out of him? I start to laugh, hard. I clutch my stomach and almost fall off the log we're sitting on. "That was absolutely pitiful!"

"Agreed," he sighs, brushing away tears from laughing. "Nah, but seriously..." he almost seems to sober up for a second. "Mason is..." He starts, swirling the content in his mug to watch it spin. "He's a really great guy, you know?"

I nod at his words, the movement making my head spin. Closing my eyes, I open one eye to focus better. "I know. He really is." I'm slurring my words.

His head whips around to look at me. "Do you know him?"

"If it's the same Mason that I know, then yes. If it's another Mason? Then...no. I only know one Mason, and his name is," I giggle. "Mason." I nod slowly in agreement with myself, feeling smart.

I take a sip of my cup, frowning when I find it empty.

Probably for the best.

I should slow down.

"Yes, you should..." Riften sighs through my mind, and I roll my eyes before searching for him. Where is that fucker?

That's another thing that bugs me. Riften won't leave me alone. He's always around somewhere. There's a constant prickling sensation of being watched just before I spot him in the crowd. Not to mention, he seems to have taken up a permanent residence in my mind, and in my dreams.

When I find his mossy green eyes, his stare is fixed on me through the flames of the bonfire. A log pops and sparks fly towards the sky with the heat from the flames. The light emanating from the fire dances across his striking face, casting half of his annoying beauty in shadows.

I want to strangle him, but where I'm from murder is frowned upon. So I refrain.

"And what do you want?" I push back. I want to see his feathers ruffled. He's such an annoyance. The way he treats me makes me feel like I'm a burden to him. Like it's my fault we share this stupid connection with each other. Like I was the one that pushed him into the lake on the day we met.

It's not that I'm not grateful that he saved my life, I am! I just wish he didn't make me feel that it was my fault!

"*Nothing.*" His voice is like a caress to my mental barriers. "*Your self deprecating thoughts are quite amusing to be honest.*"

I've actually gotten pretty good at keeping him out of my mind, but it's becoming painfully obvious that I need more training when I'm drinking.

How inconvenient.

"*Why can't I get a read on you? You seem to know everything going on in my head, but it's total silence on your end, why is that?*" I ask in my mind, and I see his eyebrow rise as he contemplates. "*Not to mention, on the first day you did everything you could to keep me alive, and now it seems like it doesn't matter to you if I live or die.*"

His posture stiffens for just a second before he takes a deep breath and shakes his head. "*Maybe I'm better at hiding my emotions than you, have you thought of that possibility?*" The light in his eyes flicker with amusement, and I scoff, gaining a sideways glance from Galen.

"You okay?"

I look at my friend and nod. "I just swallowed my drink wrong." Galen stares at me, then at the empty mug in my hand. "Sure." He frowns.

Fuck.

Riften's right.

He is better at hiding his emotions than me.

"*I told you,*" When I look over at him through the flames I find him smiling into his cup as he takes a sip.

"*I bet you would be singing a different tune if I walked over to you and dropped to my knees.*"

He chokes on his drink, and the commotion earns the attention of the others around him. I smirk, slowly letting it turn into a wide grin.

A howl pierces the air and my head jerks in that direction. It's coming from the forest. But no one else appears to have heard it. I can feel it in my chest as well. Something that tugs at my heartstrings.

Suddenly the threads on my left arm draw painfully together and I glare at it. The golden mark lights up in a gentle glow through the fabric of my tunic. I gasp in pain, dropping the mug to the ground.

"Are you okay, Salem?" Galen puts his hand at my back, immediately dulling the pain. I don't have time to dwell on that detail. My body fills me with an overwhelming urgency to jump into action. Rising to my feet, I stumble for a step before I manage to balance my unsteady feet.

"Salem, what's going on?" There's worry in his voice. "You feeling alright?"

"Yes," I brush him off with my hand, and as soon as his hand is off my body, my feet want to move towards the forest. And the pain is back.

"Riften? Did you hear that?" I don't know why I'm even reaching out to him, I just know that this concerns him too. *"Riften?"* I push at our connection, coming up blank. I can't feel his presence.

I turn to where he sits, or rather, where he sat just a minute ago.

He's gone.

I look around for him, coming up empty. He's Nowhere to be seen.

"Galen, did you see where Riften went?"

"Riften? No? He was just—" he turns to the spot Riften sat and his mouth closes shut. "He was right there a minute ago, I swear," Galen runs his hand through his hair, baffled.

"Shit," again, my mark tightens around my arm, and I can't hide my wince of pain. I grab it on reflex. Galens eyes narrow in suspicion, but I ignore him.

"I need to find Riften, it's important." My voice is filled with conviction. I know that this is what I need to do, with complete certainty.

Something is wrong.

Calm down, Salem. You need to center yourself.

Closing my eyes, I go inwards. I try to locate the pulling sensation I felt earlier when the forest called for me. In the center of my chest, I find it.

It tugs on my heartspace. I place my hand over my chest and fist the fabric of my tunic. If I follow that, I'm sure I'll find what I'm looking for.

And what if you don't, Salem? A voice in the back of my mind taunts me. It's not Riften's calm voice. It's my own demons leering their ugly heads in my direction.

Fuck you. I have no other option...I have to find him.

I grit my teeth, and follow the tug.

My unsteady steps lead me away from the bonfire. Towards the edge of the forest.

Trepidation hits me as I stop along the tree line. The forest emanates the same pulsing sensation of magic that the cave does.

As soon as I enter the first line of trees I see glowing beetles scurry across the brush of the woods. A prickle of unease runs along my skin. Beetles, that means only one thing—magic.

I was right.

I don't want to enter the forest alone, but the urgent feeling only gets worse for every minute that passes. I need to find Riften. He might be in danger.

No, it's no longer just a possibility. He *is* in danger.

My eyes widen in surprise when I see the glowing beetles form a path for me, leading deeper into the forest. "Do you want me to follow?" *That's a stupid question. Of course they do.*

Great.

Now I'm talking to beetles.

We can add that to the list of things that make me insane.

The beetles start to blink urgently, creating a pulsing pattern that lures me in the direction they clearly want me to go.

"Oh fuck it," I mutter, and I take the first tentative step, the growing unease and urgency settling heavily in the pit of my stomach.

Suddenly I wish that I'd told the others where I went. As far as I know, Galen didn't follow after me. If it had been Amadeus, he definitely would have followed; probably to drag me away from this forest since he can't stand Riften, and wants nothing to do with him.

Fuck that! Amadeus has no say in what I do.

The atmosphere shifts, and shivers run down my spine the further I walk. The chatter from the bonfire is replaced by the faint buzzing from the beetles. Unease fills me once more when I see hundreds of black birds perched on the branches above me. Their beady eyes glinting in the faint light from the moon.

That's odd.

Now and again small flaps from their wings and soft hoots drag my attention to the treetops.

I force my breathing to stay calm, despite the oncoming panic that creeps over me.

Steady, Salem. I use it as a mantra for each step that leads me deeper into the dark forest. The smell of earth is potent here. Pine and...something sour that I can't quite place.

All my senses are on high alert as I glance up at the terrifying birds above me. I swallow my nerves down and forge on, the pain in my marked arm growing worse every moment.

The silence from Riften is honestly starting to freak me out. All of this—*all of this* is so completely fucked up that I just want to run in the opposite direction.

When did I become the hero? That was definitely not a conscious decision on my part. I feel tricked into it.

The breath leaves my lungs in a whoosh when I suddenly spot a clearing. A perfect circle of boulders within a ring of trees. And in the middle stands a human figure, red tinted hair shining in the moonlight.

Slowly, he turns towards me.

"Riften? What are you doing—" I swallow a scream when I see his glowing eyes. Dread fills my body as I see what's *behind* him. Gleaming white teeth, and frosty blue eyes. Midnight black scales all over its enormous body and feathery wings.

Golden threads flow out from its chest, locking onto Riften's left arm.

Chapter Seventeen

No, no, no, no!

My knees buckle underneath me and I fall to the ground.

"No, please!" I beg.

The helplessness crashes over me, and tears start to run down my face. "Please don't take him from me."

A heartbroken sob is ripped out of my chest as I watch the Black Dragon attempt to bond with my Riften.

Dread tears at my heart, followed by the agony from the golden mark on my arm. It feels like the essence of my entire being is siphoned from my body.

All I can do is watch in horror as he starts to shudder and shake. The first sign of a failed bonding.

Why the fuck did I just think of him as mine? *That doesn't make any sense, but it doesn't matter right now!*

"NO!" I scream and reach for Riften out of instinct.

I don't know why I'm this distraught, but it feels like a piece of me is getting ripped from my soul.

I refuse to lose him.

The hairs on my arms rise from the crackling energy around them. Golden threads suddenly shoot from my fingertips, rushing for Riften's shaking form. His mouth agape, eyes glowing from the magic that tries to devour him. My golden threads wrap around him, tethering him to this plane.

I won't let him go.

I refuse to lose another person that I care about.

And I care about Riften.

An ear splitting scream rips out of me from the strain of keeping his being contained. I grab the threads in my hand, wrapping them around my wrist and yank on them. He groans, and a flood of panic fills me all over again. I have no idea what I'm doing. I might even make this much worse than it already is. But I'm acting out of instinct, letting desperation guide me.

The golden threads loosen from the dragon's chest scales and flow towards the beetle mark on Riften's left palm. He falls to the ground, unmoving.

My heart is pounding in my chest and I scramble to my feet, breaking the unmarked barrier of the ring of boulders. "Riften!"

I make a dive for him, pulling his body into my arms and shake him.

There is no reaction.

"Riften!" I scream, shaking him again. "Why?" Anger bubbles under my skin, and tears stream down my cheeks. It feels like I'm dying.

The golden threads I have wrapped around him retreat, and I start to tremble. My chest caves in on itself and I collapse over Riften, my head landing on his chest.

It's still.

There is no sound of a heartbeat under my ear.

"Get up," I sob, feeling the world crashing down on me. "Get up, get up, get up!" I shake his shoulders, trying to wake him. I grab his face in my hands, tears falling to his skin. "You can't do this to me, Riften." My voice cracks, and it feels like my heart shatters. "You're not done. We're not done!" I scream. I fist my hand and slam it into Riften's chest.

"Why?" I scream again, looking into the Black Dragon's eyes. There's a shadow of sadness lingering within them, and a small sound of mourning trickles up his throat.

I lean my head to his chest again, shaking with unexplainable grief.

Du-dunk.

I freeze.

Du-dunk.

I breathe in sharply, my tears halting in their tracks and I blink rapidly in confusion. "Riften?"

He coughs, and his mossy green eyes flutter open.

"Trouble?" He croaks, sounding delirious as he looks up at me. His head resting in my lap. I hiccup, a laugh slipping out of me as I look down at him. Tears flowing freely again, I barely manage to choke out my next words. "You asshole."

An amused laugh slips out of him. "No more than you are, Trouble," he mutters softly, a slow grin spreading across his beautiful face.

I sniffle and scoff at the same time, shaking my head as I let it fall back in absolute relief.

He's alive.

He didn't die.

Tears continue to run down my cheeks and I stifle another sob. "You're impossible," I hiccup.

A shaky hand touches my cheek, and I flinch for a heartbeat. The hand stills, before it gently brushes away the tears from my face. "Are these for me?" He asks, a slightly teasing tone entering his voice.

A shaky breath leaves my lungs and I have to concentrate on replacing it with another intake of oxygen. "No," the lie tastes like bile on my tongue, and I close my eyes to try to hide my emotions from him.

"You're magnificent when you lie, Trouble," his tone hides an emotion I can't quite place, and again I want to strangle the life out of him.

"Why do you call me that?" I whisper as another tear falls onto his face. His eyes shine with unspoken emotions and he chuckles.

"Thought that was obvious." His gentle smile reveals the small dimple in his right cheek.

Crap.

That fucking dimple.

Thank you, Golden One, A rough voice penetrates my mind and I whip around to look at the enormous creature in front of us. I had completely forgotten it was even there. *I thought he was ready. I was mistaken. If it hadn't been for you, Little Sprout, the bonding would have failed.*

Riften's body stiffens and he sits up in a rush, wincing as he does. He stares at the Black Dragon, mouth agape. "What the..." He trails off, and looks down to his left arm, eyes widening when he realizes that his beetle mark has grown.

They resemble black smoke that circles around the golden threads that already adorn his skin. Perfectly in harmony with each other, they intertwine and circle around the individual strands.

"The threads that wove our elaborate tapestry are now moth eaten and unraveling. It needs to be rectified," the dragon growls. It rattles my eardrums from inside my head and I shudder. *"That is your chosen destiny, Riften*

Tvelys. Along with the Golden One, you will weave the tapestry back together and save us all."

"My what?" Riften looks from the dragon to me, and back to the dragon. "I didn't choose this." Stunned, he rubs his newly adorned markings and shakes his head. "I didn't choose any of this! None of us did!" Desperation is edged across his face.

"You did, regardless of your knowledge of the consequences. You might not have seen all the pieces on the board, but you did choose this path. You both did." The frosty stare of the dragon fixates on me, and another shudder runs down my spine.

"How?" The question that slips out of my mouth is weak. I sound exhausted, and I realize that I am utterly drained.

"That is not for me to tell you, Golden One. Just know this; The sky will burn until dawn. The rain will fall after the drought and give life to the shadows. Monsters will come, and you will lose what you hold closest to your heart." His chest rumbles with the words, and hits me with recognition. It's the same words the White Dragon uttered to me. *"You will find strength in the flames, perseverance in the earth, tranquility in the water, and credence in the wind. They will help you to balance your opposites. Keep them close,"* Another huff of smoke envelopes us and this time we both tense.

Fucking riddles.

We both look at each other, our expressions blank.

Clearly, I'm not the only one that doesn't understand the riddle the Black Dragon has given us, even if he added some details that I didn't already know. A voice in the back of my mind tells me there is something I should ask this powerful beast, but my exhausted mind can't find the words I'm looking for.

Slowly, my eyelids start to droop, and my head feels heavier. I can barely keep my eyes open.

"Trouble." Steady hands keep me from falling over, and Riften pulls me closer so I'm cradled against his strong chest. My head nestles at the crook of his neck, and his forest scent tickles my nose. It reminds me so much of home, and the steady beating of his heart lulls me into a deep sleep.

"Is she okay?" I know her voice. It's become so familiar to me from all the time we've spent together since we met. A wave of calm rushes over me. It centers my unease.

"Yes, I think so. She's just sleeping." I hear Riften to my right.

"What happened?" Galen's concerned tone breaks my heart. I can't imagine how he feels. He was the last person to see me at the bonfire.

"She's okay, she—" Riften is cut off by a furious shout.

"What the fuck did you do to her?" Amadeus. Of course he's here too. There's a thud, and a grunt of pain. Then furniture crashes to the floor, breaking apart. "What did you do?" Amadeus growls to my right.

I want to tell them to stop. I want to tell them to knock it off. I want to tell Amadeus to fuck off. Why the hell are they fighting each other? Are they fighting because of me?

Okay, that's stupid, I might not be able to get the full picture of the situation, but I'm not an idiot. They *are* fighting because of me, but are they actually fighting over me?

"Hey, stop it!" Elodie shouts just as something else crashes to the floor and my bed shakes. "Do I have to drag Killian over here and have him touch you both at the same time? Because I will absolutely do that if you two assholes don't get it together!" She snarls.

"Please don't," Killian chimes in with a pained voice. "I'd rather not hurt them."

"Then stop this nonsense! You are both allowed to feel stressed about this, but you have both abused that privilege, now cut it the fuck out!" She growls. The scuffling and grunting from their fight finally comes to an end. "Are you done now?" Elodie sounds absolutely livid, and I want to smile because of it, but my body won't listen.

It tingles all over, it feels so, so heavy. Like the gravity around me has increased its effort to keep me tethered to myself.

"What. Happened?" Amadeus grits out, emphasizing each word, breathing painfully loud. The hairs on my arm rise in protest from the pressure that settles across my chest. The words want to spill out of me, but my body refuses to cooperate. It's almost painful.

"I don't know!" It almost sounds like his tongue is glued to the roof of his mouth. "I...I was at the bonfire...and then I was in the forest, talking to this black drag—" He gasps. "Then I couldn't move, my body just wouldn't move." The words rush out from his mouth. It sounds like he's in pain. "I passed out!"

What is going on? Why does it sound like Riften is being tortured? Is Killian somehow involved?

"When I woke up I was bonded with a black dragon, and she was there. Then she fell asleep and I carried her back here." It sounds like he spits the words out through gritted teeth, like he's trying not to speak.

I wish he hadn't told them what happened. I wish he kept it to himself.

The pressure fades from my chest, and I want to rub the center of it to ease the lingering pain.

The sound of someone getting punched, followed by a grunt of pain I'm quite familiar with fills the room.

"The hell was that for?" Amadeus growls, and another thud of a body hitting something solid reaches my ears.

"You know damn well what that was for, you slimy fuck!" Riften thunders. "You have no business using—"

"Stop it," I whimper, my voice weak and pitiful. But I've finally found the ability to speak again. It doesn't take long before I feel very crowded as I manage to pry my eyes open and peer up at five concerned faces. I frown at them through squinted eyes. "Guys, you are stealing my oxygen."

Everyone but Amadeus and Riften takes a step back from the bed, and I sigh as I try to sit up. They both jump into action to try and help me, but Riften is the only one that ignores my death glare and guides me into a sitting position.

For some reason, I let him.

He takes a step away right after and rubs his chest, giving Amadeus a sideways glance of pure annoyance at the same time. As I look over at the guys, I raise an eyebrow at the rapidly blooming bruises on their faces. Sharing a look with Elodie we both sigh.

"Men," we mutter in unison.

"How are you feeling?" Galen pushes Amadeus away from the bed to grab my hand. A warmth immediately spreads throughout my body, removing the exhaustion from my limbs. "Good, I feel good. Drained, but...good," I mumble.

"What did he do to you?" Amadeus asks, trying to push Galen away and I glance over at Riften for just a second before I answer.

"Nothing." It's the truth. Riften didn't do anything to me at all. If I had to guess, I managed to drain myself of energy from saving his life.

But I'm not going to tell them that.

I meet Amadeus's eyes. "You need to stop, Amadeus. Riften isn't the enemy, and jealousy doesn't look good on you."

Chapter Eighteen

"No, Tonak is stronger than Euna, for sure."

Forcing myself not to groan is definitely a challenge. Killian and Elodie have had this exact discussion for almost two months now.

"He is not! Euna is bigger *and* stronger than Tonak," as she tosses her braid over her shoulder it hits Amadeus across his face, making him jerk in the seat beside her. "Also, the colors of her scales are much more intriguing than Tonak's boring brown scales."

We're in the Library of Stubborn Books, and my patience is starting to run out. I don't know how many times I've written the same paragraph only to see it vanish before my eyes. The few books I've found somewhat ledgable aren't fairing any better. The words keep skipping pages, jumping all over the place and making the damned books indecipherable.

"His scales are not dull! They're practical," Killian's protest has me running my hand across my face as I stifle the urge to interrupt their banter.

The air is rapidly getting colder now that we're closer to the end of October, and darkness envelops most hours of the day. A light blanket of frost covers the grass in the mornings, and snow has settled in the mountaintops around the compound. Soon, the ground will be covered in a layer of fresh snow.

I can't say that I'm looking forward to it. The winters back home were always brutal, and the weather in Nowhere seems to be even more extreme.

"For what?" Elodie taunts, and her expression tells me that she's just trying to reel him up for the fun of it.

"Are you serious?" He scoffs. I look over to Galen for help, but he's busy reading a book. Which is just fucking perfect. They are all bonded, except for me and Amadeus. So apparently, they can read these stubborn books. "It's the best camouflage, especially during autumn."

"Guys," I warn softly.

"Sure, but during winter he's going to stick out like a sore thumb." Elodie ignores me, of course.

I can't believe the fact that our tight knit group has survived this place for five months. The hard training the older riders have put us through has been no joke. The stealth unit—my unit—is trained to become killers. Assassins. Yet I still don't know the purpose of our roles. They've started to split us up during training, because the bonded riders can share more secrets with each other than with the unbonded.

This creates a huge rift amongst the stolen soldiers.

"Not if he covers himself in snow, then he will just look like a snow-covered rock," Killian says.

I groan in frustration. "Guys."

"Tonak has no manners," She taunts him, oblivious to my declining patience.

Amadeus, who's in the infantry unit of our regiment, is destined to become a foot soldier. They're supposedly able to bond with dragons, but it's less common. At least compared to the assassins.

The dragons don't show up for our training anymore, so I'm almost certain that I won't get chosen by one. Almost. Orvin did say that he'd seen bondings happen as late as a year after the reaping. He also said that most of the unbonded ended up dead after a year or two.

I guess that doesn't bode well for either of us.

I've seen desperation before, and I know for a fact that some of the unbonded are starting to become just that. Desperate.

"If Tonak doesn't have any manners, then neither does Euna. I saw her torch a guy because he sneezed."

"That's not what happened! He got too close to her tail." Fucking hell, will they ever stop arguing?

"He was on the other side of the courtyard, Elodie!"

"Shut up!" How is it possible for them to even look surprised from my outburst? "It doesn't matter which one is the strongest, they are both equally powerful in their own ways. Don't they have their own unique abilities or something?" I ask.

Elodie opens her mouth to respond, but just as the words form on her lips, I see that her tongue is glued to the roof of her mouth.

Right. The secrecy curse.

The curse that restricts the knowledge we're allowed to have.

"It's fine, no reason to choke on it." I pull the scroll in front of me closer and start to write down some notes. I know that the hurt I feel now isn't just. It's not Elodie's fault she can't tell me anything useful, in fact it's none of their fault.

It still sucks though.

"Want me to throw rocks at them?" Galen asks. Great, *now*, he decides to get involved. After Galen bonded his dragon four weeks ago, he discovered the ability to control earth. Now he stores a handful of pebbles in his pocket for easy access. On more than one occasion we have all had a rock or two chasing us around. I'm not surprised to see a pebble hovering on either side of his head when I look his way.

"No, that's okay. I'm sure I can figure out a way to get back at them," Amadeus scoffs beside me, and I give him a glare. "What?"

"Nothing."

"It's not *nothing*. You wouldn't make that sound unless it was *something*."

He waves his hand. "No, no, continue like I'm not here."

I take a deep breath. "Spill it."

"No."

"Dude, we're not stupid. You're usually a sunshiny asshole, but the last month you've been a proper sour face." Killian leans over the desk.

"Not really. He's kind of back to the way he was back home." I scribble a note on my scroll and stare down at the paper when the fucking thing goes blank. "You got to be fucking kidding me!" I give up.

It's probably a good thing that the universe didn't bestow upon me the power of pyrotechnics. The library would probably already be burnt to cinders by now. No, I just have the annoying power of golden threads that latch onto objects and people on occasion. Leaving them dazed and confused afterwards. I still have no idea what that power does.

It's happened a couple of times now. Actually, it happened during Galen's bonding with Raleigh too. Something occurred, and I don't know *what*. All I know is that his dragon started to purr and let me pet her, which is unheard of.

Amadeus gets up so fast that the chair tips over with a loud bang, making us all startle. "What's going on?"

Instead of answering me, he grabs his satchel and stalks off.

A part of me wants to let him, but I know I can't.

"Wait up," I say, gathering my things. "Hey, Amadeus!" Where the fuck did he go? I look up and down the hallway outside of the library, spotting his retreating back on the staircase. "Amadeus." He doesn't slow down, and it's grating on my nerves. Why does he have to be so fucking stubborn?

"Vanæra!" I bark, and he freezes mid-step. Finally a reaction. I never use his last name unless I have to.

"What the fuck is wrong with you? And don't try to bullshit me this time. I want to know the truth. What's wrong?" I growl when I finally reach him.

"Am I even your friend anymore?"

His sharp tone makes me flinch. "What's that supposed to mean, of course you are."

"Really? Because it doesn't feel like it," he growls, stepping closer.

"Amadeus—"

"Do not lie to me, Vanroda," he thunders low in his throat. His eyes darken and a slight pressure settles at my chest.

"I'm not lying, Amadeus! You're my oldest friend."

He narrows his eyes and the pressure on my chest increases to the point of excruciating pain.

My eyes flare wide with shock. He's got powers. "Fuck you, Amadeus." My voice is no louder than a breath, and my eyes start to burn with unshed tears. "Why can't you trust me?"

His jaw ticks. "I do."

"No, you don't! If you did, you wouldn't feel the need to force anything from me." My words are guttural and raw, filled with emotions I rarely possess. I take a step away from him, not knowing how to express myself.

"You're my best friend, Salem. My only friend. I would never break your trust." His words cut deep, and there's a part of me that doesn't believe a single word coming out of his mouth. Because in a way, he did just that. Shaking my head, a small tear escapes from the corner of my eye.

How many times has he used his powers on the people around him? How many times has he used it on me? There've been multiple occasions I've felt an intrusive pressure at the center of my chest around Amadeus, but I never thought much of it.

Quickly I brush the tear away from my cheek and take another step away from him. I can't, I just...can't.

"Salem..."

"Don't touch me!" I wrench my hand away from his grasp as he reaches for me. "Don't you dare touch me."

His eyes fill with pain, but he jerks his head in a sharp nod. "I wish I could make you understand..." He trails off when I start to shake my head, wrapping my arms around myself.

I don't want to listen to his reasons. His fucking excuses.

"Everything okay over here?"

A wave of relief washes over me from the sound of his voice.

On pure instinct I turn and, for the first time, I seek his comfort. I let myself fall into his embrace and breathe in his comforting scent of home. His strong arms wrap around me, and he holds me close to his chest.

Riften.

He always shows up when I need him the most, even when I don't realize that I do.

"Trouble," he whispers against my hair, and a silent sob makes my body tremble in his arms. "I've got you." His voice is filled with a truth I feel on a cellular level, and another silent whimper leaves me shaken. "Breathe through it."

There's an unspoken promise hidden within his words. That everything will be okay, that I will get through this betrayal.

I should have seen this coming. I shouldn't be so blindsided by this revelation.

But I didn't see it coming, and I am devastated.

"I would leave, if I were you," Riften's chest vibrates against my ear as he speaks, and I can clearly hear the underlying threat in his voice.

"Why do you always show up when you're the least wanted?" Amadeus sounds almost deadly, and a chill trickles along my spine.

"Why do you always pick fights you can't win?"

I don't want them to fight each other. I just want to leave. *"I know, give me a moment and I'll get you out of here."* Riften's soothing voice in my mind calms me. I manage to take a breath through the restricting pressure at the center of my chest.

Trust has never come easy for me, given my childhood. It took me *years* to trust Amadeus, and I thought that he would be the last person to betray me. And I can't help but think that I kind of deserve this for the way I've been treating him these past months. He might have a point that it doesn't feel like we're friends anymore—

"Darling, you're spiraling. Nobody deserves to have their choices taken away from them, regardless of the intention behind it. Compulsion should never be used on friends unless it's a matter of life or death."

"You think I can't beat you?" Amadeus asks.

Riften chuckles softly. "Oh, I know you can't."

The invading pressure latches onto my chest again, and I fight the pull. It feels like he's putting a spell on me, making me almost willing to step out of Riften's safety.

Riften starts to laugh. "You really think that's going to do anything against me?" There's a smile in his voice that wasn't there before. It almost makes me smile too, but my thoughts are reeling and my mind is spinning. I don't have it in me to smile. "My shields are too strong for that pathetic attempt. Allow me to let you in on a secret, Amadeus," Riften says, and I feel his hold tighten around me.

It almost feels like he's keeping my entire body locked against him from the tight embrace. Even my ankles. The world seems to darken along the edges, and my stomach lurches all of a sudden. A thread is pulled, and I feel myself fall, just as I hear Riften say to Amadeus. "I'm not threatened by you."

Chapter Nineteen

"Trouble, he's gone now," he murmurs into my ear.

Taking a deep breath I lift my head from his chest and tense.

"Where are we?" I ask, looking around at the small room we're in. It seems to be a storage space of sorts. Two wobbly shelves cover one wall from floor to ceiling with a wide selection of obscure objects. A wooden chest is placed haphazardly to one side along with multiple brooms in various stages of functionality. On top of the chest lays a broken scale that definitely has seen better days.

"We're in the utility closet at the end of the hallway," he says, holding me at an arm's length. He looks me up and down before asking, "What happened? Did he hurt—" I shake my head before he even manages to finish the question.

"He didn't. But more importantly; how did we get here?" I hiss in a breath from his gentle touch at my cheek.

"You're crying," he says, sounding concerned.

"I'm fine," I insist, and it's true. Physically, at least.

Gently, he grabs my jaw and tilts my head up to meet my eyes, and a wave of burning desire instantly blooms in my belly from the intensity of his gaze. His eyes have gone a shade darker, and I can clearly see the pulse thrumming in his throat. His coppery hair falls into his face as he leans in close, and my eyes zero in on his lips when he wets them with the tip of his tongue.

"Trouble," he says, his husky voice caressing my heated skin. Shit, I think he's about to kiss me. "You are absolutely stunning when you lie."

His hand moves from my jaw to my throat and my breath hitches. "Riften," I say, my voice barely above a whisper.

He hums low in his throat, guiding me up against the wall. Honestly, I appreciate the extra support. My knees are getting weak. "How did we get here?" I repeat.

The corner of his mouth quirks up. "Magic."

"Really?" I breathe. His lips hover above mine, and I look into his hungry eyes.

"Mhm," he murmurs, and I take a steadying breath. I feel his fingers tighten slightly on my skin.

"I don't know if I believe you," I whisper, and hold his stare. We were just in the hallway, and now we're suddenly in the utility closet at the end of the hallway. It doesn't make sense.

His dimple appears, and for some reason my entire body goes hot. I'm teetering on the brink of...something, and he's dragging this out. Making me impatient.

He chuckles darkly, and his pupils dilate even more. Making his eyes go another shade darker. "Am I now?"

My jaw slackens. Right, he can hear my thoughts, at least...some of them. His answering grin tells me that I'm right.

I narrow my eyes. "Are you going to kiss me or what?"

"Maybe," he smirks. "I might just want to tease you."

Well, fuck that.

He doesn't get to be the only one in control here.

I put my hand on his chest and push him back forcefully, catching him off guard. In the split second it takes him to regain his composure, I turn us around and pin him up against the wall.

He stares back at me with those dark eyes, and I can see my own desire reflected in them. I don't know who initiates it, but the next thing I know our lips are locked together in a frantic kiss.

It's a battle of wills. His hand tangles in my hair, and my hand fists around the fabric of his shirt. Teeth and tongues clash together in a fight for dominance. I lose myself in the feeling of *him.*

All of a sudden, we are moving again, and the backs of my knees hit the wooden chest. His other hand is on my hip, yet it feels like he's touching me *everywhere*. I twist us around, and push him to a sitting position. The broken scale crashes to the floor.

Straddling him, I fist both hands in his hair, needing him to be closer.

"Trouble," his voice is pure need, as he tightens his grip on my hair and pulls my head back to look into my eyes.

"Shut up and kiss me," I demand, and our lips crash together again. My hands roam his chiseled chest. His muscles ripple under my touch, and a low groan emanates from his mouth the further my fingers trek. Finding the hem of his shirt, I tug it loose from his waistband. It snags, and my impatience gets to me.

Desperate to feel his skin under my palms I rip the fabric apart, and a primal growl vibrates through his chest.

My body aches with need. He trembles under my touch with the same desperation that courses through me. And still, I can feel that he's holding back. "Let go, Riften. Please let go with me," I beg.

"You're upset," he says, his words coming out strangled. My fingers trace the sensitive skin right above the waistband of his trousers and a groan spills from his lips from my touch.

"No, I'm horny," I growl against his swollen lips, "And now I want you to fuck me raw." I can feel the heat radiate from him against my desperate body, but it's not enough. I need more. I need more of *him*. Every part of him.

With a firm grip I guide his hand from my hip, under my tunic, and up my stomach. Begging him to remove the garment that separates us. No, not begging. Demanding.

"Fuck, Trouble," he groans, his head falling back. He swallows hard, pressing his eyes shut. I track the movement in his throat with my tongue, and a desperate moan tumbles out of him.

"Let go for me," I unbuckle the harness strapped to my upper body and watch the hairs on his neck rise from my whispered breath.

A split second later his restraints fall away, and he takes off my tunic so fast I don't even register that my chest is laid bare before him. It doesn't matter, as long as I can feel his skin against mine. He watches me with hunger in his eyes, and his hand glides over my heated flesh.

"You are stunning," he whispers before his lips crash onto mine again. My stomach flips as he stands, and he holds me up with his strong arms, somehow managing to avoid all of the daggers I have strapped to my thighs. "And you are all mine," he growls, the sound low in his throat.

My back hits the wall and I lock my legs around his hips. A moan of pure hunger rushes out of me when he presses his hard length against my core. I can feel all of him through the fabric of our clothes, and I need them off. Now.

Our lips crash together again, and his teeth bite down on my bottom lip. *Fuck, yes!* A pain laced moan of pleasure bubbles up my throat and my fingernails dig into his bare back, wanting him even closer.

His body stills under me when the warning bells ring out.

Fuck!

Breaking our kiss, he leans his forehead to mine, breathing hard. In fact, we are both panting.

"We got to go," he says hoarsely, completely breathless.

"No," I whine. I don't want to stop.

Frantic steps thunder outside in the hallway. I can hear people shouting and calling out to each other and it sounds like absolute chaos on the other side of the door.

"What's going on now?" I breathe, leaning my head against the wall to look at Riften.

He's silent for a moment, and his eyes go hazy as he checks in with his dragon. "There's been a monster sighting outside the compound."

"What?" I release my legs from his hips and look for my tunic. "There are *monsters* lurking around? Why haven't they told us...?" I trail off, glaring at him with narrowed eyes. "How are you able to tell me this?" I ask poking my finger to his chest.

He opens his mouth, but he's cut off by a loud crash against the wooden door. Turning, I see something that resembles liquid smoke seeping through the cracks in the door. They almost look like physical shadows.

Riften curses through his teeth.

There's another loud bang and a scream from the hallway. As the light in the room flicker, dark shadows explode from Riften's hands.

I scream, jumping away from the tendrils of darkness that flow around me. "What the fuck, Riften!?" I gasp. I've never seen his magic before, but the fact that he controls shadows doesn't surprise me at all.

"Are you armed?"

"I can't believe you actually asked me that question," I mutter under my breath, glaring. "Of course I'm armed. I have at least five daggers on my person at all times." Which he should know by now. I gesture to the twin daggers I have strapped at my thighs.

"Then what are you waiting for, whip them out! By the Seven Gods..."

"So demanding."

"And put your fucking tunic on," he grits through his teeth.

I roll my eyes in response but grab the discarded garment off the floor, tugging it over my head. "Didn't know you were such a prude," I mutter, just as I manage to fasten the buckle on my harness.

He levels me with a glare, and shakes his head slowly. "*I know what you're doing, Trouble. I promise you that when we've dealt with these intruders, I'll give you what you're begging for.*" He quirks one eyebrow at me, letting his eyes roam my body with lingering desire.

Well, he's not wrong, I do have a hidden agenda. Unfortunately, we don't have time for that now.

The door crashes to the floor in splinters, and a shadowy figure fills the opening. I choke on the pungent scent of rot and decay. It's damp and musty, yet it holds a strange freshness to it.

The blood drains from my face, as I get a better look at the creature looming in the doorway. It has long gangly limbs with claw-like fingers and moss covered antlers on top of its head.

A memory stirs at the back of my mind, and all of a sudden I can hear Pipp's voice in my head. "*Mares are real. They are warnings from our loved ones of darker times.*"

I freeze.

My muscles lock up.

Tears prick my eyes and my hands *burn*.

I can't move. I can't fucking *move*.

Riften's shadows rush forward, hitting the creature square in its chest. It flies through the air, hitting the wall on the opposite side of the hallway.

I fall forward, gasping for air.

"You okay, Trouble?"

"What the fuck was that?" I shriek. "Why couldn't I move?"

"What?" Riften whips his head towards me and looks stricken, horrified. "Fucking hell, it's because you're not bonded." I see the color drain from his face, and there is pure fear reflected in his widened eyes. "I need to get you out of here. *Merick!*" The last word rings through my mind like an explosion and a shudder runs through my body. "*I need you to get her out of here! The Mares are paralyzing the unbonded!*"

There's panic in his voice, and the fact that I can hear his telepathic communication between him and his dragon tells me that he's losing control.

"I'm not running away!" I growl.

"And I am not having this discussion with you! You are not dying here, you hear me?" His shadows wrap around my body and he tucks me in close to his chest. The darkness envelopes us, and my stomach flips when he takes a step. When the shadows retreat, we're no longer in the utility closet.

We're in the middle of the courtyard.

My heart plummets when I look up. All around us are motionless bodies on the ground, and shadows chasing after every living soul. It's absolute chaos.

How did we get to the courtyard, and what the fuck are these creatures? Wait...he mentioned something to his dragon. Mares. These creatures are *Mares*. They are definitely not warnings from our loved ones of darker times. *They are the darker times.*

My hands start to burn again, and it feels like I'm on fire. Sweat is trickling down my spine and my heart pounds in my chest. Power is thrumming under my skin, begging to be released. I have no control of my powers. And I'm scared it will cause more damage, so I fight the urge to lash out.

"Trouble, move!" I hear Riften yell, and before I know it, I feel his shadows tighten around my waist, moving me. The gruesome smell makes my stomach turn, I'm about to throw up. Fear has settled into my bones, and I'm fucking terrified.

I don't want to die.

I see Riften in my peripheral vision fighting off a mare with his shadows, but before I manage to get a good look at the situation, another dark creature tackles me to the ground. The hold around my waist loosens as my muscles lock up. Tears blur my eyes from the overwhelming smell of rotting flesh. Somehow, it reminds me of a bog, only stronger. More potent.

I grunt as I hit the ground, and pain radiates up my spine from the impact.

A guttural rasping sound vibrates around me, and my fingertips start to tingle. The breath hitches in my throat as hollow eyes stare down at me. The creature's face is masked with an animal skull and saliva drips from its mouth. It fizzles when it hits the ground, smoke trailing up from where it landed as the creature stalks towards me. It crawls over my immobilized body and a choked scream rips from my chest.

Slowly, it opens its jaws over my head and I gag from the rotten smell permeating from its guts.

"*Riften!*" I scream through my mind. Fuck, I'm about to get eaten by this monster.

Fuck, fuck, fuck!

A dagger flies through the air, headed straight for the Mare's head. My heart sinks when the blade passes through the creature's skull. The beast doesn't stop, continuing to crawl up my body.

Claw-like fingers dig into my legs, ripping through the fabric of my leathers.

I need to move. I need to fight back!

The sound of wingbeats drifts from far away.

Pushing down the fear in my chest, I lock it down and the tingling in my hands returns. A single golden thread slithers from my pointer finger towards the dagger at my ribs. It instantly lights and warmth spreads through my body, heating my muscles.

Finally, my limbs regain motion and I unsheath the dagger, plunging it through the Mare's chest, right where the heart should be. Energy rushes to my palm, and the dagger vibrates against my skin. The Mare shrieks as the skin on its gangly limbs cracks, golden light shining through from within its depths. It explodes in a bright flash of yellow light.

The heaviness in my body dissipates, and I can finally breathe normally again. I roll to my side, coughing. The lingering fear makes my limbs move slower. Getting to my feet, I see more bodies strewn about in the courtyard. Nausea turns my stomach, as I gaze at the blood and gore littering the cobblestone.

Still there are bonded riders fighting the horde of Mares that have invaded the compound. Earth wielders using rocks to hit back. Pyro's having their flames lick up their gangly limbs making them shriek horribly loud. Their screams cleave the air, only to have water shoved down their throats to drown out the sound.

I don't recognize any of the bodies on the ground, at least the ones facing toward me. Riften is still fighting, blood trickling down his temple. I move to help him, just as the wind picks up around me. White claws catch me around my shoulders and the ground under my feet disappears as I'm lifted into the air.

A wave of terror rips at my chest when I look up to see that I'm in the claws of the White Dragon. I look down at the compound that now is encased in shadows. A final horrified scream escapes my lips.

LINNSY B. NORTH

I have to get back and help my friends.
But I'm also *utterly* fucked.

Chapter Twenty

I can't quite put my finger on how I'm feeling. Yes, I'm terrified, but I'm also quite confused. Dangling from the claws of this massive beast I contemplate my options.

Which, to be fair, isn't many. All I can really do is...well, nothing. I can't do *shit* about what's happening right now other than let the universe decide my fate.

I can't feel my fingertips from the whipping wind, nor do I have any sensation left in my toes. It's absolutely freezing up in the air, and the howling wind doesn't help whatsoever.

Nobody talks about how cold it is to fly.

I also really have to pee.

Fantastic.

"Excuse me?" I shout through chattering teeth. Why am I even trying to converse with this beast? By now I should just accept the fact that I won't survive. But I have to try. "Could you by any chance let me down?"

The dragon doesn't answer, because, of course he doesn't. Most likely I'm not worthy of the answers.

I'm so sick of this place.

"Put me down you overgrown lizard!" I yell, kicking my feet like an insolent child, but it doesn't help. I don't even know if I care about the potential consequences of speaking in this manner either.

I'm stuck.

"Answer me!" I demand, but it sounds more like begging. I'm so sick of not having the answers to anything, and my emotions are already running high. A traitorous sob leaves me shaken, and burning tears start to fall.

I feel helpless. And I fucking hate that feeling. I can't stand it. My heart is pounding in my ears, blocking out the raging wind.

After what feels like ages the ground finally seems to get closer, and a huge mountain on the ridge comes into view. Large boulders stick up from the ground.

Ahead I'm able to recognize the shape of a cave, and I just know on instinct that that's where the dragon is planning to take me.

Then a shriek pierces the air, and I whip my head to the side, spotting two large creatures flying towards us. "Incoming!" I scream over the wind, dread settling in my bones. There are two dark silhouettes on the back of each creature. What the fuck is that? It looks like—

My eyes widen with fear.

They're dragons, but…not normal dragons.

Their flesh is all eaten away, leaving only the bones and the thin membrane that keeps them airborne. They're dragons made of bone.

Behind them, more gaunt creatures follow. The skeletons of both griffins and pegasi. Seated at their backs are horrific-looking people.

Their faces are obscured by leaves and broken branches. Gleaming white fangs protrude from their mouths. And they've got *tails*.

These creatures almost look humanoid. But they're not humans.

They're *monsters*.

By the Seven Gods.

I've never practiced religion, but now...I pray to Felving, Watcher of Life and Creation. I pray that this is an illusion created by my imagination. I pray that this isn't something he made.

I've heard stories of these creatures. But I thought they were just that. *Stories!* The tales I told my little sister at bedtime are true.

All of them.

Even the worst ones.

The White Dragon swoops down, and the terrain rushes towards us. A guttural scream is wrenched out of my chest. Just before we hit the ground he levels out. We're so low now that I can almost touch the deadly stones with my feet. Then he releases me from his claws, and I hit the ground hard.

I try my best to soften the landing by rolling, managing it at least, somewhat. My body comes to a full stop as I crash into a snow-covered rock. The air is knocked out of my lungs, and I wheeze.

Fuck. That hurt.

Looking up I see the White Dragon circling around, with a terrifying glow at its chest that has my body trembling. Just as he soars over my head, I see him open his jaws wide, and a stream of endless heat pours out from his maw. Aiming for the intruders.

I shudder when they fly straight through.

I can't stay here. I have to run. I have to flee! I don't want to die! I have to stay alive.

So I do just that. I run.

Sweat trickles down my back, making my tunic stick to my skin. The sound of my footsteps is muffled from the snow under my feet. I don't know where I'm going, other than back towards the compound.

I'm lost, and I must be out of my mind to run back to that place, but I also have to help my friends. Not that I know how I'll be of any use, since the mares paralyze the unbonded.

But I have to try.

The soles under my feet are blistered and aching, my lungs are tight from lingering panic. Each breath feels like shards of glass in my throat. Every step jars my body as I flee for my life.

I have to survive.

I have to survive for *her*.

My foot catches on a rock, I stumble and fall. The air is knocked out of me, and my muscles feel raw and sluggish. Shaking through pain I try to get to my feet, but my limbs won't move. I'm frozen to the ground.

The deafening sound of my own heart screams through my head.

I can't move.

Crap. The Mares have found me. But *how?* I'm Nowhere near the compound yet. My hands start to sting again, and my fingertips tingle with power. Forcing down a deep breath, I let myself fall into the sensation. Feeling the magic radiate along my skin, covering me in a blanket of warmth.

Trembling, I get to my feet on shaking legs, the air vibrates with a guttural rasping sound that makes every hair on my body react.

Danger.

I sense danger like it's a tangible thing.

I'm not alone.

Fuck.

Slowly, I turn, and my heart just...stops. The black shadow-like creature stands hunched over in front of me with a strikingly white skull. Hollow eyes stare back at me. Foam is gathered around its mouth, glistening teeth protruding from its gums. Neon green moss hangs off the antlers on its head.

With great effort, I move my hand through what feels like mud towards the dagger at my ribs. Immediately it starts to hum with vibrant energy. My lungs expand and I can finally move my body more freely. Holy fuck. It's the *blade*. The golden flora within the metal is the exact same as the depiction on my arm.

But *how?* Heason made this blade.

There is no time to think. The Mare pounces. Its gangly limbs dart across the snow-covered ground with unnatural speed, headed straight for me.

I brace, lifting my arm up to meet the charging monster with my dagger poised. Its claws dig into the skin at my shoulders, and the putrid smell threatens to paralyze my body. Holding my breath I plunge the dagger deep into the center of its chest as we both go down.

The Mare shrieks in agony, and my face burns when acid drips onto my cheek. The shadowy skin starts to crack, gold seeps through the jagged lines before it bursts into light.

"Holy fuck," I mutter under my breath, fighting to breathe normally again.

My body feels heavy, beaten, and bruised when I get to my feet at an agonizingly slow pace. I brush off the snow from my legs and wince. My feet look almost mangled, and crimson blood is soaking my leathers. I feel the blood trickle down my shoulders, making the garment stick to my skin.

Why don't I have the power of healing or something that's actually *useful?*

The sound of flapping wings and rustling feathers makes me look up and I freeze all over again then I spot the White Dragon.

You got to be fucking kidding me!

I'm about to run, but again my legs are frozen to the ground, only, this time it feels even more forceful than with the Mares.

Oh, shit.

Oh, shit.

Oh, fucking shit!

What kind of magic is this? My muscles tense to the point of excruciating pain, my feet are on *fire*. Like I'm standing on glowing embers. I want to scream, but there is no room in my lungs.

As the golden threads start to flow from the center of the White Dragon's chest, I know what's coming. He's about to bond with me. And I'm not fucking ready for that, nor do I want to. Hell no!

I have to survive, and I don't want to risk a failed bonding.

A choked sob threatens to burst from my lips when I realize that there is *nothing* I can do in this situation, other than fucking *watch*.

The golden threads whip through the air, and as soon as the first thread grazes the skin on my left arm I know what comes next.

Death.

I won't survive this.

There is something *missing*, but I don't know what.

Searing pain envelopes me as dread replaces all rationality in my mind and I scream inwardly. I can hear the scream ring out in the deepest corners of my mind, but no sound is coming from my mouth.

Agony.

This is utter torture.

My body fights for the ability to move again, but nothing happens. *Please don't!* I beg behind sealed lips. Molten iron crawls down my forearm, towards the beetle mark at my palm. I want to scream, I want to run.

"*Riften!*"

Terror grips my heart when something slams into me from the side, knocking me to the ground. I wheeze from the multitude of confusing emotions.

Panic, dread, terror, pain...relief.

Someone is yelling, but I have no idea who.

The pain slowly subsides from my aching limbs. Air trickles down my windpipes, filling my tortured lungs with precious oxygen. Finally, I'm able to move without the heaviness. Only to feel my body tense up all over again when I hear Amadeus's voice growl beside me.

"No. You don't bond with her."

In slow motion I look up at my best friend who's facing off the White Dragon with determination plain on his face.

The White Dragon growls low and deep in its throat, heat radiates from its chest, hot enough to almost burn my skin. He bares his razor-sharp teeth at Amadeus, row after row of gleaming teeth on display. They promise death to whomever stands in his way.

Amadeus snarls back, and a golden ring appears around his irises, making him look completely unhinged for just a flash. Shadows flicker over his skin in a split second. The White Dragon roars, making me shudder in fear.

Nausea threatens to bubble up my throat when my oldest friend grabs a hold of the golden threads from the dragons chest. Twisting them around his left arm. The command in Amadeus's voice is devastating, and it rings out along the mountain ridge with the force of an avalanche.

"You bond with me."

Chapter Twenty-One

This is all wrong.

An inhumane scream cleaves the air around us. It's pained and filled with sorrow. The hairs on my body stand on end, sending pulsing waves of energy along my skin.

My fingers start to tingle. "Noooo!"

Shut up. Shut up. Shut up!

Heart wrenching sobs of true grief replace the tortured screams. It's absolutely heartbreaking.

Please shut up, someone make her shut up!

The ground underneath me vibrates. My body starts to shake violently, and something grabs a hold of my jaw. A blurry face envelopes my field of vision, but I can't make out anything else than the color of their hair. It's copper, and reminds me of sunsets.

His mouth is moving, but I'm not able to understand a single word. My gaze shifts and I zero in on the golden threads that are wrapped around Amadeus's arm. He lets out a growl I can't quite place, but it stirs something violent in me.

Suddenly my cheek stings, like someone slapped me. It throws me out of my panicked state, and I realize that I'm the one screaming like someone is dying.

"Trouble, snap out of it!" The command penetrates the fog in my brain, again someone grabs my jaw with a firm grip, forcing my face upwards. Everything snaps back into focus all at once.

Riften is standing over me, rage wafting off his body. "You good?"

"My dragon," I cry out. "He's taking my dragon."

A furious roar leaves the White Dragon's chest as he starts to flap his wings furiously to make an escape. A pained sound pierces the air.

"Fucking bond with me you useless creature," Amadeus growls, desperation seeping into his words.

"Don't, please!" I beg, and my knees buckle. My chest constricts with a grief I have no reason to feel. Then, it turns to absolute rage.

Like hell he's going to steal *my* dragon.

"Trouble? Oh shit."

My vision blurs with hot anger, and I get to my feet grabbing my golden dagger. My knuckles whiten around the hilt. Amadeus will pay for this.

I charge and let the dagger sink into his shoulder with a deep growl bubbling up my throat.

"Let him go," I twist the dagger around in his shoulder, hearing his agonized scream like a song to my soul. "If you value your life, Amadeus Vanæra, you will release him from your hold. Or I swear to you that I will hunt you down and make you regret the day you were born." I lift another dagger to his throat for emphasis, letting it nick the delicate skin under his chin. "I will break every pathetic bone in your body before gutting you, then I will shove your intestines down your throat like the animal you are."

Amadeus cries out in pain, but doesn't let go of the threads. No, he has the audacity to tug on them.

"I said—" I kick the back of his knees, rip out the dagger from his shoulder and grab a fistful of his hair. "Release him, you worthless piece of shit." Moving fast, I twist my body and knee him in the gut, making him double over from pain.

His grip loosens, and the golden threads retreat back to their source. I hear the furious roar from the White Dragon. Gusts of wind whip around us as he flees.

Amadeus screams, but I don't have it in me to feel any remorse from his tortured sounds. In some twisted way, it fills me with an immense satisfaction to hear him like this. With the hilt of my dagger I strike him in the middle of his face, making blood splatter all over me. He falls to his back, breathing heavily. He's dazed and sounds almost confused when he speaks. "Why did you do that?"

Slowly, I crouch down at his side and let the tip of my dagger prick the skin at his collar. "The bigger question is, why did *you*?" I sigh.

"You don't understand..." he pleads, trailing off into a pathetic whimper.

"I should kill you for this, Amadeus. You are meddling with forces we don't understand, and you are smarter than letting your desperation take over like this."

"What do you want to do with him, Trouble?" I look up to meet Riften's mossy green eyes before looking down at Amadeus once more.

"Let's leave him here for the Mares to feast."

I feel hollow.

It's like every emotion inside me has been stripped from my soul. The emptiness is almost choking me. I didn't realize it was possible to feel this...numb. I can't help but think that this is all my fault.

Still, I don't understand.

Why did Amadeus betray me like this? Why did he feel the need to force a bond on a dragon? Why didn't I see this coming? Have I really become so comfortable with my best friend that—

"*Darling, please stop.*"

I freeze against his chest. The complete intimacy of the way he's able to communicate with me through our mind link is jarring.

"With what?"

He sighs deeply and squeezes me tighter to his chest. "Stop blaming yourself, Trouble." He says into my ear, and my skin puckers from his warm breath. "He broke creature-law, and he betrayed you. That violation warrants a much heavier punishment than what he got."

I glance back to him with questioning eyes and he sighs deeply. "Merick doesn't agree," he says hesitantly, and the dragon underneath us chuffs out a plume of smoke that hits us in the face seconds later, making me cough. It smells like a strong concoction of charcoal and sulfur.

"How did he even find you? I couldn't sense you until you reached for my thoughts. It was like...walking through complete darkness before you called my name.

I blink.

"I didn't even realize that I called for you," I mumble, feeling my chest swell with emotion.

Merick banks towards the forest, and Riften's hold steadies me from sliding off my seat. I can see smoke in the distance, and I know it's coming from the compound. "Where are our friends? Do you know if they made it out alive?" I ask, squeezing my legs around the scaly back of his dragon.

"They're okay, they made it out," He says, but there is something in his tone that makes me uneasy.

"What are you not telling me?"

Silence stretches out between us, and it doesn't seem like he's going to elaborate. Merick makes his descent amongst the branches landing in the middle of the perfect circle of the henge. Immediately I go to dismount, but startle from the slight growl that Riften lets out behind me.

"You know better than that, Trouble," he mutters, and lifts an eyebrow when I just glare in question. He rolls his eyes and sighs. "Let me help you down."

"Excuse me, I'm fully capable of getting off this dragon without your help, sir."

"Ever heard of being a gentleman?" He quips back.

A laugh bubbles up my throat. "Yes, and I'm pretty sure you don't possess a single gentle bone in your body."

He frowns, still not letting me go. "That might be true, but it's also called common decency."

"Sure, and yet I've never asked you to be decent with me. In fact, I might actually prefer the filth you hide from everybody." I flick the tip of his nose with my pointer finger and swing my leg over the dragon's neck before gliding down to the ground.

"Oh, you want my filth, do you?" I hear the small smirk on his lips, and a shiver runs along my skin when he lands behind me on the ground.

Merick puffs out an annoyed breath, but I can't find it in me to care. Everything else falls away when I'm around Riften like this. "You *did* promise..."

A low chuckle caresses my neck and I lean my head against his shoulder for a moment, closing my eyes to feel the nearness between us. "*I did, didn't I?*"

I fucking love it when he talks directly to my mind like this, especially when it turns somewhat suggestive and sensual. It's the most intimate form of communicating. My skin puckers when he brushes a lock of my silvery strands away from my neck, and I take a sharp intake of breath. *"As much as I would like to cover you in my...filth, there are more important matters at hand."*

I groan. "Like what?" I sense his barely-there touch along my skin, it lights up a fire inside me. Turning my head to the side, I meet his eyes. I could drown in those eyes.

"If you two are quite finished with that, I do in fact have to talk to you, Golden One." I jump away from Riften and whip my head around to stare at Merick, who's now standing in the middle of the circle of stones. *"What?"* He drawls inside my head in a deep rumble. *"Did I interrupt something?"*

It's the sarcastic tone that throws me off. It feels like he's laughing at us. *"Indeed I am."*

"Wait, can you hear my thoughts too?" I can't hide my surprise, because I didn't expect it would be possible for any magical creatures to hear my thoughts. Granted, I don't know nearly enough about the strange magic of this land.

"Obviously." The dragon snorts, and if I'm not mistaken he's laughing. *"There are many things you don't understand about this land, Golden One. And even more things I can't tell you."*

Reluctantly I take a steadying breath. "Because of the curse?"

Merick dips his head, closing his piercing blue eyes. They look so familiar, hell, they look like my own.

That's...odd.

A chill settles in my bones, and I pull the fabric of my clothing tighter. I'm not dressed for this weather.

The Black Dragon ruffles his feathered wings, and a golden shimmer runs along them like liquid metal. I wonder why his wings look like that. The wings of the other dragons are all covered in a thin membrane, but the

Black and White Dragons don't have that. Their wings are covered in gold tipped feathers.

One black, one white. One dark, one light.

It feels like there's a significance there, but right now I can't think.

"It wasn't supposed to be this way, Golden One," Merick says into my mind, making me frown. I'm too tired to ask. Too exhausted to care. *"Monsters will come, and you will lose what you hold closest to your heart, Salem. Be wary of the one who lurks in the shadows; for he will do what it takes to get his way."*

"Fuck that! Listen, you overgrown lizard. Monsters are already here, they just attacked the compound!" I can't for the life of me keep the anger out of my voice. "And the guy lurking in the shadows? If you're talking about shadow daddy over here, I'm pretty sure he's...I don't even know. Fuck it, I don't really care anymore. All I'm trying to do is survive, and this—" I fling my arm out, and a fucking golden thread shoots out from one of my fingertips, headed straight towards the Black Dragon. It latches around his throat and I curse violently under my breath. "You got to be fucking kidding me, let that stupid reptile go." I yell at my magic.

Merick growls in pure anger, smoke pluming out of his nostrils. His wings flare wide, and his tail whips through the air.

This is so bad. So fucking bad.

"Trouble, let go of him." There's a warning in Riften's tone, and I roll my eyes at him.

"Does it look like I'm doing this on purpose? Fucking hell, all I'm trying to do is to let him go, you wanker!" Shaking my hand only results in entangling the Black Dragon in yet another golden string. Another curse slips out though my lips. A layer of sweat is coating my skin and my breathing is heavy.

Shit.

This is draining my power, and I can't control it. My muscles start to tremble with exertion, I'm struggling to keep myself in check. "What the fuck is happening?" I whimper, and my vision blurs.

A flood of intense sounds invades my ears, drowning out everything, even my own scream. A rush of energy washes over me, along with another wave of pain. My vision blurs again before it goes back to normal.

No. Not normal. It's sharper. The detail of the fabric on Riften's tunic is clearer, the pulse in his throat bounces against his skin and I'm able to see every single detail on his throat move to the beat of his pulse. *When did he get so close?*

Dizziness takes over, and I stumble. My knees buckle and I fall. Strong arms catch me before I hit the ground, and an intense need for *something* rushes up inside me.

Violence. *I crave it with every cell in my body.*

"Knock me out!"

"What?" The confusion on his face is almost devastating.

"Knock me out, Riften," I repeat, more urgently.

"I'm not going to—"

"Knock me the fuck out before I end up killing someone!" I feel it then. A *shift*. There's something seriously wrong with me. All my senses are running on overdrive, and I have no idea *why*.

"Oh, fuck." Pain enters Riften's eyes before a sharp blow to my temple makes me see stars.

Thank the Gods.

The last thing I hear before I'm swallowed by darkness is the familiar whisper inside my head. An ungodly voice calling my name.

Saaaleeem.

Chapter Twenty-Two

The lack of sounds around me is absolutely serene. I'm drifting through darkness. Calm washes over me, and I feel a strange sense of peace cleanse my soul. My mind is *finally* silent. After months of not having my mind all to myself, it's finally silent. I can't remember the last time I felt this peaceful.

The memories start to flow freely.

My little sister's smile is the first thing that comes to mind. I can't remember the sound of her voice, but I remember her incredible laugh. Like wind chimes and summer rain. It's the first time I've thought of my sister in a long time.

In her reality, I've already been gone for a little over two years. Twenty five months. I wonder if she's okay. If she went to Heason, or Tegner for help as I told her to. Or did she end up taking our mother's advice and chain herself to the brothel. Tears start to prickle behind my eyelids.

I don't want to cry. There is nothing I can do for her now. But still, I wish it didn't have to be this way. If I only had known there was a loophole to avoid the reaping, I wouldn't be here right now.

I flutter my eyes open, but there is only darkness in front of me.

I'm all alone. The blackness is almost choking me. There is no light here. I'm floating in darkness. My body feels weightless, and I float through the Nothing.

Pain seeps into my veins when the sound of my heartbeat gets louder. There is no end to this maddening darkness. My bones are aching.

Someone is lurking in the shadows. I'm not alone.

As I try to inhale, my lungs feel small and insignificant. Like there is no air in this place. The sound of water droplets echoes around the vast emptiness.

Am I alive still?

I feel my body shake. Pain shoots through my left arm.

Burning. Burning. Burning!

Air! I need to find air.

Everything *burns*.

I want to run. I need to flee. To get away from this torturous Nothingness trapping me here. Wherever this blackness is.

Do I even have a body?

Saaaleeem.

A whisper that's getting louder and louder, closer and closer.

I am alive. My heart is beating. Faster and faster. I have to be alive.

Louder.

Louder.

This isn't a safe place for me. I need to figure a way out. A way to get free. Back to myself.

"She's still sleeping?" A voice says, echoing around inside my head. No. It's outside somewhere. Muffled, as if in a bubble.

I know that voice. It's faint, but it's there. I can't place it. It rings true to my bones. I know this voice.

The pain pulses through my body once more, blinding hot pain. Restricting shadows wrapping around my essence. Holding me tethered to some semblance of normal.

What even *is* normal?

I want to throw up, but there is nothing there. No body. No vessel. No ground. Nothing. I'm surrounded by Nothing.

I'm drowning in darkness. There is no light. Only pain.

Pain.

So much pain.

So much burning pain.

Saaaleeem.

Another whisper. Closer this time.

All of a sudden I can move my focus. I'm all alone in the darkness. Where am I? Is this...Death? It must be, but then, why did the voice ask if I was sleeping still? There is no logic to this feeling of emptiness. This *anger* flooding my cells.

Something's wrong. I have to wake up.

If I am to survive. I *need* to wake up.

"Orvin." Another familiar voice, and the mark on my left arm tingles from the sound. Like bells ringing out their gentle song across my skin.

Calming me.

"Yes. She's in and out. Mostly out," the voice says. Who is it? I know this voice. Intimately.

He sounds exhausted. Hopeless. Small.

I know that whoever this voice belongs to isn't that. This person is strong and steady. I just can't place it. I can't place anything in this endless darkness.

I'm not alone. There is someone here in the Nothing.

Someone screaming.

They also feel this pain. They also feel their cells waste away. Piece by piece.

I'm not alone.

I wish I was.

It *hurts.*

It's too crowded in the Nothing. No one should be in this between.

Air. I need to locate air.

A sudden breeze strokes along my skin. Calling me gently to its source.

"Salem."

The whisper sounds more urgent this time. I don't have long. I know this. I feel it.

"She seems to be tethered."

The first voice says. I remember now. The second voice said his name. Orvin. My father. Is he back from...wherever he was? He's been gone for a while. I wonder how he is. If he has any new scars. Any lost battles. I know this man.

"Salem!"

I can't find the voice.

I can't stay here.

"The golden bond. Somehow you are anchoring her."

The voices are so muffled that they're hard to grasp.

Why am I here again? This is even worse than when I exhausted myself after using my magic. I didn't use my magic this time. Did I? No, I don't think I did.

The White Dragon tried to bond with me. It got interrupted.

Someone is screaming. Pain shoots through my missing body. My soul is fading. I'm losing something...vital. Something important. Anger fills me.

Kill.

I need to kill.

No!

"Tell me your theories old man," the second voice says.

"I'm not old."

"You know what I mean, now talk." Even if the voice still sounds like bells along my skin, he sounds annoyed and impatient. Why can't I place him? I know that I know this voice. He's part of me.

A scream of utter agony cleaves the air around me. I know that scream, but once again I can't remember who it belongs to. I know I've heard it before. Somewhere.

"Golden One!"

What!? I want to yell back at the voice that so clearly rings through my hazy brain. Follow it to the ends of the earth. Tether myself to the voice that chose me as its bond.

Bond?

Yes, that's right. The White Dragon tried to bond with me. It must be him calling me to him. I will my consciousness towards the enticing voice. The other voice that feels like home. It might be my only hope of survival.

"Her bonding got interrupted. It's a failed bonding, and failed dragon bonds turn the human into a husk. Her body is rapidly losing weight," my father says, halting my progression towards the alluring voice.

Is that what's happening to me?

Am I turning into a husk?

Is that what this feeling is?

I take a moment to sense myself. My body is gone, but there is an echo of it, somewhere. It no longer feels strong and capable. It feels frail and weak.

He might be right.

But there is also something else withering away inside of it. Something much more vital. Something close to my heart.

I need to find the voice that calls me closer.

Again I turn my consciousness to float through the darkness, pushing through a veil of emptiness. The familiar voices fade away into the distance as the whisper from the White Dragon gets louder and louder.

Gradually the world around me brightens, giving form to the vast darkness of shadow. Pounding rain falls through my essence as I float up, up, up.

Gaining momentum, the edges become recognizable. Majestic mountains, hills, and valleys. Lakes and villages. Beaten paths stretch throughout the strange land of Nowhere. Linking everything together like a map.

I soar across the landscape, seeing humanoid creatures engulf villages along the mountain ridge. They lurk in shadows and misery, stealing precious life with their violence. Snuffing their lights out from under their noses.

Icy plains stretch across the northern parts of this strange land, hiding secrets of ancient magic in frozen caves. Scorching deserts with deep tombs and buried cities hide strange creatures with scales and translucent wings. A multitude of breathing forests that span for ages across this dangerous land, hiding all kinds of monsters in the deepst corners of the wild nature.

Golden threads bridge the landscape together, linking everything in an elaborate blanket of beauty. Despite the violence of the dark creatures lurking in the shadows of this land.

"Golden One!"

Shadows eating away at the majestic gold, spreading sickness and misery throughout the land. My heart plummets at the realization of the destruction.

"Little One."

Without thought, my consciousness shifts towards the gentle call. The picture changes, and I'm in the cave. The watery wall that leads to terrifying depths looms behind me. Drops of water fall from the ceiling like a drizzle. The ground shakes, making stones fall all over the ground. Glowing beetles crawl on all surfaces, glinting like moving constellations across the night sky.

The White Dragon is curled up on the ground, breathing hot air into the frost. As my essence nears him I'm almost afraid I'll disappear into the Nothing, but he opens one huge green eye. Pinning me in place.

"There you are, Little One," He says. Blinking slowly, pain reflected in the deep of his eyes. There's a bottomless pain that hides behind them. But I see it through the windows to his gentle soul. *"You need to wake up."*

I want to tell him that I don't know how, but the words are lost. I'm nothing more than energy floating around in the Nothing.

"You need to wake up, Little One."

The rumbling vibration from his chest shakes my essence, making something sting and glow around me.

Still, there is nothing. Nothing of me to be seen.

"Wake up!"

The force of the words touch my soul, solidifying something in my bones. It shudders through the emptiness that is myself.

"Wake up!"

Slowly an outline starts to form, and I can see the edges in clear detail. A golden glow illuminates from my left arm and a thread flows out behind me.

Leading back, back to somewhere, and I know I have to follow it.

All of a sudden multiple golden threads lights up all around. Connecting missing pieces of a mystery I can't fathom. Twisting together in impossible knots, but the one behind me is the brightest. The purest of them all.

That's the one I have to follow.

That's the one that will lead me back to where I truly belong.

Chapter Twenty-Three

Waking up from the in between happens in stages.

I didn't realize that the five senses had an order, but they do.

Gradually my taste buds start to register the tangy taste in my mouth. It's dry and uncomfortable and has my hackles rising. It's almost metallic, like blood, but different. More pronounced. The urge to get a sip of water to wash away the taste is almost overwhelming.

My sense of smell is the next thing that registers.

A woodsy scent that tingles in my nostrils. A smell that calms me in every possible way. Making me feel both safe and at peace. It reminds me of the forest surrounding our village. Like basil and dewy moss, mingled with a different smell that feels more masculine and strong. Also familiar, but that smell feels more distant. Like an old memory from my childhood.

Then, slowly my sense of touch starts to function once more.

Scratchy fabric clings to my damp skin, restricting me from moving. It itches against my raw flesh, almost to the point of pain.

I try to focus on the scents in the room, the only thing that seems to calm me at this point. The one thing that keeps me tethered to my own sanity. I hone in on the scent of basil and dewy moss.

Muffled voices start to trickle in. Gruff, low pitched and gravely. Filled with concern.

I'm fine, I want to say, but my mouth won't move.

"Riften, she's coming back."

Strange hands grip mine, squeezing them tight. I get the urge to hit the person touching me, rip out their insides and feed it to the darkness that lives inside me.

Kill.

I need to kill.

No!

"Trouble?" The voice is filled with tortured hope. "Open your eyes, Trouble, please." His voice grounds me, making my violent urges dim to a simmering whisper in the back of my mind.

With great effort, I manage to flutter my eyelids, but they're too heavy to stay open. I feel the fatigue wash over me from that small movement. I'm so tired, and there's this...anger that has settled in the pit of my stomach. And it's not going anywhere.

Slowly I manage to open my eyes.

Mossy green pools meet mine. Worry written all over his face. Then the feeling merges into relief. He takes a deep breath, almost like he hasn't been breathing properly for days.

Maybe he hasn't.

I struggle to focus on his features. Why is he even here?

I'd thought Elodie would sit by my bed, not him.

"Riften?" My voice sounds weak and gravely. He leans closer to me, lowering his voice. "What?"

As I try to lift my head, it spins. Damn, this might be the worst hangover I've ever had. Wait, it's not a hangover. It's something else. Something much worse.

Pushing that thought out of my head I focus on Riften again. "You're too close," I mumble, and a snort from someone in the room has my eyes wandering. Only to find Orvin leaning up against the wall, arms folded across his broad chest.

I blink slowly.

Once.

Twice.

Am I supposed to call this man *dad?* Or *father?*

"What are you doing here?" I ask instead, in that broken voice. Feeling the fatigue hit me full force.

He tilts his head to the side and pushes off from the wall, walking over with a confident stride. "Got the message that you were in the infirmary." His steps falter for a moment, and suddenly, he seems a bit unsure of himself, which is a strange look on this otherwise impressive man. With his strong posture, broad shoulders, and tall build. He's a warrior, through and through.

"I'm fine," I manage, again trying to sit up in bed. Not wanting to show weakness to anyone. Especially these two.

My father is a stranger. Riften is a nuisance. I wish Elodie was here, or Galen. I wouldn't mind them seeing me in this state. Heck, I'd even take Killian's company over theirs.

Then the memories start to trickle back to me. The Mares. The attack on the compound. The White Dragon. Amadeus.

Bolting up in bed I gasp in both pain and confusion. "Where's Elodie? Galen, Mason...Killian? Are they alive?" My voice breaks, and tears gather in the corners of my eyes. "Where are we? What happened?" A surge of panic grows inside my chest, almost choking me.

"Easy, they're fine. They're here. We're at the compound, our friends are alive," Riften soothes, making calming circles at my back. "Please, lay back down. You're still weak."

"I'm fine," I protest.

"I can see that," Orvin says in a flat tone, looking over me from the top of my head to the tips of my toes, scanning me. Once again, I get the sense that he sees too much of me. That he sees everything. Past, present, and future. Shivers run down my spine and I get the urge to shift my posture.

It's not necessarily a bad feeling, just...uncomfortable. He looks at me like he actually cares about my well-being. A sharp contrast to my whore of a mother back home in Terrby.

"You don't need to worry yourselves, I'll be fine after some sleep."

"You have been sleeping," Riften interjects. "You've been sleeping for eight days, if you can even call it sleep." No wonder he looks like shit. They both do.

"You've been having fun without me?" I pout mockingly.

"Wait, what? No. It hasn't been—" he groans, running both of his hands through his red tinted hair in frustration. "Stubborn woman," he mutters underneath his breath. "You're fucking with me, aren't you?"

"Hey, I just woke up from a horrible dream, I'm allowed to fuck around. I'd much rather do the actual fucking than joking around but, alas, we can't get everything we want."

"Please stop talking about fucking," Orvin grumbles under his breath.

"Anyways, I'm fine, you're obviously fine..." I pin Riften with my stare. "In fact we are all fine here, you can all just leave my stupid alone."

"Right now, I'm incapable of *leaving your stupid alone*—whatever that means," Riften says with a deadpan glare in my direction. "I'd very much like to leave *you* alone." He looks all kinds of annoyed...and edible.

"Why *can't* you leave me alone, Riften?" I ask.

"Because my mark won't stop burning!" He growls as he rubs his left arm, right atop his golden mark. The soft glow lights up his hand, casting gentle shadows across his chest.

I frown in question. "...Why? I'm not in danger now."

"Heck if I know. My mark isn't happy, that's all I know, and I'm incapable of leaving you alone. So, you're stuck with me until it stops, I guess," he grumbles.

"Sure." I shake my head slowly before letting my focus drift to my father. "You on the other hand," I say slowly.

"I'm your father," he says.

"Of course you are, but I just met you and then you disappeared for weeks doing whatever. I don't know you at all. You are fully capable of leaving me alone."

"I don't want to."

"That's too bad. I don't care what you want, Orvin. If he isn't leaving," I point towards Riften before adding. "Then *you* are."

"Salem."

"Don't you *Salem* me. You have no right to *Salem* me. You haven't been a part of my life. You don't know me." The anger simmers underneath my skin as a physical thing. My voice gets gradually louder the angrier I get. It seeps into my voice, making it come out almost as a growl.

"That wasn't my fault!" Orvin protests, looking almost distraught.

"I don't care if you had anything to do with it or not right now!" I shout, feeling the tears prickle behind my eyelids, and cursing myself for showing any emotions in front of them. "You might have known about my existence, but that doesn't take away the fact that you weren't there for any of my childhood. I know you didn't have a choice in the matter, and I'm sorry for that. But you have absolutely no right to barge into my life now and demand a spot in it. That shit is earned, and you have not yet earned that spot, *father*," I spit.

He flinches, and a sinking feeling turns my stomach as he takes a step away from me.

His eyes fill with hurt. Then he flexes his jaw. "As you wish," he says, dipping his head in a small bow.

I know I should feel bad for what I said, but I can't bring myself to feel anything other than relief as he retreats to the door. His shoulders tense, steps heavy.

With one hand on the doorknob he stops and turns in my direction. "Whenever you're ready, Salem, I'll be here to support you." And with that he twists the knob, pushes open the door and leaves.

"That was a bit harsh, don't you think?" Riften says beside me, looking at me warily.

I give him a pointed look. "Sure it was, but it's also true."

He opens his mouth as if to say something, but seems to think better of it, and closes it again. His eyes narrow slightly before he shakes his head. "There's something—" He mutters, but cuts himself off.

My eyebrow twitches in question, but he gets up from his chair without an explanation. "I'm going to get you some water." He says instead, and with that he leaves the room too.

Thank the Gods.

I let myself sink back into the pillow and heave a painful breath. Everything hurts. At this point I'm so sick of pain, it's even difficult to remember a time when pain wasn't a permanent part of my life. There's an ache inside my chest. A hollowness that covers my heart in a festering kind of torment.

A sharp prick stings my bottom lip, and the taste of iron tickles my tongue. Frowning, I go to touch it, only to find a bead of blood on my fingertip. There's a strangeness to this I can't put my finger on, and frankly, I don't know if I have the energy to ponder over the fact.

Is it possible for someone to experience so much fucked up shit that they go completely numb?

I think it might.

"Where is she?" I hear Elodie from the other side of the door, and the corner of my mouth twitches. Fuck, I love that girl. "Get out of my way, Riften, or I swear I'll drown you where you stand." Is it weird I find her violent threat endearing? Maybe. I also don't care. I also know that Elodie wouldn't hesitate to follow up on her threat either.

Her water wielding makes her fully capable of drowning someone on the spot, as long as she has access to a source of water. No matter how small it might be. I'm pretty sure she could drown someone with a bead of sweat if she really wanted to.

The door bangs open, and a spray of water mingled around a soaked Riften comes flying through the room. Sprawled on the floor, he coughs loudly. "Why the fuck did you do that?"

"You were in my way," Elodie walks in, tossing her braids over her shoulder. She's styled it with multiple long braids that almost seem to shine silver as she moves. "Besides, you were about to protest with some bullshit, and I don't really have the patience for that."

"You can't possibly know what I was about to say," he says, getting to his feet once more. "Great, now I'm drenched."

I look him up and down for a moment before looking over at Elodie, who smirks mischievously. "Serves you right for not letting me past. Besides, you look good when you're soaked."

"Elodie Mayers, are you giving me a compliment?" He asks, sounding far from amused.

"Don't flatter yourself, it was meant as a backhanded remark more than anything," She smacks her tongue before making a face.

"Holy Gods, what happened to you?" I stare at my friend, and the angry new scar running down the side of her throat.

"Oh, this?" Elodie gestures with her hand to her neck. "Got up close and personal with a Mare, nothing to worry about. How about you? You look like death."

"Feel like it too," I grumble as I push the covers away from me.

"Elodie," Riften growls low in his throat, as if in a warning, or an attempt to grab her attention. I'm not quite sure, but she ignores the man.

"What happened to you? I saw the White Dragon fly you away," she sounds concerned, but also intrigued. "Are you—" she trails off, as her eyes roam over my left arm, finding the golden mark there. Her eyes go wide in shock. "I've never seen markings like that before—"

"It's not what you think," I say quickly, trying to hide the golden marking on my arm.

"Elodie," Riften warns. She continues to ignore him.

"Then what is it?" She walks over to the side of my bed, grabs my shoulders and guides me back to the pillows. "Stop pouting, you look like shit and you need rest. Now, please tell me what you can," she says, before grabbing a chair and sitting down.

"Elodie," he says again.

"I'm not bonded to the White Dragon, he tried but...it got interrupted," I say, feeling bile on my tongue. I can't believe I'm actually telling her about this.

"What, how?" There's anger in her voice. Shock, disbelief, rage even, but most off all concern as she looks over to Riften with a deadly glare. "Did you know about this?"

"Yes, I did, but Elodie—"

"Why the *fuck* didn't you tell me about this earlier? This is a really big deal, that shit is incredibly fucked up, you know that, right?"

"Elodie! Remove the water, before I kill you." Then he adds, like it's an afterthought, "Please."

She rolls her eyes. "So dramatic."

With a wave of her hand, the water on him disappears as steam. "Happy?"

"You have no idea."

Elodie turns to me again, before discarding the chair in favor of sitting on the bed beside me. She takes my left hand in hers, tracing my mark with her finger. "Strange," she says softly. "I've seen this pattern before."

"Where?" I ask, a little too quickly.

Her eyes move to mine, she opens her mouth to speak, but her tongue gets glued to the roof of her mouth before any words are able to form.

We both curse. By now it's becoming a real nuisance. I want answers for fucks sake! "No matter," I say, trying to hide my annoyance the best I can. Pretty sure I'm failing miserably at it though. "Tell me what happened here, with the Mares, is everybody—" I know Riften told me this, but for some reason I need her to tell me. I need her to confirm his words.

"We're okay. Killian spent a couple of days in the infirmary, but recovered quickly. There were casualties, and a lot of the unbonded disappeared. We haven't been able to find them," she swallows, looking almost pained. "Amadeus is one of them."

"I know, I left him in the mountains to die," I say, sorrow lacing my voice.

"You what?" Elodie barks out, glaring at me with evident shock. Which is understandable, honestly. "Why?"

I take a deep, painful breath, forcing myself to look at her, sadness entering my eyes. "He tried to force the White Dragon to bond with him, instead of me..."

"He did *what now?*" Absolute fury enters her eyes as she gets to her feet. She's pacing now, staring from me, to Riften, and back to me again. "This is bad. This is really fucking bad, Salem."

"I didn't die," I try to say, realizing that my voice sounds absolutely pathetic and small.

"Salem, no, you don't understand how bad this is, I—" Her tongue locks up, and she screams out in frustration, fear entering her eyes as she looks between us, before pinning her stare at mine. Then she mouths the words slowly to me.

"Salem, you're going to die."

Chapter Twenty-Four

It takes me a couple of days to regain my footing again. The healers were reluctant to let me out of the infirmary at first, but eventually they didn't want to deal with my progressively pissy mood so they let me out.

That served me just fine, to be honest.

I know I'm not fine. For some reason, I'm losing weight and my muscles are rapidly deteriorating, but other than that and my shitty mood, I feel just fine.

The fact that I'm losing all of my muscles though, that actually pisses me off. I worked hard for those, and I'm losing all of my strength along with them.

Walking up the stairs to the library takes me at least three times as long as it normally would, if not longer. By the time I'm at the top at least ten people have walked past me and some of them have already left the library after doing whatever they were supposed to do there.

Gods, I hate being weak.

"Where are you going?" I clench my teeth as Riften's voice reaches me.

Great.

Leaning against the railing I look at him with my best impression of a careless expression. "I'm taking the stairway to heaven, can't you see?" I ask him nonchalantly. "What the fuck does it look like? I'm headed to the library."

"I can see that."

"Then why did you ask?" I glare at him in question, enjoying the fact that he seems to struggle to find the words. He looks almost edible as he opens and closes his mouth like a confused fish.

"I, uh," he clears his voice. "Never mind. Can I help you with anything?"

Giving him a slow blink, I lift my brows. "Does it look like I need help?"

I want to strangle this man, so bad. He is so incredibly annoying. Always lurking in the shadows, and that was even before I ended up in that stasis kind of state! Now he's all but glued himself to my side, constantly there to *help*.

"If I'm being honest, yes. Yes it does." Again, he clears his throat.

You've got to be kidding. He did not just say that.

"Well, I don't," I say, pushing myself away from the railing. Actually, it was kind of nice to have an excuse to stop and catch my breath.

I'm not telling him that, of course.

"What's up with you?" He asks, taking a step towards me, but halting himself as I mirror his movement and take a step back.

"Nothing." Can I just kill him? Would that be considered murder? Oh, yes, it would, and murder is frowned upon.

Kill.

I need to kill.

No!

He narrows his eyes, and the corners of his mouth lift. "You lie so pretty, Trouble."

I'm gonna kill him.

I wonder if my golden marks would hurt if I did that, but I'm not sure I want to test that theory. It might be best to refrain from murdering this man. Besides, he is quite handsome.

Where the fuck did that come from?

I'm losing my mind.

He's edible. That's what he is.

My mouth waters thinking about sinking my teeth into his soft skin, feeling his blood flood my mouth.

Kill. I need to kill.

I'm about to take a step towards him when he lifts his hand to rub the back of his neck. "Anyways, let me know…if you need anything. I'm here," he says. Sounding almost shy.

That throws me off enough that the delectable picture that just flooded my brain evaporates.

Why the fuck did I want to *eat* him right now? And not in the fun way. Actually *eat* the man. He'd probably taste like death and shadows anyways.

"Sure," I try to blink myself out of my own confused state and physically force my body to move in the opposite direction of him. Towards the library. I need to find something, and I don't know what it is yet.

I can't remember why I was headed to the library. I woke up, left my bed, and headed here. Not really knowing the reason behind it. It doesn't matter. It's a hunch. I always follow those.

Unless they involve murdering people for no obvious reason. Apparently.

But if that would quench the thirst for…whatever this is, I might consider it.

No, Salem! Stop that!

With too much force, I push the door to the library open. It vibrates violently on the hinges, threatening to fall off. I curse low in my throat, glaring at the stupid door.

That makes absolutely no sense. I thought I was losing my strength, not gaining it.

Whatever.

I have a hunch to follow, and I can't do that if I'm staring at that useless door.

As I walk down the numerous shelves of stubborn books I wonder what on earth I hope to accomplish. It's not like I'm going to be able to read any of the books in here anyways. I'm not bonded. Yet the hunch is pulling me forward.

It feels like something is tugging at the center of my chest.

Picking up a book with a blank spine I leaf through it, feeling my heart sink at the empty pages. I'd hoped there would be something.

A word, a sentence...anything.

What I wouldn't give to be able to glean any kind of information about this place. Even the book of old Tales had disappearing ink, the one I found in the library back home. Such a pity that I lost it, but even those pages hid their knowledge as I started to read it.

What if the books connected to this place have a mind of their own, and really do hide the knowledge from the unworthy? But how do I become worthy?

If I'm not mistaken, the White Dragon chose me. Doesn't that make me worthy? Or do I have to actually survive the bonding?

Probably.

Well, if that's the case, I'm fucked. I wasn't going to survive that bond, I could feel that in my soul. It almost got shredded to ribbons.

Stupidly, I pick up another book further down the line. I bet it doesn't contain a single word. When I open it, my theory is confirmed with another blank page. Not even a shadow of a letter.

There is Nothing.

I hate this place.

I *truly* hate this place.

I want to go home. Back to Terrby, to my old life. To Pipp.

The longing I expected to feel when thinking of her, doesn't come.

That's odd.

Normally I'd be close to tears, but right now? It's like I couldn't care less about what happens to her. Or anyone else for that matter. In the back of my mind, I know that I should care, but I...don't.

I really do not care about anything anymore.

"*Saaaleeem.*"

I ignore the voice and continue wandering aimlessly along the various shelves of spiteful books. A glowbeetle scurries across the floor and a smile tugs on the corner of my mouth as I lift my foot and squash it flat under my boot. A strange laugh bubbles up my throat when I lift my foot and see the soft glow flicker and die.

Serves it right.

I'm about to start walking again when the small insect starts to glow once more. Becoming stronger, more steady. It seems to inflate, then it pops into its original form. Scurrying along the floor away from me in a zigzag formation.

"What the fuck?"

Frowning, I decide to follow the bug.

It should be dead, but isn't, and for some reason that makes me brim with anger.

It needs to die.

"I tell you, there is something off about her," the hushed tone of Elodie's voice says behind a bookshelf, and I stop to listen. "Ever since she woke up she's not been herself. It's concerning."

"I know," Galen replies. "My calm doesn't affect her either, it's like it bounces off her as soon as I try to regulate her," he sighs, and I can just picture the way he runs his hand through his hair as he does. "Somehow, it feels like a part of her is missing."

"What do you mean?"

"It's difficult to explain." Are they talking about me, or someone else? Because if they are talking about me, there is no reason to be as worried as they sound. I'm fine. Never better actually.

All of my worries have dissipated.

I no longer care about useless things like other people's well-being.

Maybe that's the problem. Maybe that is what I should worry about. But then again, I don't.

"Do you think it could be the failed bonding?" Galen asks thoughtfully. "Hear me out, you said she looked like death when you visited her—"

"She looked like a living corpse, Galen."

"—Right, but think about it. If the dragon that chose her started the bonding, and wasn't able to complete it, then maybe she is turning into a husk..."

They're silent for a beat, before Elodie adds. "Or something worse."

Well, if that doesn't sound ominous. Holding back my sudden chuckle I continue listening in with more interest now.

"What's worse than a husk, Galen?"

The silence that stretches out between them is almost enough for me to lose interest in them both, but I stay for a moment longer.

"I don't know, a monster?" Galen swallows audibly and I'm actually quite impressed that I even caught that small sign of nervousness.

"Yeah, but what kind? There are many monsters lurking in these lands. And we're not privy to all of it, even with our bonds."

"Saaaleeem."

"Did you guys have tales of Hulders in Kinnon?" He asks in a low tone, almost too low for me to catch. Kinnon. A city far south in our homeland. The place Elodie grew up and called home. I've only heard rumors of that place, but I know it's a city that prides themselves on their military forces. No wonder Elodie and Killian were highly skilled at fighting prior to the reaping.

Elodie sucks in a surprised breath. "You don't think—"

"Only thing that makes sense, isn't it?"

"Sure, but...it can't be. They're just stories, Galen. They can't be—"

"True? Look around you, El! We are *bonded to dragons* and currently standing in a library that decides who and what gets to read the books within these walls. I'd say it's more than likely."

I tilt my head to the side, contemplating. I've been able to glean more information from this conversation than anything else so far, though not anything that gives me any answers. Only more questions.

"Not to mention, just last week we fought off the Mares," he continues. "I think we need to find that dragon that tried to bond with her, and have it complete it." Good luck with that. "Have you asked your dragon where we can find it?"

"Euna doesn't know, neither do any of the others. It's like he vanished," Elodie snorts, probably rolling her eyes.

"Saaaleeem."

I don't want to bond with the White Dragon. I really don't. Besides, wasn't he sworn not to bond with anyone? I remember Tara—or was it Yara?—said something about that. Maybe that's the reason it failed. I'm convinced it's a good thing.

"But how will we find him?" Elodie makes a sound almost like a whine. Pathetic.

Why do they even care?

"*Saaaleeem.*"

It's getting harder and harder to ignore the dragon's call. It feels like a part of me is drawn in that direction, but the other half recoils from it. I'm not sure which path to take. It's like being in limbo, or...yes. Limbo. I'm standing at a fork in the road, and there's two paths to choose from. Neither of them seems very lucrative at the moment.

No.

Yes.

Is there a third option?

My head tells me to stay far away from the dragon's call, because by now I know it's the White Dragon calling me to him. He wants me to find him. I'm sure of it. Yet my heart tells me to follow that small tug.

They're silent for the longest time, obviously thinking about their options, or rather, their lack of options.

Spotting the glow beetle in my peripheral, I suddenly remember what I was doing before I got sidetracked listening into their useless conversation.

I was on the hunt.

About to kill that annoying beetle that apparently didn't want to die. Turning on my heel, I stride away, not giving them another thought. All that matters is killing that beetle. For a brief second I wonder just how important my new task is, but quickly push it away. The annoying call of the dragon is also pushed to the back of my mind, locked behind ironclad doors as the beetle leads me out of the library and back down the stairs.

Everything is tender. My bones are aching. The itching won't stop. Small cracks reverberate through them as they morph into something else. The urge for violence is so strong. I want to kill. I need to kill. I'm so hungry for blood. I need to find her. That is why I did this. I need to find my own blood.

Chapter Twenty-Five

I walk in a daze after the beetle through the courtyard. It looks almost drunk as it zigzags from side to side on the ground. My blood thirst gets more and more potent the longer I follow the bug. On occasion, I manage to step on it. Squashing it flat. I see the light flicker for a beat, before it inflates and the glow resumes once more. Then it continues its wobbly walk. It does nothing to quench my sudden need for violence. It just makes me fume with anger.

I think someone calls out my name at some point, but it falls on deaf ears. I'm completely engulfed by my mission. Gradually, my feet move from cobblestone to a dirt path, to mossy terrain, and then to the soft forest floor. Eventually, my feet hit stone again.

Overgrown rocks are placed in close proximity to one another. They form some kind of yard in the middle of the deep forest. My clothes snag on unruly thorn bushes that have tangled themselves into the neatly placed markers. Broken logs and shards of glass are strewn amongst the brambles.

Lifting my eyes I find myself in the midst of the small square of a ruined village.

A well stands alone in the middle, the rope no longer present, rotted away long ago. The roofs of the buildings have caved in on themselves.

No structure looks to be untouched by the atrocity that must have swept through this place at some point.

Something tugs on my heart at the thought, but it's pushed to the back of my mind immediately.

I look around for the beetle, but it's Nowhere to be found. Walking forward, I step on something soft that doesn't feel like grass. I see a small ball of fabric when I lift my foot, half decayed from the elements and time. A wooden button hangs loose from the top half of it. Picking it up, I frown at the object.

It's a doll.

Or, it was a doll, at some point.

Tossing it to the side I continue my search for the beetle, still needing to kill it for some unknown reason.

I don't think I will ever know why killing that beetle is so important. It doesn't matter. It just is.

There is no wind here, I realize. The air is stale and dead. Chokingly so. I hear wings flap from the canopies. Eyes. There are eyes on me. Beady eyes blinking from their perches. A flock of midnight black birds sits perched in the branches.

Peering silently down at me.

Lurking in the shadows.

Whispers echo in the stillness.

High pitched voices reach me, speaking in a language I don't recognize. It's melodic, and repetitive. Nothing I've ever encountered before.

Rows of sharp pointed teeth gleam in all directions from the last light of the day, as I realize that it's about to give way to the darkness.

I have a feeling I should be afraid of the creatures lurking in the dark, but I can't find the feeling.

"Look, look, look," A cacophony of high pitched voices pierce the stale air. "Touched by darkness. Touched by misery. Eating away, eating away, away, away. Soon it will consume it."

The voices are coming from all directions at once—and not.

"What are you?" I ask the creatures.

"What are we? What are we, it says. It has no right to ask such a thing," the shadows respond. I turn around in a circle, trying to pinpoint where the voices come from, but they are everywhere. It's almost like they are one creature split into multiple beings.

"It doesn't know it's turning. It doesn't know." The voices seem to come closer as glowing green eyes start to illuminate the shadows. Lighting up the outline of their long uneven noses. Dried up roots and twigs dangle from their patchy heads, moss covers their gruesome complexions. "The other one too, yes, yes, the other one too."

I whip around as something brushes the back of my leg, a shadow darts between two broken walls, disappearing into the darkness.

"What do you want?"

"It doesn't know how alluring it is, how delicious the darkness tastes. It doesn't know yet. It doesn't know." The voices echo between each other. "The King might like it, yes. The King might like it, oh, we should take it with us."

My neck prickles, and I kick out once more as there is another brush at my leg. "Piss off you pests."

"The incomplete bond will eat away its heart. It will turn it into one of us. One of us. One of us!" Their chant is eery and makes me bristle. But then again, it's absolutely enticing. It makes me want to let go and give into the darkness they speak of.

"It's grumpy, we like it grumpy. Yes, we do. Feel that anger. Be that anger. Let the anger consume you." The voices chant. I struggle to get a good look at them as the remaining light rapidly fades into darkness. Something tells me that I shouldn't be here, that it isn't safe, but I no longer care. The things these creatures say ring true to me on some level. I want to give in to the anger. The blood thirst. The violence.

As the voices bounce from one direction to the other, I can feel myself being lulled deeper into it. Into the Void of no emotions.

"That's it, deeper, deeper, give in to the Nothing."

My lower back starts to itch, and the sensation pulls me out from the Void as the pressure on my mental barriers gets almost too much to handle. Gasping, I take a step back from the creatures, away from the chaos.

"No, no, come back. Come back to us," Their voices raise to a shriek, desperate for me to give in. I blink rapidly, trying to push the fog away from my brain. "It's slipping. We want it. We need it!"

I shake my head vehemently. "Leave me alone!"

"No, no, come back to us. Let us help you."

The pressure on my chest and mind gets heavier, tugging me backwards, away from these creatures. A niggling thought comes trickling back into the forefront of my muddled brain. A distant, foggy memory that feels muffled all of a sudden, that I know shouldn't be. A voice rumbling in the back of my mind that isn't my own. *The sky will burn until dawn. The rain will fall after the drought and give life to the shadows. Monsters will come, and you will lose what you hold close to your heart.*

The memory tugs at my chest, warning me away from this place. I know I should listen to it, but I don't want to.

My foot hovers, as if it's deciding which way to go. If it's going to retreat from the potential danger, or give into the darkness. It's like I can taste the darkness, taste the power it will give me.

A shattering sensation slams into my mental barrier, demanding to be let in. I block it out and lick my teeth as they start to ache for something soft and coppery. I want to taste the forbidden flesh. I want to let go and sink into the darkness that invites me in.

"Yes, come back to us, come back to us. Yes, step into it. Let us in. Let us in." Something soft slithers around my hovering leg, up along my calf. Brushing the soft skin under my thick leggings.

My body gives an enormous tremble. Vibrating throughout my bones, settling at my core.

Don't give in, Salem. Don't. Not all the way.

I'm balancing on the tip of the Void to the Nothing, almost tasting the alluring sensation of misery. I want to give in. Get the answers I need. These creatures can give me the answers I want. They can give me the future I crave. If I just let go.

Closing my eyes, I sense my heart scream in agony and despair. My mind tells me to let go of it all. Let go of my heart. Give in to the Nothing and let these creatures lead me to their King of Misery.

"Take the step, take the step." They chant, louder and louder in their screeching voices.

I need answers, that is what I need. I realized that that was why I was headed to the library earlier today when I found the beetle. And this is where it led me.

I take the step.

And let go.

*S*oft flesh gives way to my sharpened teeth. It tastes like the sweetest nectar. My thirst for violence is finally quenched, and I can turn my attention to what's important. The need for it rings true to my bones. Rushing leaves whirls around my feet as my victim takes its last shuttering breath. Blood gurgles from their throat, sputtering out from their mouth. I need to find my own blood.

Chapter Twenty-Six

I'm almost giddy with glee as the huge boulder booms behind us. Closing up the entrance to Dover mountain. When I decided to follow the ominous creatures, I knew there would be no way back. I don't want that. I'm looking for answers.

The walls echo as we walk, and the cackling laughter from the tiny humanoid creatures bounces up and down the passageway.

They haven't stopped chanting their celebration since I took that very first step.

In an odd sort of way, they're quite charming. Despite their horrifying looks. Huge bulging eyes that glow neon green in the darkness. Sharp gleaming teeth that reflect any light cast upon them. Moss covered branches stick to their clothes, and their footsteps sound almost wet.

"One of us, one of us, one of us!" The cacophony of voices around us multiplies when we near the end of the cave-like hall. It opens up to an entirely new world.

Glowing gemstones cover the walls inside the mountain. Natural vegetation carpets the rugged stones. Huge eyes blink out at me from their hiding spots in the small caves dotting the walls. None of them look even remotely human. Yes, they have human-like features. They look almost elf-like though, with their pointy ears and long noses.

"We have it, we have it! We have the Bridge!"

More creatures gather around, creeping out from all kinds of hiding spots. The majority of the creatures reach my knees, but some come close to the height of my hips. The taller ones are extremely thin, and don't wear any clothes. The bones poke out in all directions from their skin. They remind me of rocks for some reason. It might be because of their grey complexion and the moss that covers their skin in patches. I've even seen a couple of mushrooms growing on their skin, giving them all a horrifying look.

But it's their eyes that capture me.

Their eyes have a layer of grey that fogs their otherwise unworldly beauty. Because, despite their ugliness, they are beautiful.

I don't know where my certainty comes from, but it's a fact I know to be true.

These creatures are not all evil.

They follow behind our odd procession to something that looks like a street encased in stone. The glow from a multitude of crystals makes it so we're able to see, but otherwise it's hard to make out the details of this magical place.

Gradually, the crowd grows in size, brimming with new creatures that are similar in size to myself. They don't look as gruesome as the smaller ones. In fact, the only major difference I can see is that they have tails. Their eyes are clear, and glow slightly in the dim crystal light.

Almost too scared to voice it, I brave the question. "What are you?"

Someone my own size huffs out a snort, but doesn't answer. Looking over at the person, I'm struck by his intense beauty. Teal blue hair, clear jade eyes, and a jaw sharp enough to cut diamond. He's fucking stunning. His tail flicks through the air, almost hitting me in the face, and a small smirk touches the corner of his mouth.

"Trolls, they are trolls. We are all trolls. Different kinds, but still trolls. Yes, yes, trolls. So is our King," one of the smaller creatures says, climbing up the...troll's back, settling in on his shoulder.

"Thank you, Pekwim, for the explanation," he drawls, unamused.

"You're most welcome, you're most welcome."

"Do they always repeat themselves like that?" I can't help my question.

He flicks his tail through the air again before sighing impatiently. "Only the more deranged ones do." He levels a pointed glare at the creature on his shoulder, who now has his finger up his nose, wobbling in deep concentration. There's a chanterelle growing from the bridge of Pekwim's nose, and his eyes cross as he focuses on it. "Oh, look! Look at my mushroom, isn't it beautiful?"

"Yes, yes, very beautiful. Next thing you know you start pooping out gemstones and starlight," the other troll says humorlessly.

I stifle a laugh, not wanting to be rude. "What is your name?" I ask the bigger one.

He sighs heavily before looking at Pekwim on his shoulder. Almost like he's asking the creature for the answer. Pekwim beams. "His name is Dante."

"Can you tell me anything about what's going on here, what kind of place this is," I ask Dante. Again, he sighs, looking at Pekwim who's still beaming. "We need the Bridge. We burnt one a long time ago. Had an oopsie with some wordsies. Yes, we did," it says.

Dante grumbles. "And you still call it an *oopsie*..."

"It was an oopsie, we didn't mean to cast the spell, we didn't mean to burn the Bridge." Pekwim protests, sounding like a small child on the brink of a breakdown.

"I'm sure you didn't, but you still cast it, and it has cost us a lot of lives. On both sides," Dante says, arching a brow at the creature. Now it's Pekwim's turn to grumble, but it doesn't protest further.

Thankful that they are actually communicating with me. I dare another question. "Where are we?" This time, it's Dante that answers. "Nowhere, but you already knew that."

I did. I did know that. But I was also hoping for a better answer than Nowhere. Is that the actual name of this place? Nowhere? Somehow I thought they were joking when they said that was the name of this land.

"Yes, but where exactly?" I push. Dante closes his eyes, as if to feel for the words he's about to speak. "We are inside the Dover Mountains, in Nowhere. But again, you already knew that, stop asking things you already know and ask something new."

Well, maybe they called it something else? Maybe it had a different name than what the riders of the Stolen Soldiers had for this place.

"Why can't I read any of the books here?" I ask suddenly. Odd, why was that the first question that came to mind?

Dante tilts his head to the side, smiling before looking to Pekwim for an explanation. He beams again, like a child. "Because you are not bonded yet, it is part of the oopsie that we did. Yes, the oopsie made it impossible to read anything for the ones that did not belong. But you do belong, the bond is not yet complete. But Atticus will help. Atticus will fix the oopsie. And Merick. Yes. They will both help fix the oopsie we did so long ago."

I frown. "Why won't you answer the questions, and who is Atticus and Merick?" *Does it mean the Black Dragon?* Dante nudges Pekwim impatiently with his head, swishing his tail in agitation.

"Because he can't tell you anything you don't already know. Any new information has to come from one of us," Pekwim explains, and a cacophony of voices join a new chant of "One of us, one of us, one of us."

Interesting.

Inconvenient, but interesting.

"Did you cast a curse on this place?"

Pekwim nods solemnly. "We did, as I said it was an oopsie. We didn't mean to, but we prefer to call it a spell. But yes, yes we did spell the land. We glimmer gnomes are the only ones that can tell full truths." And they also seem to speak in riddles. Great. More riddles. I fucking hate riddles.

An itch settles at the base of my spine, at my tailbone. A faint throbbing pulse through me and I wrinkle my nose in discomfort. I don't like this feeling.

"They are in fact able to tell simple truths and half truths, like metaphors and riddles." Pekwim continues, seemingly unaware of my discomfort. I'm actually not quite sure what gender the creature is. Is it a she? Or is it a he? It feels sort of rude to call the creature an *it*, even in my head. But why the fuck do I care about that? I turned that emotion off.

My mouth fills with saliva when I catch a whiff of something delicious, and fully alive. The urge to sink my teeth into soft flesh, just to quench this overwhelming thirst for blood is hard to keep at bay.

Don't give in to it, something tells me in the back of my mind. I can't tell who it is. It could be the dragon, it could be the hag, or, it could simply be my conscience. Which sort of feels…off kilter at the moment, like it's split in half. Head versus heart and all that, and I'm unsure what organ to follow.

Logic or desire. And if that, desire for what exactly?

Ignoring that thought, I halt. We've entered something that looks to be a throne room. At the front there's a dais with a throne made of golden thorny vines. It almost looks like they're woven together into this beautiful piece of furniture.

"It's as annoying as you can imagine," Dante remarks beside me, rolling his eyes. Then he tilts his head to the side and studies my face. "Not being able to tell more than half truths and riddles when you want to speak." He shrugs before smirking. "Welcome," Dante says, taking a slight bow.

"To the Dover Mountain and the Court of Misery," Pekwim finishes.

The tortured sound coming from the majestic creature in front of me fuels my inner violence. My thorny threads wrap around its soul, keeping it hostage. As our souls merge together as one, I feel the inhumane growl of victory rumble up my throat. I sense the reluctance from the beast, but my thorns have dug themselves too deep. Now I can find her. I need to find her. I need to find my own blood.

Chapter Twenty-Seven

Mouth agape I stare towards the throne and the man seated there.

His hair is pink.

Pink.

Is this their King? The King of Misery? His elbows are placed on his knees, and his hands rest casually in between his widened legs. When he looks up, towards the oncoming procession, his face brightens in a welcoming smile. Sharp canine teeth poke out from his upper lip. A piece of bone jewelry dangles from one of his earlobes, accompanied by a raw piece of smokey quartz. Only—the smoke inside the gem *moves*. I've never seen a piece of crystal do that before.

Sharp jade eyes pierce into my soul, and a shiver runs down my spine from the raw power he exudes.

He's young. Much younger than what I'd expect for a king. But then again, what do I know about kings? Nothing.

"The Court of Misery?" I ask Dante and the glimmer gnome. "Couldn't have come up with a better name for this place, huh? I mean...what about 'The Court of Stale Air' or something like that?"

Dante snorts. "That name was already taken."

"Really?"

"No." He looks at me with annoyance before continuing. "We're cursed, not stupid."

"Had to ask."

"If there had been a place called 'The Court of Stale Air', I wouldn't be able to tell you anyways, would I?"

He's got a point.

I'm suddenly struck by the resemblance between him and the King. They look so similar, like...brothers, and yet, not. I'm pretty sure they are related. No one looks that similar without a blood relation. They have that same piercing jade eyes, a jawline sharp enough to cut diamond, not to mention their noses have the exact same shape.

The King bears no crown, instead I spot a gleaming white circular object hanging off of the top of the throne. It almost looks like bones.

"My King," Dante says, startling me out of my thoughts, and he gives a slight bow at his waist towards the man seated in the throne.

The King smiles. "Dante."

Another glimmer gnome, female I think, climbs up the various golden vines on the throne—almost knocking the crown to the floor,—before she takes a leap and settles on the King's shoulder. "Hello, Piworin." His eyes soften for the small creature, and she turns a slight shade of blue from his velvety voice.

That's odd.

All of it, really. Not only the fact that her skin changes colors, but also the softness in his eyes. Not that the King isn't capable of being kind or soft, but because of the title he holds. *The King of Misery* doesn't exactly point out any softness within.

Yet, there's no mistake. Those eyes *are* kind. Maybe even kindness itself.

Piworin giggles softly, and her soft bluish skin turns a pure royal blue color that almost makes her look like a blueberry.

"Am I making you blush, Rin?" The King chuckles.

"Yes. Yes, you are, and you are well aware of it too. We have guests, can't you see?" Her soft voice flows almost like waves in the air, and it reminds me of soft bells chiming in the wind.

"I'm so sorry my dear, you know how much I love your royal blue," the King teases. "I simply can't help it."

"Oh, hush," Piworin paws his face away from herself as she titters, and the sound of her soft giggles makes a memory tug at my heart.

Pipp.

She reminds me of Pipp.

"Oh, sweetness, you were the one that decided to perch on my shoulder. Besides, our guests can wait while I banter with you, my dear." His voice sounds like velvet, soft and alluring. There's pure power hidden behind that voice. That mask he holds. It's barely contained, and yet I can feel it with my whole being. "Will you do me the honor of being my translator to this..." his sharp eyes drift to me. His eyes move slowly up and down my body, making me shiver. "Lost soul?" He finishes.

"Well of course, my King." She giggles again, and her tiny hand covers half of her face as she sways on his shoulder. "Welcome, my friend," she all but chirps. When her hand falls away from her face, needle sharp teeth poke forth, and a golden ring lights up around her neon green eyes. I almost catch myself correcting her. We are not friends. I don't have any friends.

That's a lie. And you know it.

True. I do know that. I shake my head, in an attempt to gather myself. There are too many voices in my head. Too many presences pushing in on my mind that it has me confused. At this point, I'm not even sure how many it is, or who they belong to.

"We have been waiting for you, my Bridge." Piworin chirps, like a songbird. She smoothes down her purplish tunic—it's the same shade as the King's attire. Then she claps her hands together.

"I'm sure you have many questions for us, Bridge, and they will be answered as best as we can, to the best of our language." The glimmer gnome seems to move dramatically with each word.

Dante clears his throat. "To the best of your knowledge, you mean?"

"Yes, yes. That's right, to the best of our knowledge," she smoothes down her tunic again. Giggling, she tucks a lock of hair behind her ear and I see the patch of moss that grows on her neck along with a couple of gemstones.

"My name is Piworin, but you can call me Rin." She dips her head in an awkward curtesy. Almost like she doesn't know how to behave in front of people.

"Why do you call me that?" I ask. *"My Bridge."*

"Oh," she giggles again. "Because that is what you are. A Bridge. The Bridge we need to stop this war. You see. All the pieces are gathering on the board. And you are a vital part of the game."

A low growl slips out of Dante, and he drags his hand over his face. With a groan he mutters. "It's not a *game*. It's a curse. And it's destroying our world."

"Let her speak, son," The King says in a stern voice.

Dante lifts his hands in defeat. "Fine, fine."

"As I said," Rin continues, giving Dante one impressive looking side eye before surveying me once more. "You are the Bridge, and the one that will help us end the Misery. You are the beginning, and your other half is the end."

"Excuse me?"

"You're excused," Dante leans into me, smirking. Rin cocks her head like a bird. "Yes?"

"No," I say, trying to stop my mouth from gaping like a fucking fish, and I catch the King chuckling. "I don't...I'm what? No, no, no. I'm not a bridge, or whatever you mean with that nonsense. I'm—I'm—,"

"A bridge," The king smirks. "*The* Bridge, in fact. And we need your help."

I look from the King, to Dante, to Pekwim and Piworin, then to the crowd that has gathered in the throne room.

It's packed with onlookers.

Apparently, this meeting is much more public than I'd imagined it to be. Honestly, I didn't think it would come to this. I just followed a fucking beetle.

Is this the reason why it led me here? Or was it all a coincidence?

I glance down at my beetle mark in the middle of my palm. *Stealth.* Supposedly this means I'm going to become an assassin, but I still don't know who or what I'm going to kill. "Do you know what this means?" I hold up my palm for them to see.

"It's your beetle mark. It allows you to bond with a dragon. Well, it's an activator really," she explains, rubbing her hands up and down her thighs. "It jumpstarts your own magical abilities if you have any. But your abilities come from your other mark," she glances down to my left arm for a beat. "Your power was gifted to you, I don't believe you have any other powers—" She shifts uncomfortably on the King's shoulder when he clears his throat, shaking his head slightly. The movement is so small it's almost impossible to notice.

But I do notice it.

Narrowing my eyes at them I clear my throat. "Explain."

A collective gasp rings throughout the throne room from the gathered creatures. "She dares to demand anything from our King?"

"If I'm not mistaken, you need me far more than I need you. So, spill."

Piworin gives me two rapid blinks, before glancing over to the King. He quirks an eyebrow, as if to say *'Well, you stepped into that one, you're on your own'* and waits. The small glimmer gnome rubs her small hands over her tunic *again*, wobbling a little as she hisses in a breath. "You might have two powers, no-one really knows. But what we do know is that the Old Lady gifted you her own powers in the Caves of Transition."

Who came up with these stupid names? They should be ashamed of themselves.

The King lets out a small growl of annoyance at the mention of the Old Lady, sounding more like a monster than a human. Then again. They aren't humans at all. They're trolls.

"You have now started the bond with Atticus," she smoothes down her tunic *again,* and I'm almost to the point of asking her to spit out the rest of the words so I can sort them out myself.

Then the name registers and I cock my head to the side. "Atticus?"

"Yes, the White Dragon's name is Atticus," Rin nods to herself, glancing over at the King with a nervous look before sliding it over to Dante, seeming to bite the inside of her cheek. "Anyways, his brother is the Black Dragon, Merick," Rin continues.

Dante snorts. I look to him for an explanation, who motions to Pekwim that's still seated at his shoulder. "They are all brothers," Pekwim beams. "All of them. Twins and a spare. Dragons and a square."

"I'm neither a spare nor a square, do you even know what a square is, Pekwim?" Dante turns his head so fast that the poor gnome loses his balance and topples to the floor.

He sits up, looking cross eyed at his mushroom, before his skin turns a slight shade of yellow. "You almost broke my fungi, you will pay for this you insolent—"

"Manners," The King drawls. And the word echoes through the crowd, making Pekwim's skin turn almost white.

It's fascinating to see how the glimmer gnomes change color depending on what they feel. I shake my head, confused. "Can someone, anyone, explain to me what a fucking Bridge is?"

The whole throne room goes quiet, and all eyes are on me. Empty expressions stare back at me from everywhere. I stare back, equally dumbfounded.

"You don't have bridges where you're from?" Dante asks, looking almost concerned.

"No?" You could drop a needle in the room and the sound would be deafening from the silence that follows.

Dante rears back his head, shaking it as he does, before he looks between me and the King. "Are we sure we have the right one?—" He leans closer to me, taking a whiff of me and—

"Did you just sniff me?"

Dante blinks surprised. "—When did you wash last, you stink."

I slap him across the face on pure instinct. "Of course I stink, I've been tracking through the fucking woods all evening!" I growl angrily. How dare he? "And don't give me that look, you deserved that. Now answer my question! I want an answer." I say, poison dripping from every syllable. "What is a bridge?"

Dante pinches his nose. "Even I can answer that for you, because you already know; It's a structure that connects two places. Making it possible to cross to the other side."

I stare at him like he's an idiot. "I know *that*. I mean, what do you mean that *I'm the Bridge* and what the fuck am I supposed to do about it?" I growl, frustrated. Honestly, I'm teetering on my last nerve.

A chorus of *oh's* and *ah's* trickle through the room, and my jaw slackens. "Did you seriously think I'm *that* stupid?"

"I was beginning to wonder," His face lights up with a slow grin, and his eyes darken slightly as he rubs his jaw. "I like you."

"Reel it in, son. She's bonded to another." It's a warning, and I glance at the King with a frown.

"Oh, this you mean?" I shake my left hand, taking a step towards the throne, anger brimming under my skin. "Because I have this golden curse imprinted on my arm I suddenly *belong* to someone else, huh? Let me tell you something, this mark—" I grab the dagger at my ribs and press the tip down to my forearm. "Means *nothing* to me if I don't start getting some serious answers soon!"

The rippling alarm that travels across the throne room is absolutely delicious. Maybe *this* is what I've should have done all along to get some fucking answers.

"Where did you get that dagger?" Dante trails off as he looks to the dagger that's still pressed against my arm. "Please, Salem, remove the dagger from your mark." His eyes are almost pleading.

"How do you know my name?"

He sighs deeply, holding out his hand for me to give up my dagger. Like hell I'm giving it to him. It's mine. It's part of me.

I narrow my eyes to slits. "What is the purpose of the Bridge?"

Piworin clears her throat and I jump from the sudden nearness of the sound. I look down to see the tiny gnome standing in front of me with wide innocent eyes. "You're supposed to bridge the gap between our people. And help us end the war."

Chapter Twenty-Eight

"Wait, what—No! That's impossible," I shake my head, blinking rapidly at the glimmer gnome.

"It was a part of our attempt at fixing the oopsie," Pekwim says, getting so excited that he's climbing on Dante's head. Stomping his small foot in the center of his face.

"Pekwim..." The gnome doesn't seem to register the warning in Dante's low growl and continues with his enthusiastic explanation.

"You see, after we realized that we could no longer communicate with the other creatures or the humans of the land, we spelled the twin Princes to become dragons. We did not know that they couldn't get back into their bodies, nor did we know that they weren't able to speak with anyone other than themselves," Pekwim continues, wobbling on his perch. All the while using his hands to speak, making wild gesticulations in all directions.

"Wait a second," I say quickly. "You *turned* the Princes into *dragons?*" My mouth falls open as I try to make sense of it all. "And I have spoken to both the Black and the White Dragons on multiple occasions, so that's not entirely true."

"Ah," Pekwim nods enthusiastically and beams, jumping up and down on Dante's head, making him grunt in discomfort. "They *can* speak to others when they're visiting places with an abundance of natural magic."

"That's weird, but good to know." That explains why they've kidnapped me every time they've wanted to chat. "So, the salt and pepper dragons are your...*brothers?*" I look to Dante in disbelief.

"Pekwim, get your foot out of my face before I chop it off and feed it to the Nøkk," He growls low in his throat, ignoring my question.

What the fuck is a Nøkk?

Pekwim on the other hand, still doesn't seem to register the warning in Dante's voice, and continues. "So, with the twin Princes stuck as dragons, The Queen stuck in the cave and The King stuck in the mountain, we needed to find the Bridge. Especially after what happened between the first Bridge and the King of Shattered Souls—"

Pekwim doesn't get to finish that sentence because he's suddenly no longer on top of Dante's head, instead he's soaring through the air across the throne room. The gathered trolls cheer with excitement as they watch his body fly over their heads.

"What did you do that for?" I snap.

Dante just smirks. "What? I did warn him."

"You threatened to chop off his foot, not fling him across the room."

"Would you prefer me to chop off his foot instead?" He asks, sounding puzzled.

"Yes. No? I don't know." I blink in confusion and Dante takes a step closer to me, inhaling deeply. Is he...sniffing me again? Why is he sniffing me at all?

"Interesting," he mutters, glancing over to the King. They almost seem to communicate telepathically with each other as the King's face twists into a grimace.

"We need to find Atticus," The king says, dragging a hand through his pink hair.

"Okay, hold on. Back the fuck up. What's interesting, and why do we have to find Atticus? What's up with the Queen and what do you mean about the King being stuck in the mountain? Can't he leave?" All the questions seem to fall out of my mouth at this point. "And what happened between the first Bridge and this...King of what — Shattered Bones?" That question is almost the hardest to ask. I haven't forgotten that that was the last thing Pekwim said before Dante flung him across the room.

They almost look pained at my questions. "The King of Shattered Souls," Dante leans his head back for a moment, as if he's trying to find the words to explain. "I'm sure you've started to notice some...changes," He starts, almost hesitantly. "But you are ignoring the signs of a change you—" he winces before clenching his jaw. "—shouldn't want." I see a muscle tick at his temple. Suddenly he's breathing hard.

"You're all deranged," I breathe.

"We're cursed," the King says. "I can't even tell you my own name without the help of the glimmer gnomes."

"And what is your name?" I feel the anger start to rise in my chest and again, the small itch returns in my lower back. Right above my tailbone. It feels almost tender. Painful. The King snarls, mouth moving, but no words being formed.

"Skeylfre," Piworin says sadly at my feet. "His name is Skeylfre."

The king slumps back into his throne, sadness shining in his eyes.

That surprises me.

All around, more trolls stand with solemn expressions of hopelessness. Most of them have a glimmer gnome perched on their shoulder, or tied to their back with a piece of fabric. Even if they do look absolutely horrifying, they're also kind of adorable. It must be their big innocent eyes and their childlike behavior.

"It makes communicating very difficult when we can't even tell our own people the truth about ourselves," The King says, massaging the bridge of his nose. "And my name is Skeylfre, as Rin so kindly elaborated for you. Skeylfre, the King of Misery, ruler of the Dover Mountain."

"Leader of the rebellion," Rin adds with a shy smile, as she walks back to her king and climbs into his lap.

"Pff, there is no rebellion, it's a war amongst—" groaning in frustration, the King fists his hand so hard the knuckles turn white.

"Among ourselves, and it's bled into the human world. That was why we divided it in the first place," Rin says in a timid voice. "You see, during the first bonding between man and creature, someone killed the dragon before the bonding was complete. It muddled the man's mind and biology. Every possible emotion got heightened. Anger, sadness, rage, envy, happiness...lust," Rin makes a face for a second before continuing. "When children started to be born with tails in the villages, the humans didn't want to keep them. So instead they put them out in the forest to die." She glances over to Dante who just stares at her with a bland look. A muscle ticks in his jaw, but that's the only sign of discomfort on his otherwise expressionless face.

"They birthed a new race. Hulders to be exact. The hulder people are very resilient, so the children didn't die in the woods like the humans had hoped," Rin continues, with her eyes glued to Dante, who now has started to pace back and forth whilst pulling on his own hair. Rin's voice sounds apologetic as she resumes her tale. His tale, I realize. "The more they repopulated, the less humanity was left in their bloodline," her voice trails away and her shoulders sag.

"Turning some of our people *deranged*," Dante spits in my direction. "As you so well put it."

"You were one of those children," I say, and I watch his face twist in pain. Well, there's my answer.

His shoulders fall. "Yes, I was."

"I'm sorry to hear that, it can't have been easy," I say, thinking of my own upbringing. How I had to take care of not only myself, but also my younger sister from an early age since our mother neglected us.

"It wasn't, but it is what it is."

"How is it that you can tell me some things, like their names, but not all?" I ask, not able to hold the question that has been burning in the back of my mind for a while.

"We don't know," Rin says from the King's lap. Her skin has gone back to that grey color that reminds me of rocks. "They can say our names, but not their own. They can correct something that is said if it's close enough to the truth, or give vague indications to how things are. Like half truths and riddles. But it also has to be something that you've thought might be true," she sighs, looking almost defeated.

"The sad part of it all is that we have no idea how to reverse the oopsie," she says.

Shit. That really sucks.

"Call it a curse, would you? Because that is what it is! It's a fucking curse. I can't even tell my own story to anyone, I can't make anyone believe me without my tongue getting glued to the roof of my mouth. Two hundred and fifty fucking years of this crap and I'm fucking sick of it!" Dante growls so loud it vibrates along the walls of the mountain.

"Two hundred and fifty years? You're two hundred and fifty years old?" I gasp.

"What?" Dante looks at me in confusion. The people gathered around gasp in unison, holding their hands to their mouths as they stare at one another. The King moves so fast from his throne that Piworin ends up sprawled on the floor. "How?" The question comes out as a breath before he flies down the steps from the dais.

Overwhelmed, I take a step back from the King, stumbling on my own feet. But the King grabs my arms and starts to shake me. "Did you know? Did you know how long its been?" His eyes bore into mine with an emotion I don't understand.

"No." Glancing between them I blink rapidly. "I had no idea he was *that old*. How is that even possible? Shouldn't you be like…a dried up fruit or something by now?"

Disappointingly, the King ignores my small jab, seeming almost gleeful where he stands, jumping up and down like a child.

What the fuck is wrong with these people?

An overpowering feeling of anger and bloodlust washes over me at the same time that the King announces to everyone in the throne room. "She *is* The Bridge!"

And the room erupts in loud cheers.

Everything from that point on is a total clusterfuck of events.

Trolls of all shapes and sizes grab a hold of me and toss me into the air while I flail about, waiting for gravity to pull me down again. I scream my ever-living head off, demanding they put me back down.

That unfortunately falls on deaf ears.

The trolls dance around in circles, throwing colorful dust around that gets stuck *everywhere*. Stomping around in an odd sort of rhythm that sends shivers through my body. The glimmer gnomes chant in that language I don't understand.

It's both charming and terrifying. Like my brain can't figure out which feeling to grab hold of.

I'm carried through the throne room, down a new street-like tunnel that reminds me of some kind of open-air market. Wagons and carts are tucked into nooks and crannies. Flaps of fabric cover holes in the mountain wall with signs atop them. The glowing gemstones light up the darkness of the mountain, along with mushrooms and other vegetation that glows in bright colors.

Small hulder trolls run around with their tails swishing in the air, cheering and laughing. Glimmer gnomes continue their chanting song of celebration.

It doesn't matter how loud I scream for them to let me down, they don't hear me. Or rather; they don't care.

"We have The Bridge!" They yell, over and over, overjoyed by the fact that I even exist.

My anger rises, but they don't seem to mind. They don't seem to understand. The urge to hurt them for their careless treatment of me is getting harder and harder to ignore. I'm just about to do something about it when they toss me to the ground.

Struggling to get to my feet I hear the unmistakable sound of hinges creaking. Just as I turn around, the barred door shuts. The clank of the latch echoes in the small space.

The cheering stops so abruptly that my breath gets stuck in my chest. Air is trapped inside my lungs as I study the faces of the trolls on the other side of the bars.

"What...What is this supposed to mean?" The words barely make it past the lump in my throat.

The crowd parts, giving way for the King of Misery. He strides through the passage they create for him, stopping just outside my cage. Slowly his smile spreads across his face, taking on a manic expression.

"Oh, my sweet Bridge. My dearest pet. It's supposed to keep you safe," he says and his eyes darken along with his voice. "We can't risk losing you too."

Chapter Twenty-Nine

Time is a fickle thing.

It can move so fast you hardly register what's happening to you in the moment. It takes you a while to even understand the significance of the events until long after they have passed. Other times, time moves so slow you feel trapped in your own mind.

Five minutes feels like an hour.

Your brain tries to rationalize what's happening, where you are, why you're there. How long you will be there. Stuck in time.

Five hours feels like an entire day.

Giving you all the time you need to lose your mind, getting angry and violent. It can give you a taste of your own self, maybe even your true self.

Five days can feel like an entire moon cycle.

I don't know how long I stay in that cage, trapped in my own vicious mind. Having only my dangerous thoughts for company, but it's long enough for me to question my own sanity. The anger and resentment simmers under my skin like a physical thing.

Over time, I lose count of how many times I try to convince the guards to let me out. Their stony faces has dread trickle down my spine every time

I look at them. At some point I get distracted by the pebbles on the ground, I frown.

I wonder how many pebbles there are. A hundred maybe? Two hundred? Five hundred?

Banging on the bars doesn't help either. That only makes my hands hurt, and causes my ears to ring.

Instead I start screaming.

I scream for hours before my voice gives out on me.

All the while, my captors stand motionless outside my tiny cage.

After what feels like an eternity I start to count the pebbles on the floor, but that only makes me feel stupid.

I finish though.

There are one thousand two hundred and thirteen pebbles in my tiny cage. That number should appall me. How can so many pebbles share the same space as me? How can it all fit? Granted, the pebbles are small, but still.

On more than one occasion I wish I had Galen's power of earth manipulation. Not to make the earth shake, no, more so because I want to chuck pebbles at the guards from boredom.

I was beginning to get some fucking answers, and now I'm stuck in this blasted cage. I can't remember how long the guards has been standing there. They have rotated so many times by now.

In the beginning I tried to follow their rotation, but sometimes it felt like they only stayed for a couple of minutes before they changed shifts. From one minute to the next, they'd switched. Other times it seemed like they stayed for hours, if not days.

The ache in my body hasn't let up either. It only seems to get worse.

I can't trust them, none of them. And I'm so sick of everything happening to me, without it being my choice.

If the hag was here, she'd probably tell me that I *chose* all of the things that happened.

I didn't.

I didn't choose to get reaped in the first place.

Ever since I was ripped out of my little sister's embrace, hearing her parting scream for days afterwards, I've had no control of my life.

I got thrown into a lake through a *cave wall* for fuck's sake. Then blindsided by the realization that there are *dragons, griffins and pegasi* living amongst us.

No.

Not among us.

Because this land is Nowhere.

It might as well be the Nothing. As deep and endless as the Nothing in the Void. A place I got a small taste off not too long ago. Or maybe it was forever ago it happened.

I have no way of telling how long it's been.

And there again, we come back to the fact that time is a fickle thing.

Unpredictable.

Ruthless.

Malicious.

Even traumatizing.

They say that *time* heals all wounds. But when it comes to a festering wound on the soul, it only lets the disease spread.

It eats away at your very being. Your sanity. Your mind. Your hopes and your dreams. Crushing them to an unrecognizable pulp at your feet.

My magic is useless. I can't even feel it. No tug at my chest. No golden threads leading me away from this mess.

I'm powerless.

Weak.

I hate being weak.

Determination starts to emerge in my muddled mind, forming, not necessarily a plan. But a vow.

I vow to make these creatures pay. This land to pay. I vow to destroy—

Time is a fickle thing.

It can move so fast you hardly register what's happening to you in the moment. It takes you a while to even understand the significance of the events until long after they have passed. Other times, time moves so slow you feel trapped in your own mind.

Five minutes feels like an hour.

Your brain tries to rationalize what's happening, where you are, why you're there. How long you will be there. Stuck in time.

Five hours feels like an entire day.

Giving you all the time you need to lose your mind, getting angry and violent. It can give you a taste of your own self, maybe even your true self.

Five days can feel like an entire moon cycle.

I don't know how long I stay in that cage, trapped in my own vicious mind. Having only my dangerous thoughts for company, but it's long enough for me to question my own sanity. The anger and resentment simmers under my skin like a physical thing.

Over time, I lose count of how many times I try to convince the guards to let me out. Their stony faces have dread trickle down my spine every time I look at them. At some point I get distracted by the pebbles on the ground, I frown.

I wonder how many pebbles there are. A hundred maybe? Two hundred? Five hundred?

Banging on the bars doesn't help either. That only makes my hands hurt, and causes my ears to ring.

Instead I start screaming.

I scream for hours before my voice gives out on me.

All the while, my captors stand motionless outside my tiny cage.

After what feels like an eternity, I start to count the pebbles on the floor, but that only makes me feel stupid.

I finish, though.

There are one thousand two hundred and thirteen pebbles in my tiny cage. That number should appall me. How can so many pebbles share the same space as me? How can it all fit? Granted, the pebbles are small, but still.

On more than one occasion I wish I had Galen's power of earth manipulation. Not to make the earth shake, no, more so because I want to chuck pebbles at the guards from boredom.

I was beginning to get some fucking answers, and now I'm stuck in this blasted cage. I can't remember how long the guards have been standing there. They have rotated so many times by now.

In the beginning I tried to follow their rotation, but sometimes it felt like they only stayed for a couple of minutes before they changed shifts. From one minute to the next, they'd switched. Other times it seemed like they stayed for hours, if not days.

The ache in my body hasn't let up either. It only seems to get worse.

I can't trust them, none of them. And I'm so sick of everything happening to me, without it being my choice.

If the hag was here, she'd probably tell me that I *chose* all of the things that happened.

I didn't.

I didn't choose to get reaped in the first place.

Ever since I was ripped out of my little sister's embrace, hearing her parting scream for days afterwards, I've had no control of my life.

I got thrown into a lake through a *cave wall* for fuck's sake. Then blindsided by the realization that there are *dragons, griffins and pegasi* living amongst us.

No.

Not among us.

Because this land is Nowhere.

It might as well be the Nothing. As deep and endless as the Nothing in the Void. A place I got a small taste off not too long ago. Or maybe it was forever ago it happened.

I have no way of telling how long it's been.

And there again, we come back to the fact that time is a fickle thing.

Unpredictable.

Ruthless.

Malicious.

Even traumatizing.

They say that *time* heals all wounds. But when it comes to a festering wound on the soul, it only lets the disease spread.

It eats away at your very being. Your sanity. Your mind. Your hopes and your dreams. Crushing them to an unrecognizable pulp at your feet.

My magic is useless. I can't even feel it. No tugging at my chest. No golden threads leading me away from this mess.

I'm powerless.

Weak.

I hate being weak.

Determination starts to emerge in my muddled mind, forming, not necessarily a plan. But a vow.

I vow to make these creatures pay. This land to pay. I vow to destroy—

Don't. Please don't give into it. Not all the way.

My head snaps up.

It's been so long since I heard anything of reason in my darkened thoughts.

I tilt my head this way and that, trying to locate the small voice. Trying to understand who it comes from. What it wants me to do.

Give in to what, exactly?

The Nothing. Don't give into it all the way.

Is it the White Dragon calling to me again? Didn't he want me to find him? And didn't the hulder people tell me that they needed to find him for me too?

I want nothing to do with them. They can burn in hell for all that I care.

Don't!

The voice almost seems to scream. A feeling of foreboding enters my mind by the strange command. Why shouldn't I give in to the Nothing? The blissful peace of The Nothing is incredibly enticing.

I can't remember a time when I wasn't worried about something. Not that I show it, and whenever the feelings come creeping, I'm quick to push them away. Forbidding myself to dwell on it.

It hasn't done me any good.

Dwelling over my fucked up life hasn't put any food on the table or a roof over our heads. I had to harden my heart and stop caring so much about the unfairness of life.

That didn't take away the tears though. Or the worry.

Now?

By giving in to the Nothing, I won't feel anything.

I don't really care that I'm stuck in a cage, well, yes, I do. But then again, I can get out. I think. I hope. No, the fact that I'm stuck in a fucking cage just makes me angry.

You silly girl...

"Oh, shut up!" I snap, startling myself from the sound of my unused voice. It croaks and cracks a bit at the end.

A chuckle fills my mind, and I know it's not mine.

Am I going mad?

I don't feel mad. Maybe a little.

I still haven't figured out *who* this mysterious voice belongs to, because at this point it could be any number of options. The old Lady, the White Dragon, my own conscience...Riften.

All of a sudden, my heart swells with a deep longing I don't understand, followed by a tug on my heart. Without thought I fist the fabric over my chest, and feel the sting in my nose that spreads up behind my eyes. Soon after, salty tears trickle down my cheeks.

Lifting my left hand to my face, I touch the tears, and bewilderment settles in my belly. My golden marking starts to glow. It's a gentle and beautiful illumination that brings the shadows closer. So close I can almost touch them.

"Riften," I sigh, not really knowing why his name enters my mind.

"*Trouble! Holy shit, where the fuck are you?*" His panicked and urgent voice fills my mind. He almost sounds...scared. At the same time, I feel an indescribable annoyance.

"Stop calling me that," I all but growl under my breath.

"*Where are you? Are you hurt?*" Again, his voice flows through my mind, pressing past my mental barriers. It knocks them aside with so much force that I'm unable to block him out. It feels like he barges through a door, blasting it off the hinges, and leaving it in splinters in the depths of my mind.

A sharp sting crashes into the side of my brain and I hiss from the pain, but it's gone as soon as it comes.

"No, I'm not hurt. I'm just pissed," I mumble, rubbing the side of my head, inspecting my hand right after, expecting to see blood. But there is none.

"Where are you?" It almost sounds like he cares about my well being or some shit. Why? He's just bonded to me, it's not like he's in love with me or anything?

"In a cage?" I say, and it sounds more like a question than an actual fact. I know I'm in a cage, but I wonder why he wants to know. My thoughts are interrupted by the deafening boom of his voice.

"A CAGE? WHO THE FUCK PUT YOU IN A CAGE?"

Wait, it might not be normal to spend your time in a cage when I really think about it. Up until now I've only been annoyed by the fact that I've been locked up in here, but now I'm beginning to think it's a bad thing. I think.

Not that I care anymore.

"Trouble, answer me! Who put you in a cage, and why?"

"Fuck if I know. Okay, I know *who* put me here, but I have no idea *why*," I mumble, rubbing my forehead again. "And please stop screaming. I feel like you are going to burst a blood vessel in my brain when you do."

The growl he sends in response to that makes me shiver, and my body temperature rises.

"Don't pout. I'm perfectly fine. It's quite cozy in here actually," I say, turning around in my barred box. "I've got one thousand two hundred and thirteen pebbles to keep me company." Why did I tell him that? It makes no sense to tell him that.

"Answer me!" He growls, in that dangerous tone I've heard him use a couple of times. And again, the sound makes me shiver. *"This is the last time I'll ask you this:* Who *put you in a fucking cage, and* why?"

I smirk. "How awfully protective of you."

"*Trouble...*" The warning in his voice makes my temperature rise even higher. I can't explain it, but a weird sense of joy spreads through my body at this odd conversation. Now, if I only cared about...anything, I might think twice about what I say next. But, I don't. "Tell me, are you jealous that someone else caged me before you did?"

There's a pause.

There's a fucking *pause*.

"Riften?" I coax softly.

"*I don't know how to respond to that.*" Another pause, and I prod his barrier with an imaginary finger. "*Are you trying to make me beg, Trouble?*" He all but sighs in my mind.

Honestly, I don't care if he does, but it would be quite satisfying to hear.

"Not really," I say softly, before I lean my back into the metal bars of my cage and smile. I search for the words to tell him what he wants to know, but the words won't come, the thoughts fog over as I try to think of them. Therefore he can't read them from my mind either. I'm forced to do something I'd never thought I would do. Something I hate. And that is to give him a *riddle*.

"You should ask a beetle."

"*A what?*"

"A beetle."

"*That's what I thought you said.*" Another pause. "*Have you lost your mind yet?*"

That makes *me* pause.

Have I? Maybe I have. I sigh softly. "I don't think so."

"*I'll find you. I always do.*"

And with that last statement, I can feel him retreat from my mind.

It's just in time too, because heavy steps echo through the tunnel. Heading this way.

I take a deep breath as I close my eyes to gather myself once more when the steps halt just outside my tiny cage.

"Are you ready?"

Staring down at my fingertips I try to ignore the deep voice.

"Have you ever tasted blood before?" I ask instead.

"I literally can't tell you that."

"Of course not, because you can't tell me the truth, that means that you have, doesn't it?" I huff, leaning my head against the bars and look up to meet Dante's piercing gaze.

Sighing, he huffs out a breath. "I have," He says, letting his tongue glide across his sharpened teeth.

"How are your gums?" He asks.

Frowning, the response slips out of me. "They're fine."

"Are you sure about that?"

I knit my brows together in confusion, and let my own tongue glide over my teeth. A small gasp slips out of me when I feel the sharp tooth poking down. What the... "Do I have canines now?"

"You do," he says. "That's why we need to find Atticus. Do you know where he is?"

I wave a hand at him. "In a cave somewhere."

"A cave?"

"Yes, a cave. I saw him. Don't ask me where, I couldn't tell you anyway," I click my tongue for emphasis.

"Ah, yes," Dante chuckles. "Now that you're—" he shakes his head. "The curse seems to affect you in a greater way than before," he finally says, leaning against the bars with his arms folded.

I stretch my fingers in front of my face, turning my hand this way and that before I look at him. "You know I wished I had the power of earth the other day?" I ask him and a slow smile crosses my face.

"Really? What's so great about that affinity?"

I smirk. "I wanted to chuck pebbles at the guards."

A laugh bubbles out of him. "Yeah, I would have wanted to do that too if I were you." Tapping his finger on the metal bars he smiles. Looking almost sad. "Your power is so much more though." His eyes meet mine, giving me a meaningful look.

"Is it? I don't even understand the half of it," I snort, letting my hand drop between my bent legs. "I can't access it anyways, not after my bond—" My tongue gets glued to my mouth all of a sudden and I almost choke on the sentence.

"Not the most pleasant feeling, is it?" Dante smiles, pushing himself from the bars. He puts his hand in the pocket of his trousers and pulls out a white key.

"Wait," I say, almost in a laugh. "Don't tell me that it is carved out of bone."

"Fine, then I won't tell you," he answers with a soft smirk.

How does anyone smirk softly? Apparently *Dante* is able to manage that. "By the Seven Gods, you're serious?" Baffled, I pushed myself up from the ground, walking stiffly towards him.

"I couldn't say if I wanted to, and I don't necessarily want to. So I guess, you'll never know," he says, and flashes me a breathtaking grin. Showing off his incredible canines.

"You're talking me in circles," I complain.

He shrugs, before he puts the white key into the keyhole and turns it over. "I am," he agrees.

"Where are you taking me?" I ask, tilting my head to the side.

The lifted brow on his face makes me sigh.

He can't tell me where he's taking me. He's not able to. "Where is Pekwim?" I ask instead, almost hoping for a translator to our conversation.

"Around somewhere, he's not always with me, you know," He chuckles. "Now come on. Let's walk."

He opens the barred door, making the hinges scream in protest.

"What is he to you?" I ask, cocking my head to the side as curiosity takes over.

He laughs darkly, looking me up and down. "Why? You interested or something?" He glances down to my left arm. "And here I had the impression that you were already taken."

The smirk stretches across his face, and I feel the overwhelming urge to punch him. My hand even twitches, but before I'm able to do anything, he grins. "I wouldn't, if I were you. It will only make it worse. Anyways," he says, taking a step to the side to let me out. "He's sort of a pet."

"A pet? You're kidding."

"I'm not."

"Thought you could only tell half truths?" I point out to him in challenge.

"Ah, yes. Therefore the '*sort of*' statement," he smirks.

"So, Pekwim is a pet?" I ask, giving him a look.

"Yes, and no. A friend too, but yes. A pet."

"That's disturbing," I mutter underneath my breath, glaring at him in disgust. The expression on my face makes him burst out laughing. It takes a moment for him to calm down, then he leans in closer to my ear. "Not that kind of pet, my Bridge." His *voice* makes my breath catch in my chest and I take a step away from him, feeling weirdly vulnerable for some reason.

"I didn't—I—What? No, I didn't think—" I sputtered back. That only makes him laugh harder, and his grin flashes once more. "Now, let's go find my brother, shall we?"

Chapter Thirty

"I feel like we are doing something we're not allowed to." My voice comes out in between heaving breaths as we make our way through the pass of Dover Mountain.

Straight up.

Dante is walking in front of me, tail swishing from side to side with each step he takes.

"I'm a prince, the rules don't apply to me." His retort is so cocky it makes my fist twitch again in sudden anger.

"Ha ha, very funny."

Grinning, he tosses a look over his shoulder and wags his eyebrows. "Ew, stop flirting with me. I'm not interested," I mutter.

That comment earns me a boisterous laugh. "You're not my type anyway, dear. You're too..." he looks me up and down before he clicks his tongue and his eyes twinkles a little. "Brash," he settles on.

"I'm not brash." I tort.

"Oh, you're not?" He chuckles. "So you're not self-assertive, rude, and noisy?" He asks, smirking.

I grumble. "Fine, I'm brash. But there is nothing wrong with being that way."

"No, there isn't, but it becomes a problem when it's as easy to hear you as a thunderclap from the sky. You walk and breathe so loud that a deaf person could hear you."

"What does that have to do with being brash?" I ask, confused.

"Nothing, really. Rude is fine. Rude is good. I actually like that part of you," He says as he walks. "Being self-assertive isn't bad either as long as it isn't too much. The *problem* is that you are as noisy as a jøtte, and we are not alone in these mountains."

"As a what?" I ask, and I see his tongue glue itself to the roof of his mouth for a second.

I'm really starting to see the problem with this curse. And it's only the two of us on this weird journey so I won't be able to get any answers from him.

Dante growls in frustration and continues walking with me panting behind him. He's right. I am loud. I'm so fucking weak from everything I've endured these last couple of days, that I stumble on every single rock on this remote path.

The mountains are beautiful though, even if the climb is fucking deadly.

As we reach the top of the steep incline, the landscape stretches for miles. Rolling hills of rocks and moss lay before us, and I immediately feel a prickling sensation at the back of my neck. The same feeling I've felt numerous times near these mountains.

Someone is watching.

Or rather, *something*.

"Do you need me to carry you?" Dante hisses through clenched teeth. He turns to me so fast he's almost a blur. Stumbling back, I struggle to keep my footing, but the stone under me wobbles and I fall to my ass.

He shakes his head in disappointment. "Useless human."

"How do I know you won't kill me?" I honestly don't know why I'm following him. Willingly, even. It makes *no sense*. After they locked me in that cage I *should* either be terrified or trying to kill every single one of them.

And it's not that I haven't been tempted to do the latter. I'm tempted all the time. Constantly. But there is something in the back of my mind that keeps me from giving in to that urge. There is something about that act that makes me think it's a very bad idea.

"Simple. You don't." His eyes darken as he steps closer. He towers over me, looking more dangerous than I imagined he could. Then he crouches down to my level and takes a lock of my unruly hair between his fingers. "But I'm pretty sure your instincts tell you that you can trust me."

I smack his hand away from me, which earns me a deep chuckle. That bastard. Doesn't anything phase this fucker? He's so annoying. He seems nice, but then he shows a different side to himself that makes me think he's one of the deadliest predators I've ever encountered. Even more dangerous than the majestic creatures that choose to bond with humans.

A slow grin grows on Dante's beautiful face, and his eyes twinkle with a hidden emotion. "See?" He straightens his back, glancing around. "Come on, we need to get to our destination before dark," he says before getting to his feet once more. Then he reaches out a hand to me.

"Why?"

His snort makes me think he won't answer my question. But then he rolls his eyes and gives me a sad smile. "Monsters will come, and you will lose what you hold closest to your heart."

*

Nightfall comes far too quickly. Dark clouds roll in over the mountains and engulf us in twilight. A mile back or so Dante started walking faster, cursing under his breath with every step. I've noticed that his hand twitches from time to time too.

So does mine. It's not a conscious act, it just happens.

Behind the dark clouds is a fiery sunset that makes half of the sky seem to burn red. The wind is picking up, making my hair fly everywhere, and the clouds roll unnaturally fast overhead.

"Jøtte," Dante breathes, and the way he says it makes it sound like a curse. Maybe it is. "Hey, princess, get your ass moving. Time's running out," he yells back to me. And when he turns around, his eyes glow like illuminated jades.

"Holy shit, what's wrong with your eyes?" I ask. Okay, it's not the first time I've seen glowing eyes, the glimmer gnomes have glowing eyes too, but I haven't seen it on the hulder people. Maybe it only happens in the dark?

"Your eyes glow too."

"What?" I touch my face in disbelief, blinking rapidly. My vision blurs all of a sudden and for a couple of seconds it's like the world has gone completely dark. The colors are gone, and it's hard to make out *anything* in the fading light.

"That's one of the more useful changes," he says. That cryptic fucker.

"What the fuck do you mean about that, I'm blind!" I protest, because it feels like I am.

"Relax, it will come back," he mumbles reassuringly. Yeah, right. Have I mentioned that I want to kill this guy? Because I really want to.

Slowly, my vision gradually gets brighter, and his somber expression comes into focus. His eyes are sad, almost lifeless. Almost defeated. It changes in a split second as a deafening howl pierce the air. "Shit. Salem, run!"

He still hasn't told me how he knows my name, and I have no time to ask any questions. I know for a fact that I haven't introduced myself to this idiot, but I do as I'm told. The panicked command in his voice forces my feet to follow him as he bolts across the open terrain.

"There's Nowhere to hide!" I yell.

"Don't be an idiot, there are a billion places to hide!" He shouts back. "Shut up and fucking run!"

Confused, I glance over the open terrain. There is not a single tree in sight, not anything else than a flat mountain. "You better not be fucking with me!" I warn.

"I'm not, I promise I'm not!" He sounds *pained*. As if the words actually hurt him physically or something. A grunt slips out of him when a shadow leaps towards him, tackling the prince to the ground. "Fuck!"

"Dante!" I scream, almost stumbling over them.

"Run you idiot!" He growls as he wrestles the shadow. It hisses and growls in animalistic rage. Soon after, it whimpers in pain, and a jerky movement from Dante's hand reveals a bloody dagger. It glows dimly in a golden sheen, a faint pattern swirling behind the crimson blood. Dante gets to his feet and picks up speed once more. This time I'm the one running in front, and I have no *fucking* idea where we're going.

"Watch out!" He yells, and another shadow moves and jumps. It hits me in the face, hissing with that horrible sound that reminds me of a rabid animal. The shadow smells of rotten flesh and death. I go down with a thud and a scream of sudden terror. Its teeth are needle sharp, dripping with some kind of liquid that makes the air sizzle.

"Holy shit!" I gasp. It's a fucking Mare.

"Salem!" Dante screams, then he grunts in pain. Followed by another thud and a curse. "Use your powers!" Dante screams.

"I don't—" I start, cutting off when something sharp bites into my ankle and I howl in pain.

"Use your fucking powers!" Dante roars.

More shadows jump on top of us. Soon we're both covered in shadow like lumps of creatures, hissing and growling in their animalistic rage.

Panic.

That's the first emotion I register in myself. Fear is next. I have no idea what is happening.

I struggle to open my eyes from the crushing shadows that bite into my body. The pain is so intense. It's killing me.

I don't know *how* to use my powers, and the frustration makes my blood boil. No one has taught me anything. It just happens! There is no rhyme or logic to it. It just...does whatever the fuck it wants to! I don't know what I did when I grabbed onto Riften's soul and forced it back into his body. Or that time I tangled the golden threads around that dead branch, and when I got out of that cave...

Holy shit.

The memory slams into me.

The blooming tree.

The pressure inside me builds to a dangerous level, and I slam my hand to the ground underneath me with a deafening scream.

Golden threads explode like a spiderweb on the ground around me.

The creatures scream in pain as the threads wrap around their shadowy figures. Cocooning them in a tight web of glowing gold.

The Mares that aren't tangled up in my golden web flee like ants set on fire, shrieking in horror.

A relieved groan slips out of Dante, and he falls back to the ground, panting. "Thank fuck," he breathes.

"What the fuck did I do?" I gasp, horrified as I watch the golden threads wrap themselves tighter around the shadowy creatures.

"Give me a minute, and I might be allowed to answer that question," Dante says, pushing himself to a sitting position. "Watch," he encourages.

I do.

Horrified at what I'm seeing.

Seven shadows are struggling in my webbed bond. One Mare stays motionless. I stare in shock as six of them shrink in size, before a small burst of powder explodes inside the cocoon threaded around them. Black dust falls to the ground from six different places in my golden web, but the last remaining creature lingers.

Dante's attention is placed fully on the Mare that slowly starts to change into something more tangible.

A body.

A black powder-like substance falls away from its form, revealing bare arms and legs. Then, a head is revealed from the shadows, and it slowly sinks down to the ground.

The golden threads retreat from the naked body in front of us, revealing a young, beautiful woman.

A soft moan slips out of her, as she slowly sits up.

I'm mesmerized, and terrified of what's happening in front of me. And so...so utterly *confused*.

What the actual fuck?

Dante lets out a long sigh of relief, then he takes off his tunic and walks over to the naked woman and hands it to her.

"Thank you," she says, as she takes the tunic in her hand and tugs the garment over her head to cover herself.

"Can someone explain what just happened?" I shriek through my panic. Because this is just utterly fucked up. This *woman* was...*inside* the Mare.

They both look at me.

"Salem?" The woman blurts, confused.

I *glare* at her. *How the fuck does she know my name? Who is she?*

"Yes..?" I croak hesitantly, taking a shaky step backwards as she fully sits up. My blood freezes and my heart stops as the recognition hits me like a mallet.

It's Teagan.

Amadeus's sister.

There is nothing sweeter than the taste of dwindling humanity. Letting my sharpened teeth sink into the warm flesh I feel the pure magic of life seep into my veins. This was what I needed. Another fill of the forbidden flesh. A rumble echoes from the mountain and my blood sings in response. It tingles through my veins, calling for me. My own blood. I can finally find my own blood. So I turn in that direction, and take off.

Chapter Thirty-One

"Teagan..." I breathe, and my vision blurs. I blink away the tears gathered in the crooks of my eyes, letting them fall freely down my face. She looks exactly the same as she did the day before her reaping five years ago. Maybe a bit more toned, but still the same. She still has that warmth in her brown eyes. That sweet heart shaped face, that perfect bow on her upper lip.

"What..." Alarm enters her eyes the second before our bodies collide, and I hug her body tight to me. She stiffens slightly, before her arms wrap around me in return. A breathy laugh escapes her. "You've grown."

I start laughing. "A few more scars than the last time you saw me, but I don't think I've changed that much since I was nineteen." Her arms tighten around me, and she takes in a deep breath before releasing it. "True."

Holding me at an arm's length she surveys my face, her finger tips brush the small scar above my right eyebrow. "Amadeus gave me that. He's been looking everywhere for you! He will be so happy to—"

Shit.

The blood drains from my face, and my smile fades when I realize the *huge* clusterfuck we find ourselves in.

Teagan starts to shake me. "Is he here? Is my brother in Nowhere? Is he alive?"

I feel nauseous, water gathers in a rush in my mouth as my stomach turns. I manage to push her away from me just in time. My stomach cramps, and I vomit bile until I dry heave on the ground.

"That's disgusting..." I hear Dante mumble behind me, and he's right. It absolutely is.

"Salem," Teagan's voice sounds strangled, and I'm not sure if it's pleading or disgust, could be both. "Please, just tell me." Holding up my hand for her to give me a moment, I wait until my body settles enough for me to lean back on my haunches. In slow motion I lift my face to the sky before wiping my mouth with my sleeve.

"He's...around." Is all I can say. More tears roll down my cheeks and an involuntary sob slips out of me. How the *fuck* am I supposed to tell her what happened to her little brother?

I could lie, but for what purpose? It would only make the situation worse.

Another heartbreaking sob threatens to escape as I try to find the words. "I don't know how to tell you," I say with honesty, hesitant to continue.

"How about you tell me the truth?"

Well, fuck.

I can't help the defeated laugh that comes out. "He tried to steal the dragon that chose me, so...I stabbed him in the back, literally. Kicked his ass to a bloody pulp and left him in the mountains for the Mares to take."

I wait for a reaction. For her to start yelling, or screaming. I wait for her to hit me, or stab me with my own dagger. Strangely enough, they didn't take away any of my weapons when they caged me.

But it's not her reaction I should have worried about. No. It's the dangerous low growl coming from Dante as he asks "You did what?"

The threat in his voice makes my breath hitch, goosebumps erupt along my skin from the underlying violence laced within the words. This is the first time I've felt true danger in the company of a Hulder.

My gaze darts to him, and my eyes widen in sudden fear. The power that whips around him slashes through the air, hitting the ground around him as he shakes from barely contained rage.

Shit.

I didn't tell him about that little detail.

I'm struck by the incredible sight in front of me. Blue and green tendrils of light burst from the Prince in waves of beautiful destruction. The magic moves around him like the northern lights. It's a sight to be seen for sure, if his murderous eyes weren't locked on me.

"I—" my face twists in agony, and the tears fall freely down my cheeks as I try to continue speaking. "I—I couldn't do anything."

"Are you telling me that there is a person that started a *bond* with a creature, and he was left *alive?*" He takes a slow, calculated step towards me, and I cower. I fucking cower in front of him. Who the fuck am I? I don't cower for anyone. Not even royalty.

I grit my teeth and meet his furious gaze with my own. "Yes."

The northern lights explode from him in a quick devastating burst of power. The wind knocks me to the ground and pain coats my skin. Teagan is blasted away from me, hitting the ground hard a few feet away.

"In fact, there were two failed bondings that day." With great effort, I get to my feet, glaring at the Prince. I match his anger head on, fisting my hands to balls at my side.

Anger is easy.

My whole life I've been exposed to situations that provoked this exact feeling. The harsh childhood I endured with a distant prostitute for a mother, the lack of a father figure due to the reaping, watching friends and families get ripped apart every five years. Having to pick up the slack at home, raising my little sister and myself to adulthood. And for what? Only to get ripped out of her arms when I reached the age of reaping myself.

I thought I'd lost my best friend, only to find him and be betrayed in the worst way possible. My heart has been hardened by the unfairness of life, and becoming one of the stolen soldiers hasn't softened it.

No. It's only paved the way for the anger that I've collected over the years.

My hands start to itch and burn. Simmering with impatient magic that begs to be let loose. My vision shifts, the edges blurs together, and yet all I can see in vivid detail is Dante's fury. Northern light brightens up the shadows around him, slashing through the air like he's the epicenter of destruction.

The wind rages around the both of us, whirling up a hailstorm of rocks and twigs. Golden rings illuminate his jade eyes as our magic collides. A heavy boom rings out along the mountain ridge, shaking the ground under our feet.

Yes. Anger is easy, but rage is so much more fun.

I open my hands, and the golden threads rush towards him. They pierce through the colorful display of his magic, knocking it away by the force of the heavy emotions in my mind. Gold snakes around his throat and his eyes bulge. He opens his mouth in a silent scream, pain edged on his face as my threads dig deep into his skin.

I hear my name being called, and I ignore it as I will my magic to dig deeper.

Yes, that's it. Kill the Prince. Let go. Give in to the Nothing.

In the distance I hear a roar that has my body trembling. It's filled with fury, and I can't help the outrageous laugh that bubbles up my throat.

"Salem, stop! Please!" Teagan begs beside me, her words finally penetrating the raging wind. "Don't give in to it."

I want to grab it for myself and taste the dark power. I want to bring pain and destruction down upon this land of Nowhere. I want to rip it apart and see it all burn to the ground.

Kill.

I need to kill the Prince. Let me taste the forbidden flesh. Let me bask in the hidden secrets that lie within.

Don't, not all the way. Keep your heart true.

I pause and tilt my head oh so slowly to the side. Who does this voice belong to? I know I've heard it before, but the memory seems to have fogged over with a festering substance.

"Who are you?" I ask the voice, but there's no answer. Only silence.

Kill the Prince. Give in to the Nothing! Join us on the other side.

That's a different voice. One I know I've encountered on multiple occasions. A powerful presence slams into my mental barrier, demanding entrance. My mind tells me to resist, to keep them at bay. My heart tells me to let them in.

"Make a choice!" Teagan screams over the raging wind, and her face appears in front of me. Tears glittering in the warmth of her eyes. The same shade of brown that Amadeus has. Multiple cuts adorn her skin, the tunic she borrowed from Dante hangs in tatters on her form. Her dark hair whips around her face from the strong wind.

Am I the source of the wind? I think I am.

"Make a choice, Salem." Teagan takes a step into the eye of the storm and the wind stills, but rages everywhere else. "You are in control of your own actions." My eyes dart to Dante, how he almost seems to be suspended in the air by my golden grip. Unmoving, eyes bulging, not breathing. My vicious gold seeps slowly into his skin, lighting him up from within. A web of connected threads lights up underneath the surface in bright gold. Except the area around his heart, which is black as night.

The infested blackness stretches up his throat, and around his spinal cord.

"You can choose to end his life here and now, Salem. Or you can make the choice to help him. Like you helped me." Her eyes are fixed on me and I see determination enter her expression. "You alone can make the choice to become something wicked. Just make sure to stay true to your heart."

I blink rapidly.

Claws dig into my psyche, slashing through the withering barrier on my mind. How easy it would be to just let the darkness swallow me whole. To float away into the Nothing. No feelings. No worries. No consequences. To be one with the absence of responsibility. I want that. But my heart...

Reluctantly I reinforced the barricade and let my gold turn warm. My rage ebbs away into small embers. Wiggling my fingers, I let the gold threads around Dante move. There's a gentleness to my magic now that I haven't felt before as they slowly start to untangle the dark veins from his spinal cord. Sweat has broken out on my forehead by the time they've let go around his heart. A shuddering breath leaves Dante and his eyes roll back in his head. His body starts to shake violently.

A tear escapes the corner of my eye, trailing down the right side of my chin. It's warm and sticky. Taking a deep breath, I let the magic fall away.

I lift my hand up to my cheek, and I blink. There's a bead of blood there.

Dante collapses to the ground, no magic emanating from his body. He's not moving, nor is he breathing. Maybe I should go over and see if he's alive, then again I don't really have the desire to do so.

"Did you kill him?"

I give Teagan a look of disdain. "Don't know." The horrified expression on her face makes me want to laugh, honestly. "Do you need me to check?"

For some reason she just stands there with her mouth agape, not making any signs of moving in either direction. Rolling my eyes I walk over to the Prince and tilt his head with my boot to see if he's...alive. He's completely still. Maybe I did kill him? If so, I don't think I did it on purpose. Right now I'm a bit more concerned about the fact that I'm leaking tears of blood to care too much about Dante's wellbeing. What kind of bullshit is that? Tears of blood? Never heard of that before. It's not even a thing.

"Looks dead," I say, and I can't help but notice the lack of emotion in my own voice. There's just...Nothing.

"Why...?" She breathes, taking a tentative step. Her entire body trembles under my unamused gaze.

"Why what? Why does he look dead?" I gesture to his still form on the ground. "Well, he's not breathing. I think that, you know, that's something that makes him look dead. He's also kind of pale."

"No! Why did you—" Teagan is interrupted by the sudden, obnoxiously loud, breath of air Dante heaves.

I can't for the life of me hide my disappointment. Letting out a huge sigh, I look to Teagan. "Never mind, he's alive. Still looks a bit pale though."

I crouch down beside him poking his cheek with my finger. "Oh, that's new," I note, studying my hand. "Are these...claws?"

"Ouch, that was less than pleasant," Dante groans as he lifts his hand to his face. His eyes flutter open, but they look distant. Teagan stumbles over to him in a rush on her bare feet. Why was she naked when she turned back from that Mare-thing? And how did I manage to turn her back? There's so many questions, and not enough answers.

"Now you move," I mumble under my breath.

"Are you okay?" Her shaking hands roam over him, not daring to touch him as he slowly sits up, rubbing his head.

"Can't you see that he's breathing? Obviously he's fine. What?" I snap when I see them exchange looks with each other before glancing over to me.

Dante blows out a breath. "Nothing. I feel fine, just a bit dazed," he rubs the back of his neck, before shaking his head to clear it. With a slowness that would even impress a turtle, he gets to his feet. He wobbles on his legs, staggering like a newborn deer before he abruptly turns around in a circle.

"Dude, were you today years old when you learned to walk or what?" Frowning, I stare at his horrified expression as he turns around one more time.

"What the fuck did you do?" He turns to me, face pale and eyes wild with fear.

"What do you mean?"

"What the fuck did you do to me?" He all but screams, and there's panic in his voice. Real terror. *The fuck is going on now?*

"To be entirely truthful I have no clue what I did to you. What did I do?"

"My tail!" He blurts, making another circle. "Where the fuck is my tail?" This time when he turns around I see what's bothering him.

"Oh," I blink in confusion.

His tail is gone. What the fuck did I do to him, indeed.

Darkened landscapes rush beneath me as I glide through the clouds. Moonlight casts ominous shadows below. The rustle of leathery wings flutter as my magnificent hostage follows my command. I'm close. So close. I can feel it in my bones. My own blood sings in the distance. All the promises it holds, all the secrets. I need to find her. I need to find my own blood.

Chapter Thirty-Two

"Can you *please* stop fumbling around like an idiot?" I snap, after the millionth time Dante trips over a damned rock, or a cursed twig.

"Try losing your tail and see how well you walk after!" He growls back.

"I don't have, nor will I ever have a tail, you blundering foal," it comes out as a hiss between clenched teeth.

"Jøtte!" He says it like a curse as he trips again.

I roll my eyes. "Tell me who's the loud one now." He turns around, and the look he gives me has me biting my tongue. If looks could kill—wait, can they? I mean, we're in Nowhere. It might just be possible—

"Can you two stop?" Teagan asks from behind us, and we both turn to look at her. I kinda wish I had some more clothes to give her. Now, why would I want to help her? There's something wrong with me, but in what way? It doesn't matter. Nothing matters anymore.

"Are we there yet?" I look to Dante for the answer. I don't even know where we're going. Didn't he mention some kind of cave? "I think the lady needs clothes."

"I'm fine," she says through chattering teeth and we both give her a deadpan glare. "Keep telling yourself that, and it might come true. And yes, we're here," Dante gestures to the rocky wall beside us.

I blink, making a somewhat agreeable sound in the back of my throat. "Are you sure about that? Because that's—what is that, a cliff?" I think he's lost his mind too.

"Must I do everything myself?" Grumbling he stumbles a couple of steps, almost crashing into the wall. "Oh, come on!" He slams his hand flat to the stony surface a couple of times before moving further ahead.

"I think we should run," I whisper to Teagan, as I study the fumbling Prince. "He's incapacitated, I'm sure he can't chase us down."

"Salem, are you feeling okay?" She looks me up and down with a deep frown on her face.

"Yes, of course I am, I just—"

"Found it!" Dante shouts.

I roll my eyes, and mutter a silent *'never mind'* under my breath. When I see the upper half of Dante's body lean through the cliff wall, I'm quite sure I'm about to piss myself. His lower half is nowhere to be seen.

"What are you waiting for?" He gestures for us to join him.

I shouldn't be surprised anymore by this place, but I find myself baffled all the time. This isn't normal, at least not where I come from.

When we reach the upper half of his body that sticks through the wall, I clear my throat. "A mirage, how quaint." I want to slap the cheeky grin off his face. He looks so proud of himself right now, and I can't fucking stand it.

"Come on, Salem," he smirks. "You can admit to being a little impressed by me, it's okay."

"I regret not killing you when I had the chance," As I step through the vale, a sense of foreboding enters my body, and a chill spreads along my spine.

Saaaleeem.

He flashes me his canines and winks. "There's still time for that."

My eyebrow lifts. "You really don't care about your wellbeing, do you?"

"I'm two hundred and seventy years old, the only things I really care about are food, my tail, and fucking." He stills, looking confused. "What did you do?"

"This again?"

"No, seriously, Salem. What did you do?"

"What did I do now?" I snap, feeling my hand twitch.

"My tongue," he starts, trailing off, looking even more confused.

"I haven't done shit with your tongue!"

His eyes twinkle with a smirk and my hand flies before I'm able to stop it. "A-ah," he grins as he catches my wrist before I'm able to land the blow. *Well, that's just perfect.* He leans in closer and his musky scent tickles my nostrils, it's not unpleasant, but it doesn't smell like...home. "So violent."

"You have been reckless, Little One." The sound vibrates through my being. No, it's coming from further in. The walls are covered in small gems that illuminate the path forward. That voice, that chuckle. That *pet name*. I immediately know where I am.

"Oh, I have a bone to pick with you," I growl through clenched teeth. A rumbling chuckle emanates from the deep, and I pull away from Dante with murder in mind.

Stomping down the wide path, I'm not even surprised when I find the White Dragon curled up in the middle of the cave.

"You!" I point angrily to his scaly face and growl. "What the fuck?"

"Do not be coy with me, girl!" The deep rumble inside my head makes me choke on air, and my anger deflates. *"Do not meddle with things you don't understand. You have been reckless with your magic. Has no one told you not to use it when you're not bonded to a creature?"*

"No one has told me shit and you know that!" My anger rises once more to a boiling point.

"They should have. Do not risk your wellbeing for the fun of it. You risk much more than you realize, Little One."

"Whatever, I don't care about—"

"We need to bond," The White Dragon cuts me off and I wrinkle my nose in a silent protest.

"Would you rather lose your humanity completely?" Dante asks upon seeing my face, and I whip around to glare at him.

"What?" I gape in shock. "Is that what's happening to me?"

He drags his hand through his teal hair and makes a face. "Yes, that's what's wrong with all of us. My father and my brothers have more humanity than most, because we're more *human*. But some of our people don't have any, at all. And all they do is kill, torture, and rape their victims." His frown deepens. "Shit, the curse. You—I can speak!" At the same time that Dante takes a step towards me, I'm suddenly airborne. Then I feel a scaly chest that vibrates with a deep angry growl.

"Oh, come on, Atticus! We need her to break the secrecy curse so we can actually communicate with the humans that hunt us! You know this! I don't care—" He's cut off by Atticus's loud growl again, and I feel his threat.

"Do not interrupt me, *brother*. I have no qualms with killing your scaly ass. Where the fuck is Merick when I need him? He would be on my side." Grumbling, Dante throws his arms in the air, looking more like a petulant child than the Prince of Nowhere. "I don't care about your personal opinion on her *safety*, Atticus. I'm thinking of our people," Dante says. "Or have you forgotten that you're actually *one of us?*" He growls angrily.

Again, Atticus makes a furious rumble in his chest. Which I feel through all of me, and I see the air stir around his jaws. Heat waves permeate from his entire body. I wince.

"Hey, asshole, Salem and I aren't fireproof, so don't even think about it! You know as well as Dante and I that we have to get rid of the curse that's plaguing this land, so that we can end this war," Teagan says.

I narrow my eyes at Dante. "Wait, so, you knew where to find Atticus the whole time?"

"Kind of, you said he was in a cave, and I happened to know which cave, but I couldn't tell you where I was taking you. Good thing you didn't ask too many questions about it, or we would never have gotten here."

Atticus chuffs, and I can almost picture him quirking an eyebrow at his brother. That still sounds weird to me to be honest, them being brothers. Some part of me thought it was a lie.

Maybe the glimmer gnomes actually did tell the truth all along. At least part of the truth, if not the entirety of it. I don't have time to dwell on it. I have to get to the bottom of this clusterfuck and figure out how to get away from it.

"You can't," Atticus says into my mind, and I feel a deep rooted sadness in the words. Slowly, he bends his neck and turns his large head to meet my gaze. *"We need to bond, Little One."*

"Why?" I ask. There is no way I can describe his expression, but his eyes move with deep emotions that hides a plethora of knowledge.

"I can't explain it to you just yet, the curse is still affecting me."

"Because if you don't, you will lose parts, if not all of your humanity, Salem," Dante explains. "The bonding isn't supposed to get interrupted, that was how my father became the first hulder. His dragon got killed during the bonding, making it impossible to complete it. He lost his humanity, and became what we are. Hulders. Part troll, part human. The less human blood we have in our biological system, the less human we are. That's why some of our people don't have a shred of humanity left. They're the reason we are at war. The glimmer gnomes tried to cast a protection spell over us, but it backfired. They're not particularly good with their words, so they accidentally made the spell into a curse of secrecy. Making it impossible to tell anyone about ourselves. You know this already, but it's important," He takes a step closer to me, looking at me with defiant eyes.

I turn to Teagan. "How did you end up as a Mare?"

I feel the urge to hurt someone. Preferably her at the moment. But that isn't possible, because Atticus is still holding me in his claws. Probably because he knows I'm prone to violence. Even though I haven't hurt anyone physically in a long time. The last person was Amadeus, and I still think he deserved that. "What even is a Mare?"

"It's kind of what it sounds like," her cryptic response has my hands twitching. "They are essentially nightmares. How I ended up as one...I don't know," she says thoughtfully.

Bond with him, girl.

I shake my head and frown. Who does this voice belong to? It's not the same voice every time, or, maybe it is. It doesn't appear to have a specific gender, it only...is. I have so many questions, and I need them answered.

"Well, I did learn some things when I was at the compound, and being bonded to my pegasus, but I learned more after," she says. "I don't have a lot of answers, but I do have some."

I roll my eyes. "That's not at all helpful," I mumble with a mix of surprise and annoyance lacing my words.

Teagan shrugs, and it makes me bristle in irritation.

"Why are you so hesitant to bond with Atticus?" Dante shoots in, diverting the subject to the matter at hand, the very thing I don't want to discuss.

"I—," closing my mouth with a loud snap, I sigh. "What if I die?" Hesitation creeps into my voice and gives away my feelings in a way that makes me extremely uncomfortable.

Dante tilts his head to the side, looking at me with a soft expression. "But what if you live? Besides, death is just another beginning."

He's got a point, and it wasn't that long ago I didn't care if I lived or died. Ever since I got stuck in Nowhere we've all been faced with so much death that no-one really cares about it anymore. Me included. And yet, I'm so hesitant to bond with him. Would I be this scared if I'd grown up knowing that dragons, griffins and pegasi existed?

Probably not. If I'm being honest, I don't know why I'm so hesitant about bonding. It just...feels wrong.

Taking a deep breath I voice another question. "Is that my only option?"

Dante meets my gaze with the same soft expression, but this time it hides a small tinge of something that reminds me of danger. "You have two options." He says, as his voice darkens. "You can choose not to bond, and become a monster. That would end in your death though, because...if you become a monster, Salem, I will kill you," he says, and I can hear in his voice that he's serious.

"So, what you're saying is that if I don't go through with the bonding, I will die. And if I do complete the bonding, there is a chance of me dying?" I ask, sounding bored now.

"Yes. But having a chance of dying is better than certain death, isn't it?" Dante's face lights up in a boyish grin. I pinch the bridge of my nose in irritation, letting out a loud groan.

"Fine, I'll bond with him," I mumble in defeat.

Dante grins. "Good, then let's start," he says, clapping his hands together.

All of a sudden, something powerful slams into my mental barrier with the force of a boulder, and I can't help but gasp. My stomach lurches and there's an unmistakable *tug* at my chest.

I realize that I'm about to throw up again, when the thread gets pulled and I'm *yanked* backwards. I fall to my ass inside a cave tunnel. Glowing beetles crawling on all surfaces. *You gotta be shitting me.*

Atticus, Dante, and Teagan are gone, and in front of me stands the old hag. Her long nose is still stuck in the petrified tree stump. "Haven't you learned anything by now, Salem Vanroda?" She asks in a chilly voice.

Closing my eyes, I have to concentrate on *not* hurting this motherfucking hag when I ask through gritted teeth. "Learned what, exactly?"

Her chuckle grates on my last nerve. *I'm so close to killing this woman.*

Balling my hands into fists, I force myself to stay calm. I can't take this anymore. When I *finally* agree to bond with the White Dragon, I'm yanked away from him, and the old hag has the *nerve* to ask me *anything?* I'm not having it.

My patience has reached its limit.

"There is a piece missing. He's close, and on his way. I had to stop you," She says matter-of-factly. "Don't worry, I won't keep you for long."

Glaring at her I shake my head in disbelief. "Who're you talking about?"

"You'll see, little girl," she says, and I'm almost surprised that the tree stump doesn't get peppered with frost from the chill in her voice.

The air around me stirs, it almost shimmers in the dim light from the glowing beetles around us.

"Remember, girl. You're more special than you might think. Your part is greater than you can fathom," she warns as my stomach lurches again. Shit, I'm about to get sent back.

"What do you mean, what part do I play? What is my purpose here?" I rush the questions, then the thread in my chest tightens once more.

"You'll see. Besides, I can't give you the answers. Listen to the niggles. They won't lead you astray."

What the fuck is a niggle?

The thread gets pulled, and I'm slammed back to where I was. Pressed up against Atticus's scaly chest, his claws gently holding me in his grasp.

As if I'd never left.

Maybe I didn't. Maybe it's like that time she came to visit me in the fighting ring with Tegner. He knew something was up with me then.

Glancing up, I spot Teagan looking puzzled. Dante leans up against the cave wall with his arms crossed over his muscular chest, looking almost bored.

"So, what did mother dearest have to tell you?"

I can almost taste her blood on the air now. All the potential it holds, all the secrets. I need it. I crave it with every fiber of my infested body. I force my majestic hostage to descend, and a tingle settles in my bones. I need to find her. I need my own blood.

Chapter Thirty-Three

I choke on words.

A small quirky smile fills every corner of his chiseled face. "What? Is that so hard to believe?"

"That she's your *mother*? Yes!" Teagan winces from the sheer volume of my voice, but I don't give a flying fuck about her. The old hag is his *mother*? *Their* mother, I should say. *The* mother.

The old hag is the mother of hulders.

"Wait, I thought you were left outside in the forest to die," I say stupidly.

Dante rolls his eyes. "I was, but that's beside the point." He says, then he shrugs.

A muscle in my jaw ticks.

"Stop shrugging, it makes me want to kill you," I growl, and Atticus's claws tighten around me, restricting me from doing any harm.

The flapping of wings outside the cave has all of us turning to the opening. The ground underneath us shakes. Pebbles loosen from the cave ceiling, and I feel a small tingle at the back of my neck.

I know instantly that someone has entered the cave.

Weirdly enough, my boiling blood calms. It cools to a manageable simmer.

The scent of forest permeates my nostrils, filling me with a certainty I haven't felt in a while. Followed by the calming scent of basil and dewy moss.

Heavy footsteps approach, followed by slow thuds that make the cave vibrate from the weight of them. There's a rumble, and a deep growling voice fills my mind. *"I've never understood why he prefers these confined places instead of the Stonehenge."*

I recognize that rumble.

It's the Black Dragon.

Soon after I feel his grounding presence. His red tinted hair and his beautiful green eyes. The color of home.

Without thinking I gasp. "Riften!" I push Atticus's claws away from me and rush to him, wrapping my arms around him as our bodies crash together.

The air whooshes out of his lungs and he stumbles a couple of steps, but manages to regain his balance.

His arms lock around me, and he buries his nose in my hair.

"Trouble," he breathes, sounding a tinge confused.

My eyes fly open, and before I know it I push him away from me again, making him stumble. I'm sure he'd have fallen on his ass if it hadn't been for the Black Dragon behind him putting his large head behind Riften's body to steady him.

The Black Dragon chuckles and chuffs softly.

"She's trouble, that one," he comments, his icy blue eyes twinkling in the dim light.

Riften rubs his chest and sighs. "Don't I know it," he mutters.

"What are you doing here?" I ask, and I'm sure I look as confused as I feel.

He looks puzzled too, but the Black Dragon behind him moves closer. *"We need to be here,"* he says in my mind, giving me another riddle-like explanation.

"He's not wrong." Atticus chimes in, moving his head closer to my back, mirroring the Black Dragon perfectly.

"Hold on," I say, looking from one dragon to the other.. "You're brothers, aren't you? This is Merick, your twin?" I ask the White Dragon, and he puffs out warm air behind me.

"He is, yes. Haven't seen you in a while, brother." Atticus rumbles.

"Likewise."

I can't tell if either of them are happy to see each other, but this family reunion is starting to get strange. I can't get the picture of strings being pulled out of my head. It all feels very orchestrated.

"This is all very touching, but let's get this bonding over with, shall we?" Dante drawls from the darkness of Atticus's shadow.

"Who the fuck are you?" Riften asks, glaring at Dante with a protective edge in his posture.

"Dante. Nice to meet you," he says with an almost mocking bow in Riften's direction. "As I said, very touching, all of it, but I sense that time is running out. You need to start the bonding, Atticus."

"You're right. Are you ready, Little One?"

Turning around, I inhale deeply. "Yes." As ready as I can be at least.

"Wait, what's going on here?" I swear I can hear a hint of panic in Riften's tone.

Rolling his eyes, Dante turns to Riften and gives him an exasperated look. "They are bonding, so kindly step out of the way and do not interfere. If you have any issues with it I suggest you look away and keep your mouth shut, or go somewhere else," he says in a bored tone before a slow smirk enters his expression. "Preferably both."

I hadn't realized that Riften had stepped in between me and the White Dragon. It makes me feel oddly comforted.

"Is it safe?" Riften asks.

"Who cares if it's safe? It needs to be done. Just as your bonding with Merick needed to happen," Dante throws his hands in the air, clearly getting irritated by our stalling. "Look, this bonding is well overdue. *They* need to bond, right now. Before we get swamped by Mares again," Dante growls impatiently.

Riften opens his mouth to protest, but thinks better of it and steps aside. "Fine, but we are not done discussing this." His warning is crystal clear.

Dante rolls his eyes again. "Obviously."

A golden glow starts to seep out from Atticus's chest, flowing out from underneath his beautiful white scales. His feathery wings flutter gently and the golden threads start to move through the air towards me, seeking my beetle mark in the center of my left palm.

They tingle across my skin, leaving a slight burning sensation from their touch. It hurts, but not as much as it did the first time his threads touched me.

My feet are firmly planted to the ground, keeping me in place for the magic at hand. It sizzles in the air, making sparks fly.

As the threads latch on to my arm they move with perfect precision to the center of my beetle mark, lighting it up from within.

I gasp, utterly immobile.

Tremors make their way through my body, making me twitch as the connection between us gets stronger.

Then a loud *boom* reverberates through the cave and large boulders fall from the ceiling around us.

"Crap!" I hear Dante growl, it sounds muffled, as if he's behind a barrier of some kind. "I thought we had more time. Keep bonding! We'll be back."

I hear them move, but I have no idea what's going on. My heart leaps in my chest as I feel the air around us move with unnatural shadows. The prickling sensation pierces my neck again, and I know we're not alone.

Something has infested the cave, and it almost feels Void of any life. A darkness so deep it feels…familiar.

Immobile and vulnerable, I can't do anything other than stay put as the cave around us starts to crumble. Atticus spreads his feathery wings above me, protecting me from the worst debris that falls from the ceiling.

Another *boom*, and I swear I can hear bone rattling as it happens. The ground beneath my feet shakes violently. Bile starts to rise in my throat as my body shudders and shakes.

Panic seeps into me. I remember what that means.

There's a ruckus that breaks out behind me. Tangible shadows whirl around us, before a deep raspy laugh echoes in the cave. A laugh that feels as familiar to me as my own shadow does.

"Well, well, well," A deep voice behind me drawls, coming closer. "Didn't you learn your lesson the last time, Salem?"

I want to scream as the pain starts to settle in, making my body burn with immovable pain. Tears stream down my cheeks. My body twitches violently. There's a bone-deep understanding in me that tells me that the bond is about to fail. I sense my body slowly start to wither away.

I'm about to die, and there is nothing I can do about that.

"You don't get to bond with a creature," the voice says, sounding smug and full of jealousy. Dread fills my veins as the person moves into my line of sight.

Gasping, the overwhelming feeling of nausea hits me just from the shade of his skin. It's paper thin, tinged with green. His eyes no longer hold that warm brown color they did before. His teeth have turned to sharp points.

All that's left of his impressive build is skin and bones. Now he looks gaunt, sickly and...*dying*.

"Amadeus," I whisper quietly through the pain as my body twitches once more. "Please don't. Don't do this."

In his hand, he holds a sword that he points towards Atticus's throat.

The blood drains from my face.

Where is Riften? Dante? Teagan and Merick?

Why did they leave?

Muffled sounds of fighting outside the cave give me the answers. They left to fend off the danger, not knowing that the biggest threat slipped through their defenses and found its target. Atticus and myself.

Atticus growls angrily towards Amadeus, but it's followed by a low whimper. A sound I hope I'll never hear from such a majestic creature again. Turned or not.

"Please," I beg, and all I can do is watch Amadeus stroke the tip of his sword along the thin skin under Atticus's jaw.

"You know, I wasn't drawn here by you," he says, glancing between us as his smile grows into something gruesome. "But I'm not complaining." He presses the blade to Atticus's thin skin, and a trickle of blood begins to pool. "Besides, we both know that I can find you whenever I want, regardless." Movement behind him has my eyes flare wide.

A tail snakes up around Amadeus, curling around his waist. It almost looks to be a lion's tail.

What the...How in the Seven Gods' names did he end up getting a *tail*?

Blinking rapidly, I try to focus on the situation at hand, I don't have time to wonder about mysterioustails that suddenly appear on my best friend. No. He's no longer my best friend, nor is he my friend at all.

I realize that I'm absolutely helpless in this situation. I can't do anything other than watch, while I slowly wither away to Nothing.

I try to strain my muscles to move, but they're completely locked up, trembling with cramps, but immobile.

I'm *helpless*.

"What happened to you?" I ask, even though I know parts of what happened to him. What I don't understand is how he's changed this much. Or *why* he's changed this much. Is this essentially what could happen to me if I don't bond with Atticus?

It doesn't seem like Atticus can do anything either in this situation. The dragon is so focused on letting his bond blend with my soul as quickly as possible. It's like he's just as vulnerable as me during the process.

It won't matter either way, and I cry out in pain as my tremors get worse. I feel my soul start to let go. *Help me.*

All of a sudden something grabs a hold of my being. Something dark and powerful. It's Void of all light but holds on to my soul as it's about to leave. I feel a presence push at my mental barrier. Giving in to it, the being fills my entire existence, holding me close to him.

Riften.

A sob is ripped out of my chest, it gets harder and harder to breathe as my body struggles to stay alive.

"Don't let me go. Don't let me die." I beg.

"*Never.*" His response has a finality that shatters my heart as he grabs a hold of me, and I feel the black tendrils of shadow cling to my soul. "Dante!" Riften commands. Something shiny flies through the air in a blur. A dagger embeds itself in Amadeus's hand. His sword clangs to the ground, singing its defeat. Sparks of shimmering light and shadow scatter across the stones.

Amadeus howls through his anger and pain before he takes a step away from Atticus who growls threateningly. "This isn't over," he hisses, then he whistles loudly and a bone-rattling *boom* has stone and debris explode in every direction. The wall behind Amadeus explodes. Sending rocks and dust flying in all directions. I scream in horror as the bony figure of a dragon comes into view as the dust settles. Stark white, no scales, no eyes.

Amadeus, what have you done?

An ear splitting shriek permeates the air from its mouth.

My eyes widen in shock.

Holy shit.

The entire dragon is made out of bones, the hollow sockets almost seem to bore into my soul. My heart splits open from the tortured sound it makes as Amadeus takes a leap, jumping onto its skull. Thorny red vines whip out from Amadeus's palm. Curling along its spine. Yanking the thorns harshly, the Bone Dragon retreats, spreading its tattered wings.

Several heavy, rattling footsteps later it takes off with a pained shriek that has my throat closing up.

He didn't. He just didn't!

My heart falls to my stomach in sorrow.

Another ear splitting scream slips out of me. The shadows wrap themselves around my soul even tighter as the last remnants of the golden threads flow into my beetle mark, forming a black swirling tattoo with the same floral depiction of my golden one. Dancing together in perfect harmony.

That's the last thing I register before everything goes dark.

Chapter Thirty-Four

Riften

Salem's body goes limp in my shadow's hold. I feel it, and I force my shadows to grab on to her soul and keep it here.

Just like she did with her light during my bonding with Merick.

"Trouble," I breathe, rushing over to her. Atticus growls protectively with his head hovering above Salem's body, and I smack his snout away from her. "Don't be stupid, I'm not going to hurt her."

His head jolts away from my unexpected attack and he seems stunned for a moment, unable to decide how he's supposed to react.

I guide her body gently to the ground. Her silvery hair fans out underneath her like the finest silk. This woman affects me more than anyone else has ever done. Ever since I felt the tug on my arm on the day of the reaping. Forcing me to jump into the lake for a second time, only to be led to Trouble.

She's completely taken over my life.

This troublesome woman has invaded my mind and has me *pining* after her. And she doesn't even know it.

I've come to the conclusion that it has something to do with her smell that makes me so enthralled by her. It's a perfect combination of smoked cherrywood and rosemary, and a hint of ripe orange.

It smells like the orchard back home.

Her smell isn't the only thing that has me intrigued. It's her personality, even though that has been off the rails lately, but her obvious strength, even through that. Her heart. And the bond we share. The vulnerability that she doesn't share with anyone but her inner most thoughts of insecurity.

Leaning over her still body, I feel my heart still in my own chest as the golden bond between us tightens. The constant pain I've felt since her failed bonding heightens, and I have to bite my tongue not to scream in agony as I feel her life start to ebb away from me.

The threads are taut and threaten to tear apart.

"Trouble, please," I beg, flattening my ear to her chest to listen for her heartbeat.

It isn't there.

"She's not breathing," I cry out, panic lacing my every word.

"What?" Dante growls as he crawls over fallen rubble and dirt to get to us.

I sit up and push down at her chest hard to force the blood in her veins to move around, supplying her brain with the nourishment it needs to survive. Her soul is still wrapped tight in my shadows.

She isn't gone yet, and I refuse to let her slip away from me.

It isn't time for her to leave me yet.

"Move over!" A female says. The girl that fought beside me against the mares. She pushes me to the side and the cave fills with growling from every angle.

"Seven Gods, roll in your titties guys, we don't need a cockfight."

I blanch for a second, glaring at this woman in shock as a memory slams into me. The odd sentence that she's uttered is so like Salem that I get the feeling that they know each other. *Is she from Terrby?*

My hesitation gives her the chance to put her hands onto Salem's still chest, and the smell of sulfur burns my nostrils as the air starts to crackle. Her brown hair rises from her scalp and I can taste something metallic in the air.

Then, her hands light up with a blueish light, and every muscle in Salem's body locks up from the energy the woman pushes into her before they release once more. "Do not touch her or you will get zapped too and your heart will stop." She snaps, just as I'm about to grab a hold of Salem.

Strange.

I didn't feel the power through my shadows.

Again, her hands light up with the strange light and Salem's body locks up.

It feels like time has stopped. Every agonizing moment she doesn't breathe is torture. The worst part of it is that I'm not able to do anything.

"What are you doing?" I choke out, my voice gruff with unshared emotion.

"Saving her life," the woman replies curtly, not even looking at me. Her focus is on Salem, where it should be.

I swallow, and I send up a silent prayer to the Seven Gods. My eyes burn, and my nostrils flare as the pungent scent of sulfur fills them once more. I'm not opposed to begging the Gods, even if I don't think they will listen. I just know that I need her alive.

An almost blinding light brightens underneath both our sleeves as our golden bond comes to life. For the first time since I got this cursed thing from the old man in the cave, it doesn't hurt.

It grows underneath my skin and stretches up my arm, across my shoulder and spreads towards my chest and back. The light from our bonds gets so bright it's almost unbearable to behold.

"What the..." I hear Dante breathe before he falls silent.

"By the Mother," The girl whispers in disbelief.

Instinct guides me towards Salem's still form, and I watch as one of my tears falls to her pale face. It's almost like time stands still as the tear spreads across her skin and slowly trickles down her temple.

Gently, I grab her left hand in mine and instantly feel our connection strengthen. "Come back to me, Salem," I whisper softly into her ear, feeling my nerves tremble under my skin.

Her eyes flutter under her eyelids. Then, *finally*, the most beautiful sound fills my ears as she takes a precious breath and her chest lifts, filling her lungs with air.

Slowly, she opens her eyes and her glacier gaze pierces mine with confusion, then a slow smile spreads on her face. "That's the first time you've called me by my name," she whispers.

A choked laugh slips out of me, and my eyes blur. "Yeah, I think so too," I whisper softly.

Her hand lifts towards my face. I don't flinch away from her gentle touch as she wipes away my tears.

"Are these for me?" She asks, and I can't help but laugh. The irony isn't lost on me, I asked her the exact same thing when our roles were reversed.

"Yes, Trouble. They're for you."

Her face fills with mischief, and she smirks up at me, eyes twinkling. "Am I still Trouble?"

"You will always be my Trouble," I say. Then I lean down and kiss her.

Chapter Thirty-Five

As his lips touch mine, goosebumps erupt along my skin. Traveling along my entire body. Making the air around us crackle with soft energy. I wouldn't be surprised to see sparks in the air.

His lips are firm on mine, it's not gentle, but passionate. Filled with unspoken emotions. And I feel him *everywhere*. His entire presence fills my being as his lips move over mine.

At first, I'm not sure how to respond, but my body seems to know what to do. I return it, giving in to his demanding lips. His hand cups the back of my neck as he tilts my head back to gain better access, and a soft moan slips out of me.

Immediately, he deepens the kiss, letting his tongue delve into my mouth, coaxing my own into a slow dance that makes me shiver. The marks under my skin grow, traveling up along my arm leaving a tingling sensation in their wake.

His sharp intake of breath has me smiling, he seems to have lost all control, and yet, he's in complete control. It feels like he's been waiting forever to kiss me like this.

And it makes me weak. I'm surprised that this feeling isn't something I despise. I'm actually hungry for more, and just as I'm about to demand just that, he slows the kiss, slowly retreating.

I whimper in frustration, and he chuckles as he gently nips my bottom lip with his teeth. Leaning his forehead to mine, he waits and catches his breath once more. "Don't do that again, Trouble," He whispers to me.

I swallow before I ask. "Do...what? Kiss you back?"

He laughs, then he shakes his head. "Oh, you should definitely do that again," he says, and his torturous dimple appears. "What I mean is, don't die on me again," he breathes.

Blinking, I breathe slowly. "I didn't—"

"You did, and you can't do that again," he says vehemently.

"Oh," I breathe. "I'm sorry."

His eyes glitter from the soft luminescence of the glow beetles that have slowly surrounded us in a perfect circle. The light moves across his face in all the colors of the rainbow, and I'm absolutely entranced by his chiseled features.

This man...

I have no idea how this man has invaded my life, and somehow gotten entangled in my impossible knots.

"How do you feel?" He asks, leaning his forehead to mine as he works on catching his breath.

"I—" my words halt in my throat as I contemplate his question, actually checking in with my own body. How *do* I feel?

The pain is gone, and my mind feels less...crowded. The tingle at the back of my neck is still there, but not too pressing. Otherwise, I feel good. Really good, actually. I would almost go so far as to say that I feel *balanced*. Which is something I haven't felt since before the reaping. "I'm good," I settle on.

Riften narrows his eyes as he studies me, and I roll my eyes. "I really am good, at the moment. Ask me again in a couple of days and the answer might be something different."

"I'll be sure to remember that," he mumbles, shaking his head.

A throat clearing has me almost jumping, and in the process I push Riften away from me as if his touch burns my skin. I look to the others in the cave, which no longer is a proper cave. Open sky lies above, and around us are huge boulders and debris from the mountain that crumbled during the attack. Somehow, the place feels dead now.

How the fuck did we survive this?

"Are you done being all lovey-dovey and all that crap? I'd like to get back to Dover Mountain. When we're safe, we have a lot to discuss and figure out, and Salem needs to rest up after the bonding and magic use." We all look to Dante who brushes off some of the dust from his sleeve. Not that it helps that much, he's filthy.

Blood, dust, and grime cover his otherwise flawless skin, and his lip is split in one place. It looks to be healing already though. So, there's that.

"Are you going to cage me again?" I grumble feeling a bit salty. The smirk on Dante's face only stays in place for about a split second before he literally *pales* from Riften's outburst.

"What? Is this the asshole that *caged* you for nine fucking days?"

"Shit." Dante breathes.

Riften's anger isn't the only one that flares up, no, *Atticus* growls dangerously at his brother as he moves his massive white head closer to Dante. Pressing him up against a huge boulder with his snout as he bears his teeth to him.

"There, there, brother," Dante says soothingly at the White Dragon. "I wasn't the one that put her there."

Another devastating rumble emanates from Atticus's chest, and for some reason that warms my heart. At the same time I feel the anger boil. But this isn't mine. I feel it trickling along the second bond that adorns my skin. Making the magic underneath ripple and surge.

"Atticus," I say, and my voice has a finality I'm not used to hearing from myself. "They didn't hurt me." At the same time I place a hand on Riften's arm to stop his advance toward the hulder. Pushing myself to my feet I walk tentatively over to Atticus and touch his white scales. As soon as my touch brushes over them they ripple with a golden shine in waves. "Stay calm, he's an asshole, but he's harmless."

"...Sure," Dante says after a beat, glaring at me indignantly. "The nerve." He mumbles, before he lifts his hands in a gesture of surrender as Atticus growls again.

"Harmless," Atticus scoffs in my mind. *"This asshole is not harmless, Golden One. He's one of the most deadly assassins there is."*

"Spill all of my secrets, will you?" Dante growls, before blanching completely. Glaring at his brother, then sliding his glare over to me with puzzled eyes. "How...?"

"She's the Bridge you blubbering fool," Merick suddenly chimes in, startling me out of my skin.

I can feel the shadows stir around us, and they aren't friendly.

"I don't know what you're talking about, and frankly, it doesn't really matter either way. Dante is right. We should get out of here and to a safer place. The shadows are impatient," I say, trying to urge them into action.

"It does matter, Golden One," Merick urges. I wave him off like he's a meek fly, and not the huge terrifying dragon that he is. I mean, he could technically tear my body apart like I was a sheet of paper.

"We can discuss this at a later date, right now the shadows are stirring. It isn't safe here," I say curtly.

"What in the world are we waiting for? Let's get a move on," Teagan says and turns away from us to start tracking down the darkened terrain.

"And where do you think you're going?" Dante asks stupidly after her.

"To the Dover Mountain?" She throws a glance over her shoulder at us.

Dante quirks an eyebrow, then gestures to the two enormous dragons in our strange ensemble. "I mean, why use your legs when these handsome shitheads have wings?"

"Watch it, little brother," Merick growls.

"You do not decide who rides on our backs, princeling," Atticus growls. *"I hope you're not too attached to your head."* The threat is clear in both his words and his tone.

Dante just rolls his eyes and looks over at his brothers. "In fact, I'm quite attached, so I'd prefer not to depart from it. You're just a grump."

"Am not," Atticus snaps, and he lets his teeth shut with a sharp clap that has me almost shuddering.

"Are too," Merick says, voice vibrating through my mind.

"Stop bickering, let's just get the hell away from here and find shelter Somewhere," I cut in, stopping their bickering. "And then, it's time for some fucking answers."

Looking towards the Dover Mountain in the distance I see it in all its majestic pride. The Northern Light lingers around the two peaks. There's a huge dip that is carved into the top of it, leaving smaller ridges that almost resemble teeth marks. As if something has taken a bite of the top and left a chasm. I don't even want to know what could have made it look like that, or how enormous it might be, seeing how huge the marks are.

I bristle in discomfort from the thought before pushing it away and let Atticus take the lead. He's headed straight for the indentation in the middle of the mountain.

I walk over to Atticus in preparation for our departure when I spot the gold tipped feathers on his wings. "Why are your wings feathered?" I ask.

"Because we are turned dragons, not hatched like the others. We are more civil, too, if you can imagine." I really can't. *"But the glimmer gnomes' magic isn't foolproof, as you may already know. And they aren't the best with their*

words. Neither are they with their runes or symbols. The word for leather and feather is too similar for them to know the difference. Especially in the written language."

My jaw slackens. "Are you telling me that *everything* is just a mistake made by the glimmer gnomes?" I ask, disbelief flooding into me. That *can't* be the case. I don't know enough about the glimmer gnomes to say much, but they don't seem like malicious creatures.

"Not all, but...most of it."

I frown, because it seems too easy. That everything wrong with this land has to do with the unpredictable magic here.

"Even the smallest pebble can make big ripples on the surface of a lake, Golden One."

Well, he's not wrong.

"There is a lot that doesn't make sense to me," I sigh, glancing back to look at Teagan and I give her a sad smile. "Like the fact that you're here, why you were a mare, and what we will do now, especially what we will do with Amadeus."

Amadeus has always been the one I leaned on when shit went south and I couldn't fix it myself. The one that I sparred with to get better at fighting in the ring. The one I made a blood pact with after his sister got taken. Promising each other to always look out for one another. He was my everything. Now, I don't recognize him at all.

"I don't have an answer for that," she says, sounding defeated. "I don't remember much, it's all kind of blank," She says through chattering teeth. No wonder, she's half naked. Only clothed in Dante's ripped up shirt.

"What do you remember?"

She's silent for a long moment, her eyes dimming slightly when she answers. "Hopelessness," she says, and her voice breaks. "An endless hopelessness that was all consuming," she whispers.

"When did you turn, do you know?" I ask quietly, and I feel her shake her head. "Were you bonded?"

There's an audible swallow coming from her, then she nods. "Yes, I was bonded to a beautiful brown pegasi. I don't even know if he's still—"

I understand what she means. What she fears. Though I'm newly bonded to Atticus, there's a strange protectiveness blooming in my chest. Even the thought of him not being alive anymore is completely unthinkable.

"The fact that someone would dare force a bond onto a creature is devastating to me," Teagan says.

"I know...what Amadeus did is...unforgivable." After we left him in the mountains in September, I thought I'd never see him again. I thought, or rather hoped that the rumors about monsters in the mountains would take care of him. I never thought I'd see him again. And now?

I don't know what to do.

There's a prickling sensation running along my skin like a ghostly touch, and despite my lack of religious belief, I find myself praying that we get some answers soon.

"You smell better now," Dante says, coming up beside me.

"What happened to his tail?" Merick muses.

Riften tilts his head to the side. *"Good question."*

"Don't mind what happened to his tail." I'm pretty sure I'm blushing. I really don't want to tell them what happened to Dante's tail at the moment.

I can't help but stare down at my newly adorned dragon bond, and how the two marks almost seem to interact with each other in perfect harmony. For the first time, I let myself study the marks in detail. The only difference between the patterns is the color.

I've noticed that the dragon bond usually depicts something that has to do with what type of magic you hold. Elodie's mark depicts flowing water.

Galen has small pebbles that almost seem to play under his skin. Killian has thorny vines, and Riften's mark illustrates black smoke.

They all point to their respective powers. Water, earth, pain, and shadows.

Then there were the red plantlike barbs on the guy from the courtyard the first time a bond was attempted, and the red thorny vines Amadeus used to control the Bone Dragon. What if... "Does the color on the markings mean anything?"

A slow grin spreads on Dante's face. "I believe so. I've long suspected that there's a connection to the colors of the mark and the corruptness of the heart. Black meaning it's a normal bond between a creature and a human. When the mark is red, the human tends to be somewhat rotten within. Then we have the King's faded mark since his dragon was killed during the bonding and the gold...I still don't know what gold means. It certainly makes the two of you quite special."

I realize that I've seen it before, on multiple occasions. Even before the reaping.

It's the exact same pattern that's embellished on the blade of my dagger. The one Heason made.

My eyes fly wide and I turn to Dante. "Does our world still exist?"

"Of course it does."

"No, what I mean is, is it Somewhere else, or does it exist as a separate layer to this world?"

A smile spreads across Dante's face as he looks me up and down. "What are you thinking, Little Bridge?"

"There was a comet, a burning stone that made the sky burn until dawn back home. It came out of Nowhere, and landed in the forest that surrounds our village. The blacksmith used that stone to craft my dagger. It's the same pattern, and it moves just like our marks."

The grin on his face widens. "Yes?"

"I—" What am I thinking? It sounds ludicrous that the different worlds exist as separate layers at the same time, and yet, it makes sense. In my delirious dream, there were interconnecting threads that bridged everything together. The nature, the wildlife, even the monsters.

Atticus stretches out his front leg for me to climb. When I'm seated on his back, I turn to the others with a somber expression on my face. "What if the spell the glimmer gnomes did...fractured reality?"

"*Easy my love,*" *I soothe the beautiful creature under me and tug on the crimson barbs keeping him under my control. The bone dragon whines softly. "Hush, my sweet. Soon, we will have everything we desire. Just you wait." I glance over to the boy beside me when his beast lets out a sore cry, and the crimson blood dripping from his hand. "Foolish. You can't even follow instructions." The boy flinches from the sound of my voice inside his head. I look down the hill to where the shadows guided me, and the two that have become the bane of my existence. "They look so safe, wouldn't you say?" Again, my beast yowls. "Let's go for a hunt, shall we?"*

Acknowledgements

This book would not exist if it hadn't been for my Book-Community that I found on TikTok two years ago. I want to show my thanks to all of them.

Though some might not be mentioned, they are not forgotten.

First and foremost, I want to thank you, Ashtyn Turner, who has been a steady sounding board from the very beginning. Ever since this story was written in a different language. You were patient whilst listening to my poor translations on the fly and still enjoyed my writing. You have become a dear friend to me, and I hope you know that. And remember, *"Shit splatters!"*

Thank you, Roxanne, that read through a very rough draft of madness and nagged me for an ending. I'm sorry for the cliffhanger. Well, not really.

My alpha reader Sami Rae, that read through another rough draft, patiently waiting for each chapter. Even taking the leap to help edit my abundance of S's that were all over the place and Nowhere to be found at times. Constantly showing your support and love for this story and these characters through your engagement.

To my beta readers, that took a chance on reading the unknown story of Nowhere and fell in love with this world. And became fiercely protective of my work and encouraged me to keep writing through the storms.

Thank you, S. E. Zell for editing this story, helping me find better solutions and reminding me that my story is worth telling.

Casiddie Williams, for helping me find my author voice.

Pricilla Stone for brainstorming with me through the dark middle-part of my story, the part that had me stuck for weeks-on-end.

To all of the amazing narrators in our community, that has helped me voice some of the pivotal parts of the story. Giving me the opportunity to share my author voice long before I finished my debut novel.

And to all my ARC readers, thank you all for your endless love and support.

From the bottom of my heart.

Thank you all.

Printed in Great Britain
by Amazon